PRAISE FOR KIM LAW

"*Montana Cherries* is a heartwarming yet heart-wrenching story of the heroine's struggle to accept the truth about her mother's death—and life."

—*RT Book Reviews*, four stars

"An entertaining romance with a well-developed plot and believable characters. The chemistry between Vega and JP is explosive and will have you rooting for the couple's success. Readers will definitely look forward to more works by this author."

—*RT Book Reviews*, four stars ("Hot")

"Kim Law pens a sexy, fast-paced romance."

—*New York Times* bestselling author Lori Wilde

"A solid combination of sexy fun."

—*New York Times* bestselling author Carly Phillips

"*Sugar Springs* is a deeply emotional story about family ties and second chances. If you love heartwarming small towns, this is one place you'll definitely want to visit."

—*USA Today* bestselling author Hope Ramsay

"Filled with engaging characters, *Sugar Springs* is the typical everyone-knows-everyone's-business small town. Law skillfully portrays heroine Lee Ann's doubts and fears, as well as hero Cody's struggle to be a better person than he believes he can be. And Lee Ann's young nieces are a delight."

—*RT Book Reviews*, four stars

HARD

DEEP IN THE HEART

HEADED

HARD

DEEP IN THE HEART

HEADED

Kim Law

Montlake
Romance

Published by Montlake Romance, Seattle

www.apub.com

Amazon, the Amazon logo, and Montlake Romance are trademarks of Amazon.com, Inc., or its affiliates.

ISBN-13: 9781542047838
ISBN-10: 1542047838

Cover design by Pepe *NYMI*

Printed in the United States of America

To Terri Osburn. You said "she-sheds," and I suddenly had my story. Thank you!

Chapter One

"A drill does not belong in a tool belt."

—Blu Johnson, life lesson #11

Jill Sadler smiled for the camera as she stood posed beside the backyard garden shed, one hand splayed on the rough-hewn cedar planks of the outer walls, the other wrapped around the handle of her heavy-duty cordless drill, and she wondered how she'd ever come to this. How had any of them?

"A half step to your left, Jill."

She shuffled closer to the building until the photographer quit motioning with her hand. As she moved, she made sure not to glance at either Heather or Trenton. Otherwise, she'd likely catch her foster sisters silently laughing at her. This was the third time she'd had to be repositioned for this shot alone, and every time, she'd have sworn she was in the exact spot she'd been told.

"And don't forget to smile!" The white of the photographer's teeth flashed bright.

Jill gripped her drill tighter and decided that she hated the woman. But still, she smiled. Free publicity and all.

At least, that was the company line she'd been feeding herself.

But the thing was, this *wasn't* the kind of publicity any of them wanted. Not entirely. They'd take the positive light it would shine on their business—that was always good. And they were more than happy to give back to the community. But what they hadn't fully thought through when Trenton came to them with the idea for the fund-raiser was how this would also generate the exact opposite outcome from what they'd been working hard to accomplish. Which was to *kill* their current reputation.

Four and a half years ago, Jill and her two foster sisters had started what they'd thought of as any other construction company in the small town of Red Oak Falls, Texas. They'd planned to take on general maintenance and renovations to start, growing the business by flipping houses as income allowed, and had hoped to scale into new construction before any of them turned thirty—which would be *Jill* in two short months. Their construction skills had begun to develop when they were teens, thanks to their helping with an addition to their foster mother's home, and they'd thought the uniqueness of being an all-female crew would intrigue people enough to give them a chance.

Yet business hadn't exactly gone as planned.

Eighteen months after hanging out their shingle, they'd tossed a Hail Mary by building the shed they were currently being photographed with. Sitting thirty feet outside Blu Johnson's back door, it had been constructed as a test idea for side projects until the "real work" picked up. A last-ditch effort to keep the company afloat. Only, they never could have predicted the results from raising the walls on this quaint little garden shed. Women now called from all over central Texas wanting their own backyard retreat, and they were willing to pay a pretty penny to get one. Seemed Bluebonnet Construction had developed a reputation for producing one-of-a-kind designs.

All the accolades, however, hadn't scored them the more substantial renovation projects they'd been hoping for. Instead, it had set them up as being known for doing nothing *more* than she-sheds. Queens of the

She-Sheds, in fact. The local paper had even run an article proclaiming them as such.

But they didn't want to be women building projects for women. They wanted to compete.

They *wanted* to prove that they were just as good as their male competition. Or *better*.

Yet here they were: Jill with a drill held at an angle across her chest, Heather on her haunches, wearing a hard hat and wielding a hammer, and Trenton standing at the opposite corner of the building, circular saw held aloft. As if anyone would willy-nilly slice a board in two in the middle of the air.

Aunt Blu was also in the picture, but she'd been positioned in a rocker inside the open door. The four of them were doing their best to showcase how it had all begun—all the while knowing that the calendar being created to raise money for the elementary school would only garner them more calls. For more she-sheds.

"Got it." The photographer lowered her camera. Her voice was way too perky for that early on a Sunday morning. "Now let's do one last shot. Something a little different this time."

Jill stood quietly, awaiting her next directive and wishing any other photographer could have been chosen for the project. She'd never met the other woman in person before today, but Jill had been aware of her. And she'd certainly seen her around town.

Marci Hammery. The daughter of the senior partner of the town's largest law firm.

The woman currently dating Jill's ex.

Jill narrowed her eyes as the other woman puckered her mouth—seeming to contemplate how she wanted to pose them next—and had the thought that lips like Marci's couldn't possibly be that naturally full. Though the brunette was several years younger than Jill, surely she'd had work done to get that mouth.

"I want Trenton on the roof," Marci decided. "A nail gun in hand, straddling the top."

Jill frowned. "The roof wasn't installed with a nail gun. It's aluminum and glass."

She was ignored.

"And Heather on a step stool. I want you dusting off the plaque with one hand," Marci told Heather as she moved a rustic-looking stool into the shot and handed over a feather duster, "while holding a watering can over the window box with the other."

A watering can appeared, and Jill's blood pressure spiked.

The picture was going to look stupid. And not just because Heather would have her body contorted in two different directions.

They were a *construction crew*. They shouldn't be dusting anything.

But as Heather shot a pinched look, first at the duster and then at the plaque hanging above the door christening the shed as "Blu's Business," Trenton murmured a sound of agreement and moved a ladder to the side of the building. She grabbed a nail gun and began climbing. The jeans and fitted tee she'd worn for the photos were her norm for work, but she'd let herself be talked into using hot rollers on her hair. Blonde waves fell over her shoulders, giving a softer, more romantic look than the no-frills version Jill had always known Trenton to wear. This wasn't them.

Nothing about this setup was real.

"And for Jill"—the photographer turned back to her—"I want you standing just inside the building. At Blu's side."

Aunt Blu had barely uttered a word throughout the morning, and though she sat in the midst of the starter plants she was known for, Jill knew her foster mother had to hate how the rocker—that had also shown up with Marci—portrayed her as a quiet, soft-spoken "little woman." Blu was anything but someone's "little woman." But she *would* do anything for her girls.

She also had a weak spot for every child in need, so participating in a fund-raiser for elementary school children was right up her alley.

"Put your left hand on the back of the rocker, feet shoulder-width apart," Marci instructed Jill as her focus dropped to resetting the dials of her camera, "and tuck the drill into your tool belt. Hold it as if you're holstering a gun."

No one said a word.

The instructions, however, finally brought Blu to her feet. Marci looked up at the sound of movement.

"A drill doesn't go in a tool belt," Aunt Blu informed her.

Marci blinked. "Pardon?"

"A drill does *not* go in a tool belt," Aunt Blu repeated. She stepped onto the cobblestone path that led from the house to the door of the ten-by-twelve building. *A drill does not belong in a tool belt* had been one of the first lessons they'd learned after arriving at Bluebonnet Farms. Jill had been fourteen, Heather only six months behind her, and Trenton twelve. They'd all shown up within the same week, the first girls Blu had taken in, and their foster mother had wasted no time starting what she called their must-have lessons for life.

Lesson #11 had come about when Jill had snagged a drill and tool belt from the workshop, then had pranced around with the drill hanging through the hammer loop of the tool belt, announcing how "tough" she was.

Aunt Blu had not been amused.

"I just—"

"No," Aunt Blu interrupted Marci. Her gray eyes were hard as she took the drill out of Jill's hand and motioned Trenton down off the roof with a quick snap of her fingers. "And as Jill made clear, the glass panels didn't get *nailed* in. They were attached with screws. These three ladies won't be put into a photograph looking as if they don't have the first clue about what they're doing."

Aunt Blu took the water pitcher from Heather's hand and flung it across the yard. It made a sliding sound as it came to a stop next to Marci's hybrid. Aunt Blu's late husband, Gerry, had built the two-story farmhouse on the sprawling one-hundred-fifty-acre farm, and though Blu had never mastered the skills of her construction-company-owner husband, she'd picked up plenty of knowledge along the way. And she got instantly bent out of shape over the illogical use of any tool.

"For this last picture, we'll stand side by side," Blu announced. "As one."

They'd been trussed up like performing monkeys for the last two hours, when their hopes for today had been simple: capture the vision that had started it all, along with the tight-knit bond held between the four of them. This would be the cover shot for the calendar, while eighteen of Bluebonnet Construction's most original designs would fill the interior pages. Proceeds from the sales would go to fund new playground equipment over the summer, with the Bluebonnets installing the equipment themselves. The previous playground had been decimated by a tornado at the beginning of the year.

But Marci wasn't ready to give in on the setup of the photo. "As a professional with an eye for—"

"Together." Aunt Blu didn't budge.

Marci stared at her a moment longer, but Jill could see the fight go out of her. Her gaze flicked away. "Okay, then." Marci licked her lips. "You'll stand together."

She sounded less than enthused, but after Marci spent a couple of minutes studying the angle of the morning light and considering how best to position the four of them, they ended up in a slight arc off to the left of the shed's door. Bluebonnet flowers burst with color in the background, while Jill and the others linked together, arms around waists, wearing the kind of smiles that no one would ever have to force. It would make a picture that Jill would hold dear.

The camera whirred as the final shots were snapped, then Marci called it a wrap. She may have ended up annoyed with her subjects, but Jill knew that her photography business would garner as much attention from the fund-raiser as Bluebonnet Construction would. Therefore, Marci couldn't be too disappointed with the way the morning had turned out.

After the other woman finished loading her car and drove away, the climbing sun slashing bright rays of light through the whirls of dust wafting up behind her vehicle, Aunt Blu ushered the rest of them into the house. Jill and Trenton dropped into the straight-back chairs at the kitchen table, groaning as if they couldn't stand to be on their feet one second longer, while Heather headed for the marble countertop outlining the other half of the room.

"I'll pour the coffee," Heather announced. Jill could smell the freshly brewed, life-sustaining liquid, and practically foamed at the mouth.

"And I'll sit here and sleep," Trenton muttered. She folded her arms in front of her, and dropped her head. Neither she nor Jill were what anyone would call morning people, no matter that six days a week they were up before dawn.

Today, however, was Sunday. The day of sleep.

And they were *not* sleeping.

"No sleeping yet," Aunt Blu responded. She'd crossed to the rolltop desk and shuffled through a stack of papers.

"You got a new girl coming in?" Jill glanced toward the hallway as she spoke.

The house had been empty since the last two foster girls were returned to their biological mother, but as with everything else, Blu was always prepared to take in more. She always got asked, too. Since opening her doors fifteen years before, Aunt Blu and Bluebonnet Farms had only grown in popularity. Requests now came from as far out as Dallas, and Blu never turned a girl away.

Nor did she look the other way when any of them reached adulthood. She'd proven that when Jill, Heather, and Trenton had shown up back at the farm several years after hightailing it out of there, each dragging their injured pride behind them.

"No girls," Aunt Blu answered. "But there is something I need to tell you about." Her voice was tighter than normal, and all three of them looked over at her. Trenton even lifted her head from the table. "I signed you up for something," Blu told them.

Jill stifled a groan. She was all for volunteering, but after getting to the farm before sunrise that morning, she'd rather lay off the pro bono work for a bit.

"Just say we don't have to do it today?" she pleaded.

"Not today." Blu returned to the table. She held a single sheet of paper in one hand and a legal-sized envelope in the other.

"What is it?" Heather asked. She placed steaming mugs in front of Jill and Trenton.

"It's a contest."

Aunt Blu slid the paper onto the table, and Jill, Heather, and Trenton all leaned forward, each silently reading the words on the flyer. But it was Heather who reacted first.

"*Yes.*" Her eyes rounded as she looked back up at Blu. "This is exactly what we need. You signed us up for this?"

Aunt Blu nodded. "A couple of months ago."

"Do you really think we could get chosen?" Trenton's gaze remained glued to the paper. The exhaustion that had previously marred her expression had vanished.

Jill was at a loss. "What's *Texas Dream Home*?"

"Good grief, Jill." Heather dropped to a chair and scooped up the flyer, holding it up in front of Jill as if she hadn't already seen it. Heather then jabbed a finger at the early-twentieth-century home pictured in the middle of it. "It's only the most popular show on television right now."

"Which you'd *know* if you ever bothered to *watch* television," Trenton added.

Jill wanted to roll her eyes—and she would have if Aunt Blu hadn't been in the room. Because they covered this argument at least once a month. Additionally, due to Heather's rose-colored glasses, she had a habit of claiming anything she was currently enamored with to be "the best" or "the most popular." But Jill *highly* doubted that a show about renovating homes in Texas was the most exciting thing on television right now.

"I doubt it's—"

"The. Most. Popular," Heather repeated before Jill could finish her protest. Heather gave her a just-try-and-test-me look, her head angled with attitude, and Jill gave in. She rolled her eyes.

But she used her hand to block her foster mother's view.

"Like she doesn't know what you're doing behind your hand." Heather smirked.

Jill kicked her under the table.

"Girls," Aunt Blu chastised.

Trenton sat on the other side of the table batting her eyelashes, because for once, it hadn't been her who got called out, and Heather turned the flyer back around to look at it.

"I'm just saying," Heather tried again, "that it makes no sense in this day and age to be so unaware of popular culture. How can you stand to live like that?"

"And I'm just saying that having no TV is a perfectly valid life choice," Jill responded. And it had been *her* choice since returning to Red Oak Falls. She had a habit of being hardheaded, she knew, but she also had a perfectly good reason for this particular decision.

Not that she'd ever gone into specifics on that reasoning.

Aunt Blu didn't interrupt their argument again, but Jill could feel her foster mother's steady gaze on her, so she plucked the paper from between Heather's fingers and reread the details of the competition. The search for teams would be conducted statewide, two teams, two homes, with renovations to span six weeks.

Which would be *fast* renovations for an entire house. Not that they couldn't handle it.

The renovated homes would then be donated back to the community, with town leadership to decide how best to use them.

Jill stared at the words, but she still didn't get it. Why should *they* do this?

The donation to the community would be great, sure. For whatever community the chosen houses resided in. But there was no guarantee that would be Red Oak Falls.

Granted, their time and effort wouldn't be a mere donation. A stipend would be provided for each team so no loss of wages would be incurred. But that didn't take into account the existing customers already slated for work. And *not* meeting the deadlines of those paying clients while instead spending six weeks gallivanting around who-knew-what part of Texas—*pretending they belonged on some television show*—seemed like a death sentence to Jill.

"It's *exposure*," Heather finally said, her voice implying a metaphorical roll of her eyes.

"And exposure is what we *need*," Trenton added.

"But we can get exposure with ads," Jill reminded them. "Radio plugs, billboards." She took in the others as she fought against her rising heart rate. They'd talked about this. "We don't have to go on TV."

"But this would be *good* exposure, Jilly," Trenton clarified.

"*And* a lot of it," Heather added.

Panic suddenly pierced Jill, a blistering hole threatening to open wide inside her. She refused to let it show, though. She didn't show fear. Not even to her foster sisters.

She also didn't want to be on TV. Or think about being on TV.

Or think about all the years she'd once tried to be on TV.

She didn't say any of that, though, because only Aunt Blu knew that she'd wasted six years of her life attempting to be something she'd never been meant to be.

Jessica Grant.

She almost laughed at the thought—as if she'd ever actually needed a stage name. She'd been a failure from day one. But she was neither an actress nor a wannabe actress these days. She was a grown-up. One-third owner and project manager for Bluebonnet Construction. Not a girl with stars in her eyes.

Forcing herself to visualize the billboard standing in the prime location out on Highway 71, she pulled in a deep breath for a count of five. The advertising they'd tried through their social media accounts hadn't paid off, so they'd been discussing other options. And that's what they were going to do. Billboards. With any luck, they'd even outbid We Nail It Contractors, replacing each and every one of their biggest competitor's ads with giant Bluebonnet ones.

Irritation bloomed at the thought of the other company—*and* its owner.

Then she wondered if Cal had signed up for the competition, too.

Her heart suddenly thundered. Surely not. We Nail It stayed so busy, they didn't need the added publicity. They just needed more laborers. And maybe to let someone else in town win a bid or two.

"Everyone in town sees the billboards," she argued when the others remained silent.

"But everyone in the country would see this."

Jill stilled at Heather's words, then she slowly turned to face her foster sister. "The country?"

Was she really that out of touch?

Heather nodded, and Jill swallowed around the lump in her throat. There was a highly popular television show that filmed practically in their backyard, doing the very thing that Jill was now putting her heart and soul into? She refused to think life could be that ironic.

But what if it was?

And what if Heather and Trenton were right about the attention that they could get?

Could they finally show the town that they were more than foster sisters playing construction crew?

She turned to Aunt Blu. "How would we justify spending weeks doing this? Assuming we could even get chosen, of course. We'd have to delay projects that are already lined up. Wouldn't we risk moving backward instead of forward?"

"Yet that risk could bring in hundreds of jobs for every one project we'd have to delay," Trenton answered before Aunt Blu could form a response. Trenton reached over and covered Jill's hand. "This is a good idea, Jilly. I know we like to be unanimous in major decisions, but I think we might need to take this one to a vote."

"We're not voting." The finality in Aunt Blu's tone brooked no argument.

"Fine." Trenton made a face. "But if we really want to be known as more than Queens of the She-Sheds, this is our shot."

"We need the chance to *prove* what we can do," Heather supplied. "And this show would do that for us. Even if we didn't win"—Heather stared at Jill, her gaze as earnest as her words—"I promise you, just being a competitor would boost the company into a new realm. And I am *not* just talking about being sought after in Red Oak Falls."

Jill looked from Heather to Trenton. Could they possibly be right?

Even if the show only got Texas viewers . . .

She thought about the size of Texas. About the number of homes that likely *did* have televisions, even when only considering Red Oak Falls. Many of the locals would watch—if for no other reason than to see if "that little Sadler girl" really had turned out okay. And that's when she, Heather, and Trenton could win their way inside other people's homes. Because from the way the flyer read, the teams wouldn't be stuck building a froufrou she-shed out in a backyard somewhere. They'd be tackling a full-sized renovation.

They'd either prove themselves capable—or they'd know they should give up for good.

Hope replaced the burn of panic. Bluebonnet Construction could finally be heading in the direction they'd worked so hard to attain. While at the same time, she'd get the chance to validate herself in front of the camera once and for all.

She could do this. She was older now. More mature.

She wouldn't have to do anything "untoward" to get cast on the show.

It would be a win-win for all of them.

But then her gaze landed on the fine print at the bottom of the page, and the optimism that had just begun to glow shriveled like a dried-out twig. She sagged in her chair. "The date for notifying finalists has come and gone, Aunt Blu." She pointed to the stated date. "We apparently didn't make the cut."

Aunt Blu slid the legal-sized envelope onto the table. "Except you did. Interviews start this week."

Chapter Two

*"If it walks like a skunk and smells like a skunk . . . plug
your nose and head for the door."*

—Blu Johnson, life lesson #28

"And . . . cut."

At the three-letter word, Calhoun Reynolds let the overdone smile
fall from his lips and stepped from the circle of lights set up on the
back porch. The *Texas Dream Home* film crew had been at the house
since early that morning, capturing footage for the opening credits of
the upcoming competition. They'd slapped makeup on him, traipsed
through every inch of the seventy-year-old Craftsman where his grandparents had once lived, and asked more questions than he could have
imagined. Yet he sensed they remained less than satisfied with what
they'd gotten.

He wasn't sure what else he could offer, though.

Of course, there was the fact that he was sitting on a farm no one
knew about. They'd be all over that.

Single, eligible bachelor, with his own three-hundred-acre ranch?
And renovating the original log house himself? They wouldn't be able to
resist. They'd likely even encourage him to strip down to his jeans and

drive in a nail or two—just for the women viewers. No one had been shy about stroking his ego today, nor about how they'd love to play up his looks for the viewers.

"Hey, Cal." His uncle Rodney stepped through the sliding back door, a practiced smile on his face, as his gaze sought out who might be in charge of the madness going on in the secluded backyard. This was the first Cal had seen of his uncle since the other man had left for a date the night before. "I didn't realize filming started today."

Rodney could be an exceptional liar when he wanted to be. His dark hair was freshly trimmed, plaid shirt tucked into his best jeans, and he'd even brought out his lucky boots. The ones he typically only wore when he wasn't positive a date was a sure thing.

"They wanted to get a few shots before everything starts Monday morning," Cal told him.

The cameraman had once again stepped behind his equipment, and as Rodney's smile swung toward the glowing red light, Cal wouldn't have been surprised to see his uncle whip out a cowboy hat and plop it on his head. He'd been looking forward to this.

"It's all still hush-hush," Cal reminded him. He turned his back to the lens. Though word had leaked out about the production company's purchase of the two one-and-a-half-story bungalows over on Pear Street, it remained a secret just *who* had been selected to compete in this year's competition. Or if *any* local company had. *Texas Dream Home* typically chose one team from the area where the houses were to be renovated, as well as one crew from another part of the state. Therefore, rumors had been running rampant.

"Not a problem for me," Rodney assured him. "My lips are sealed."

He zipped his finger across his lips as if to prove his words, while Cal took a step closer to catch a better look at his uncle's eyes. Not bloodshot.

At least not yet.

"Any way I could get in on the action?" Rodney asked. Lack of subtlety was another of his charms.

"I think they're—"

"Mr. Reynolds!" Patrick Whitaker, the show's producer, caught sight of Rodney and made fast work of eating up the distance between him and them. He easily maneuvered Cal and Rodney so that anything said or done would be caught on tape, and thrust his hand out in greeting. A boom mic hovered above them. "We were hoping you'd show up today, sir. Good to see you again. Since you started We Nail It Contractors, we absolutely want to get you on screen. Can you stick around?"

"For however long you need me."

Cal kept his features blank. He'd been so close to getting everyone out of the house.

"Will you be doing any of the work with Cal for the show?" Patrick asked.

"I'm pretty much out of the game these days," Rodney informed the producer. "Cal and I still talk business and I jump in when needed, but I mostly prefer spending my time . . . giving back. I'm either *giving* to the horse races down in Selma—or I'm *giving* the ladies who've yet to have the pleasure of Rodney a firsthand chance." Cal's uncle gave a wink, and Patrick responded with the appropriate guffaw. "My nephew is perfect for the cameras, though, don't you think?" Rodney slapped Cal on the back. "Boy's got the Reynolds charm on his side. Not to mention the looks."

Another round of laughter came from Patrick.

Rodney was right about the Reynolds charm, though. At least where it concerned *Rodney*. The man was in a league of his own. It was how he'd managed to get married three times.

The divorces, however, were another story.

But even with multiple exes, Rodney still had no problem reeling in the ladies. It was impressive, actually. There'd been a time when Cal had thought he wanted to be just like his uncle.

"Maybe we can talk you into stopping by the house," Patrick went on. "Swing a hammer to show where Cal gets his skill. We like the episodes to be about family as much as the renovations, and I know the viewers would love seeing you two together."

Cal remained silent. He didn't point out that his skill had actually started as a kid. Back when his grandfather had been alive. Nor that neither he *nor* his competition would have much in the way of family on camera. Rodney would be it for him. And Cal planned to do his best to limit the amount of time that attention would be pointed his uncle's way.

"Sounds good to me." Rodney put an arm around Cal. "I'd do anything for this one."

Cal kept his own arms at his sides, but he did fire a winning smile at the camera. Rodney was mugging for the potential viewers, he knew, but Cal didn't doubt the sentiment. They'd lived together in his grandparents' house for thirteen years now, Rodney having once provided Cal both a roof over his head *and* a job in his business, and in that span of time, any pretense with the other had fallen away. Cal could have moved out years ago, but he liked being surrounded with childhood memories. He also liked his grandmother knowing that her house still had life in it.

Plus, Rodney needed him here. Rodney wasn't someone who handled being on his own well. Nor was he someone who handled the business side of things well. Which was why Cal had taken over the company several years back. They'd made a gentleman's agreement. Cal would purchase Rodney's remaining portion for a single dollar bill—while also providing Rodney a salary for life. It had been a win for both of them.

And though his uncle had practically run the company into the ground, since taking ownership, Cal had made it his mission to turn We Nail It into what it was today. Which was a thriving business that stayed so busy both in and around Red Oak Falls that he certainly had no time to be filming a reality show. Nor had he applied to *be* on one. Yet when *Texas Dream Home* had come calling, he'd found himself signing on the dotted line.

"We start filming at the houses on Monday," Patrick was saying to Rodney now, his words cutting into Cal's thoughts. "We'll interview you here today, but let's also plan on talking to you at the jobsite before the week is over."

"I'm in," Rodney confirmed. He shook the man's hand. "Just tell me when and where."

And not to be drunk, Cal thought. His uncle had a problem that was fast becoming harder to hide.

Patrick and his uncle moved away from the porch as they continued to talk, and Cal returned to his thoughts. He still couldn't believe he'd agreed to do the show. The last thing he'd ever imagined for himself was being the "star" of a television show. That had been his ex's so-called dream. Therefore, when *Texas Dream Home* had sought him out, he'd refused. Even when Rodney had pointed out the obvious. That if Cal truly wanted to be the best in the business, it wouldn't do to shun an opportunity like this.

And it was a heck of an opportunity. Cal could admit that. We Nail It was already the most well-known construction company within a one-hundred-mile radius, and they'd been voted Red Oak Falls' Best in Biz three years running. But if they were to be on TV . . .

If Cal was on TV, even his father would have to take notice.

Still, Cal declined. He had too many irons in the fire to take on the additional role of reality-television personality. Not to mention, Cal didn't make decisions based upon his father.

Ever.

But then the executive producer had played his trump card. *Jill.*

And everything had begun to look different.

Unbeknownst to Jill, Cal would be his ex's competition. And he swore, nothing could have gotten him interested faster. Because, dammit, he might have been the one to walk away from their twenty-four-hour marriage, but she'd been the one to throw down the gauntlet. And *then* she'd had the nerve to sashay back into town six years later and open a competing business.

Texas Dream Home had been aware of all those facts, though how, Cal hadn't bothered to ask. They'd even waved around the knowledge that Jill had refused to speak to him in the five years she'd been home. They felt they had a gold mine on their hands by pitting two exes together for this year's competition, and they'd made it clear they would do whatever it took to sign Cal.

Shamefully, it hadn't taken all that much. A chance to finally put Jill in her place?

Done.

Bluebonnet Construction would have to concede that they simply couldn't compete in the same arena. Construction was *his* game. And the fact that Jill would be spitting nails when she found out she would be going up against him? Icing on the cake.

He did feel a tiny bit bad about his part in it, though. Keeping this from her *did* make him a bit of an ass.

But then, genetics and all, he couldn't help but be an ass.

He had a sudden vision of his ex completely livid, her eyes snapping with heat, and her body coiled and ready to snap. The girl had a temper. And he'd always loved it.

Cal groaned at the unbidden thought. Surely that hadn't played into his agreeing to be on the show. *Just* to get her mad? To see it directed at him?

What in the hell was wrong with him? Would making her finally speak to him again—*winning* the unspoken battle she'd declared between them—give him a sense of power? Or would it prove him a complete moron for putting himself in her line of fire to begin with? Because the fact remained that he'd never been able to resist her particular brand of fire. And he suspected it would engulf him just as fiercely today.

What an idiot.

He turned and slipped inside the house. There were still hours of daylight left. His uncle could entertain the crew however long he wanted, but it was time for Cal to get to work. *And* to quit thinking about Jill.

~

"Two breakfast specials, half a grapefruit on the side, and . . . uh"—the waitress's too-wide smile faltered as she stared unblinking at the third plate in her hands—"one . . . *uhmmm*"—her hands shook as she clearly fought to regain her thoughts—"one veggie omelet," she finished in a rush of relief. She quickly distributed the plates, her smile once again too bright.

"Thanks, Harley." Jill touched the back of the younger girl's hand. Harley had been doing her best to ignore the cameras scattered around the local diner, but her best hadn't quite been doing it for her today. The abrupt appearance of the production crew had overwhelmed the girl.

"I'll be back with your . . ." Harley froze again as the overhead mic dipped closer.

"Coffee," Jill whispered, and Harley's gaze shot to hers.

She blinked. "Coffee. Yes. I'll be right back with refills."

She spun on her heels and was gone a second later. Jill knew Harley would be okay. She'd worked for Bluebonnet Construction over the last two summers, and though she sometimes let her nerves get the better of her, she always managed to pull it together. She'd started college the previous fall, and Jill had already seen her confidence begin to climb.

Picking up her fork, Jill eyed the plate of bacon, eggs, and hash browns in front of her. Should she have chosen something lighter since this was being filmed?

"How long do we have to sit here pretending to eat?" Heather asked under her breath. Both she and Trenton peered across the table at Jill, each holding her own fork the same as Jill, and Jill felt a momentary pang of guilt.

"He didn't say," she murmured. They were looking to her for direction because the night before, the *Texas Dream* crew had gathered them together and "explained the situation."

Yes, Bluebonnet Construction had been chosen to compete on the show, and yes, they wanted all three of the owners available for filming, and most definitely for the renovations. They were looking forward to seeing them working together as a team. But the majority of the attention would be focused on Jill. She'd come across best during the screen test.

"I'm sorry," she said again. She'd been apologizing since last night. "I didn't want it this way." She'd even tried to talk the producers out of it.

"We're fine with it." This came from Trenton. She looked from Heather to Jill, nodding as she did. "Seriously. Whatever it takes to get the job done. Plus, you were amazing in the clip they showed us. I didn't know you had it in you."

Jill had been a little amazed herself. She hadn't lost all the things she'd once learned.

"We can't control how they want to set up the show," Heather chimed in. "All we can do is manage the outcome." She flashed deep dimples before poking a bite of omelet into her mouth. "Which means our business name splashed all over and our phone ringing off the hook," she said around the egg whites.

Jill could get behind that.

And the fact was, as soon as it had become public knowledge that homes in the area had been purchased for the show, the number of calls had already increased. No one knew that Bluebonnet had been picked to compete, but people *did* love to speculate. Not to mention, the entire town had been abuzz with excitement not only at the prospect of their little town being "put on the map," but that one of their own might be the star of a national television show. This alone had upped the chatter among everyone.

Because of all the extra excitement, Jill and her foster sisters had brought in Aunt Blu to man the phone, allowing them to keep moving forward with scheduled work. A handful of the calls had been people merely hoping to get their own fifteen minutes of fame—*if* it turned out that Bluebonnet would indeed be on the show—but the largest percentage had been legit business inquiries. Many people hadn't even been aware that Bluebonnet did renovations until an article about all the local construction companies had run in last week's newspaper.

Aunt Blu had reassured each and every one of them that Bluebonnet Construction was *more* than capable. She'd then sent photos of some of the more recent work the company had done, as well as the full renovation on the farm's original homestead—where Heather still lived. All three of them had moved into the three-bedroom cottage upon first returning to town, and as a way of paying Aunt Blu back, they'd given the place a major overhaul.

That renovation, in fact, had led to the creation of Bluebonnet Construction. They'd started the company in honor of Big Gerry, as well as Aunt Blu's three young daughters, all of whom had been killed in a car wreck with her husband.

Along with providing manual labor, each of them filled a specific role in the business. Jill handled schedules and personnel. She made sure the jobs got done. Heather was the spokesperson. She was hard to ruffle, so she worked directly with potential clients and spent time publicly promoting the company. While Trenton preferred to deal more behind the scenes. Trenton took care of the finances, but mostly, she just wanted to get her hands dirty and build things. She was their workhorse.

Though no new contracts had been signed of yet, the phone calls had gone well, and all they had to do at this point, it seemed, was to *not* screw up the upcoming six weeks. Do that, and a booming construction business would soon be theirs. And surely they could manage that.

Six weeks, one renovation? They wouldn't even have to split their time between other jobs thanks to some stealthy rescheduling on Jill's part. This would be a piece of cake.

"Ms. Sadler." The nearest cameraman got her attention. He'd poked his head out from behind his camera, a big guy with a thick copper-colored beard and eyes the same kind of see-through blue as Heather's. "We're going to need you three to actually *have* a conversation we can use on tape."

He looked mildly uncomfortable at having to make the request, but off to the side of the room, Patrick Whitaker nodded with an encouraging smile.

"Like we talked about last night," Patrick said.

Right. Like they'd talked about last night. Jill glanced around at the faces of the patrons packed into the café, noting that no one seemed to be eating, even though everyone had food on their tables. Last night Patrick had given an overview of how the next few weeks would go, while letting them know the crew would be looking to *her* to take charge during most takes. To keep things rolling smoothly.

She put her fork back down. She couldn't eat when so much was at stake.

Patrick had promised that by the time the episodes finished airing, the entire country would not only be begging for Bluebonnet

Construction to renovate their homes, but they'd have fallen in love with the three of them, as well.

Only, Jill didn't want them to love *her*. Her heart pounded at the thought. Then she mentally corrected herself . . . she didn't want to *want* to be loved.

But she sure had at one point in her life.

"Can you do that, Jill?" Patrick asked. He'd come a step closer, concern dimming his smile, but his gaze never left hers. Patrick was the complete opposite of the camera guy. Smaller in stature, sharply dressed. His eyes missed nothing.

"We can do that," Jill assured him. Only, her heart thudded so hard she wasn't sure she could say anything more than the four words she'd just uttered. All she could think about was how she'd once poured everything she had into making it in Hollywood.

There had been few people from Red Oak Falls to ever make it "big" outside of the small community—one person went on to be a senator several decades ago, another had a music career, and a third had been hired by NASA—and none of them had returned to live in their hometown once finding their rightful place in the world. After Jill's birth mother had died, Jill had promised herself that she'd be the fourth to make it onto that list. Only, she'd do it by going into acting. As, *apparently*, had been her father's career of choice.

Janet Sadler had never come off a name for the man who'd gotten her pregnant, but from the first time Jill had asked, Janet had claimed him to be a Hollywood star. Janet had spent a few months in LA the summer after her senior year of high school, and Jill had been born nine months later.

"Aren't you excited to finally get a firsthand look at the house we'll be working on?"

Jill stared across to the other side of the table, hearing Heather's words, but none of them made sense.

"I've driven by both houses every day for a week," Trenton added. Her gaze pinned Jill's as if trying to impart an urgent message. "Just hoping I could catch sight of *anything*."

"As has everyone in town." Heather chuckled. The sound came out slightly forced, but not so much that anyone who didn't know her well would notice. "Pear Street hasn't seen that much excitement since Bobby Gatlin decided to streak down the middle of the road for Halloween three years ago."

Jill continued to say nothing. It was as if her throat had been glued shut.

Patrick circled his index finger in the air, telling her to get to it. And for crying out loud, what *was* her actual problem? She'd had acting classes for years. She *could* do this.

But mixed in with the hope for the company's growth—of not wanting to once again have hope for anything more for herself—was also flat-out terror. Because if anyone *could* screw up this kind of hand-gifted opportunity, Jill knew it would be her.

Trenton's gaze narrowed. "How many times have you been by the houses this week, Jill?"

Under the table, one of them kicked her.

The kick did the trick. Jill jerked, glanced around the room once more, then stared straight at the redheaded cameraman. He'd pulled out from behind the eyepiece again and was giving her a poor-thing look. His lips tugged down at the corners, and that alone was enough to tick Jill off. She didn't want pity. Least of all from some stranger who thought she didn't have the guts to play a role on camera. *Or* to pull it off like the pro she'd once wanted to be.

So with a determination she hadn't managed to dredge up in years, she shoved her emotions aside and mentally cracked her knuckles. She not only *could* do this, she *would* do it. She had to, because this opportunity wasn't only about her. If she screwed this one up, she'd be taking Heather and Trenton down with her.

She returned her attention to the table, and as if she were no longer inhabiting her own body, all nerves simply vanished. Her facial muscles eased, and she gave a teasing shrug. "This week?" She let out a snippet of laughter, recalling from her training what would translate best on screen. "Probably only a hundred times or so during *this* week. But if you're talking about *last* week . . ."

Her words seemed to ease the tension at the table, and the three of them spent the next several minutes discussing potential design ideas for the hundred-year-old houses they had yet to see the interiors of. They also chatted with patrons of the diner after Patrick sent them over. *Texas Dream Home* had a script in place for how they wanted the next few days to go, starting today with "breakfast with the locals." They'd drive to the houses next, where both teams would meet, and then they'd finally get a firsthand look at the condition of the homes.

Design plans and pulling permits would be the priority over the next two days, and on Wednesday, the show's regular hosts, Bob and Debra Raines, would arrive to film the "official" meeting of the teams. Bob and Debra wouldn't return after that until renovations were complete, at which point they'd choose the winner and gift the deeds to the city.

As Jill listened to Bonnie Beckman talk about how she'd taken her Pomeranian for a walk down Pear Street just last week, and how her precious Winston had made it known to her that the Cadillac House would be *the* home to choose, Jill let herself wonder about their competition.

It would be an all-male team, but that was all she knew. Men versus women was how they were billing it.

She'd been hoping to find out more the previous evening. At least what part of Texas the others were coming from. But Patrick had held firm. Teams would meet for the first time in front of the houses today. That way, neither could gain an advantage.

She supposed that made sense.

However, Patrick's gaze had drifted away from hers more times than not during that part of the conversation, and Jill had been thinking about that ever since. She didn't like entering into situations with only partial details, nor did she deal well with being "handled." And though nothing up until now had indicated there was anything off about the setup of the show, she couldn't help but feel she was missing a key part of the picture.

She couldn't help but consider calling a stop to everything, and just walking away.

"So that's when I knew," Bonnie was saying now, her eyes round as she clutched her black patent leather purse in her lap, and Jill realized that she'd missed a huge chunk of the other woman's story.

"What did you know?" Heather asked, her tone as awestruck as Bonnie's.

"That it was my Winsti who brought *Texas Dream Home* to town in the first place. And that allowed them to choose *you*." She placed a hand over her heart. "Because you didn't just build *me* a retreat earlier this year, you built the best vacation home for my baby that any sweet puppy dog could ever ask for."

Jill stared at the other woman. And she ignored the boom mic hovering over them.

Bonnie's dog had communicated to the producers of *Texas Dream Home* by telepathy, telling them not only to come to Red Oak Falls, but to choose Bluebonnet Construction to be on the show? *And* the backyard shed Bluebonnet had built for her had been a . . . *vacation* home? For the *dog*?

None of those things was the vision Jill would have chosen to start viewers off with.

She made a mental note to beg Patrick not to make too big a deal of this.

"We'll be sure to mention that to the parade committee," Heather assured Bonnie. A parade had been in the works for a week now, even though until that morning no one had known who the featured guests would be. "Winston will need to be recognized."

Bonnie beamed at Heather's words—while Jill wanted to reach across the table and strangle her foster sister.

There was no way the producers wouldn't follow up if Bonnie and her dog made it into the parade. And if that happened, Jill could already imagine what their next career rut would be. That of building doggie vacation homes for the rich and eccentric.

But at least if the crew checked out the retreat, they'd have to agree that Winston's vacation home was one of a kind. A cushy bed, a mirror to groom himself in, window seats on either end of the rafters so he could watch outdoor activity. But the crowning glory was the two-chair "throne," where Winston and Bonnie could watch "their shows" together. Bonnie's husband wasn't a fan of the daytime dramas that Winston preferred, thus the real reason for the "vacation home."

Harley appeared at their table then, a decanter of coffee in one hand and to-go cups in the other. This was the third time she'd shown back up since the cameras had started rolling, and finally, the smile gracing the younger girl's lips was that of a confident young woman. "One for the road, ladies?"

"Please." Trenton was the first to answer.

Jill glanced at Patrick, knowing he must have sent Harley over to communicate that things at the diner would soon be wrapping up, and as she did, the cameraman nearest to Patrick began to move. He slid out from behind the producer, repositioning his lens to point toward the café's front door, just as a swooshing sound came from behind Jill. The smell of morning dew and sunshine filtered in to mingle with that of freshly brewed coffee, and as Trenton's outstretched hand closed around her to-go cup, her gaze snagged over Jill's head.

Her jaw stiffened for a split second before she quickly averted her gaze. She brought it back to Harley and forced a bright smile. "Thank you." Trenton's voice was pitched too high.

"What?" Jill mouthed, but Trenton ignored the question.

Heather had caught the interaction, though, and her gaze followed the path Trenton's had taken. And then *her* jaw stiffened.

And with nothing more than that to go on . . . Jill instinctively knew.

Pressure settled in her chest as whispers immediately started around her, and she didn't have to look to confirm that her ex had just walked in.

"What do you give her, five seconds?"

"My money's on three."

"There's a camera on her. I say she breaks a record. I'm going for two minutes."

Jill stared across the table, seeing nothing but the blurred edges of her anger. They were betting on how quickly she would depart from the building now that Cal had entered.

And she *so* wanted to get up and leave.

But instead, she sat there. Because dang it, Cal was a jerk. And she refused to give him the pleasure of a victory today. It wasn't enough that he corralled all the business in town for his own, that he had every last person eating out of his hands thanks to that stupid "Reynolds charm" that he and his uncle were so proud of, *or* that he'd lied straight to her face when he'd talked her into marrying him.

He had to one-up her on this, too?

Oh hell no. This was *their* opportunity. She'd keep the attention on them if she had to strip naked in the middle of the room and climb on top of the—

Trenton's gaze lasered to hers as if reading her thoughts. Trenton and Heather knew Jill had a bit of a hair trigger when her ire was up.

Heck, the entire town knew it, though she *had* done an excellent job of reining it in over the last five years.

But Cal had a way of making that hair trigger exponentially worse.

"Just don't look," Heather muttered behind her coffee cup.

"Trust me. I don't intend to." But she didn't miss when the cameraman moved closer to Cal. She barely kept herself from crushing her own to-go cup in her hand. "Why is he even here?" she gritted out. "And what in the world is he *doing* over there?"

"Just sitting at the counter." Trenton watched through her lashes. "Greeting Loretta."

And no doubt Loretta was greeting him. Probably after losing the top two buttons of her top. She and Cal had a long-term on-again, off-again thing—which was *off* at the moment since he was dating Marci—but from everything Jill had heard, Loretta was determined to turn it back *on*.

Of course, Marci sang a different tune. She was busy running around town, telling anyone who would listen, that she would be the one to finally snag the youngest Reynolds.

High-pitched laughter trilled through the room, followed by a deep rumble that could only come from Calhoun Reynolds, and . . . *dammit* . . . Jill couldn't help it. She turned. Because he should *not* be in—

He was staring at her.

He sat on a stool at the far end of the counter, his dark hair slightly mussed by the spring winds, and the scruff of his beard shadowing his face in a way that only accentuated the strong line of his jaw. Loretta batted her eyelashes at him while he carried on a seemingly normal conversation . . . but the deep-brown depths Jill had done her best to avoid since returning to Red Oak Falls were focused on her.

The camera covering Jill moved in tighter.

"Let's just go," Trenton whispered behind Jill.

But instead of taking the advice of her youngest foster sister, Jill took in the rest of the dining room. Because she was stubborn like that. Her eyes roamed over women, men, even all the babies who would normally have already been dropped off at day care by that time of day. And she noted that every last one of them was looking from her to Cal.

And she knew that every last one of them was fully aware that she and Cal didn't speak. Ever.

That she and Cal had once run off to Vegas to get married.

And that Cal had returned—*alone*—after only one day.

With cameras now positioned on both her and her ex, the crowd seemed to be hovering on the edge, waiting to see what would happen next. As if wondering if Cal's appearance in the café was by chance—or if her past with him would somehow be worked into the show.

And then Jill's stomach sank. She faced the lens that was now practically in her face, imagining she could see through the layers of glass to the blue eyes on the opposite side. Then she slowly turned her head to seek out Patrick. But as had happened the night before, the producer's gaze didn't quite meet her own. And Jill finally had a full understanding of the situation.

Texas Dream Home hadn't merely wanted Bluebonnet Construction for the novelty of them being an all-female crew. Or because they were foster sisters who'd been thrown together in the worst of circumstances. They'd also unearthed Jill's marriage. As well as her quickie divorce. And they were looking for drama.

She turned an accusing stare on Cal. What a sellout. That was why the focus of the show would be on *her*. Had he made them pay him to show up at the diner today?

Or maybe he had done it for free. Because he was such a "good guy."

And just *what* was he supposed to do now that he was there?

The bastard. He'd been out to ruin her since she'd come back home. The two of them might never speak, yet somehow, he was always there. Putting in bids on every renovation job Bluebonnet tried to get. Charming the ever-loving pants off anyone who so much as *considered* giving them their business.

So what was his plan now? To pop up wherever she happened to be for the next six weeks, simply to keep her off balance?

Or would he take it a step further? Was he there to make her lose her temper?

She pressed her lips together at that thought. If they'd brought him in to make her lose her temper, that meant the producers were also aware of her past anger issues. *And* that they intended to exploit them.

A low growl began in the back of her throat. What would they do next? Have Cal show up on the set?

Her stomach pitched. This whole thing was nothing but a joke to them.

Just as it had been in Hollywood, little was as it seemed. Everything was about taking. Using. It was "what can *you* do for *me*?" She'd known something had been off about the setup for the show. She should have listened to her gut. *If it walks like a skunk and smells like a skunk . . .*

She glared at Cal. And he *definitely* had a stench about him.

His returning look gave nothing away, his features masked with stoicism. But at that point, she wasn't looking for anything from him. The show clearly knew the facts. And for the sake of entertaining television, they couldn't pass up the opportunity to work juicy gossip like her and Cal's past into the episodes. She wouldn't pass it up, either, if she were producing the show. Especially when that juiciness was all twisted up with another local contractor—

Her mouth went dry before she could finish the thought. Surely they hadn't . . .

She jerked her gaze back to Patrick, but this time, the man didn't even pretend she was still in the same room. He'd turned his back to her.

They *had*.

Bile rose to the back of her throat.

She fought the urge to put her hands over her mouth, clenching them in her lap instead. *Damn him.* He had no right. Cal wasn't just a plant to get under her skin. *He* was their competition.

She stood then, without another word or a backward glance to anyone, and she walked straight out of the building. Except, she didn't quite make it out as poised as she would have liked. Because right before slipping into the bright morning sunshine, she kicked the crap out of two empty chairs.

Chapter Three

"Be a lady. You are from Texas, after all. But when the occasion arises to kick some rear, never show mercy."

—Blu Johnson, life lesson #97

Trenton's four-door Titan sped down Highway 71—a camera crew following closely behind—as Jill sat stewing in the middle of the front seat. Over the last week, she'd heard time and again that *Texas Dream Home* chose *one* team from the community where the houses were to be renovated. Not two. The producers had even hinted at this same thing when she'd first talked to them.

And Bluebonnet Construction was the *one*!

Yet clearly, that wasn't always the case.

She growled under her breath as she had at the diner. She couldn't believe she'd been played like that.

It'll put your business on the map, Jill.

You'll never want for anything again.

Both those things had been said to her before she'd agreed to sign the contract. Though Heather, Trenton, and Aunt Blu had already convinced her to jump in with both feet, she'd requested a phone call before putting pen to paper. She'd wanted to talk specifics.

The producers she'd spoken with had answered all her questions, saying what Jill needed to hear, and in all honesty, everything had come across as aboveboard during that call. They'd even been up front about their intentions to use Jill's, Heather's, and Trenton's backgrounds as personal interest stories. The unusualness of the three of them having all been orphaned late in their childhoods would show their connection, while *how* they'd come to arrive at Bluebonnet Farms would endear them to viewers.

Jill had expected that. Their years in foster care would have to be part of the story. It was how they'd met. Why they'd ended up starting a company together. Just as Aunt Blu would eventually be interviewed, as well. Viewers would find it heartwarming to know that out of such tragedy, happy endings could be found. And she was prepared for all of that.

Yet for some reason, she had not been prepared for Cal. At all. Once they'd been chosen to be on the show, Cal hadn't crossed her mind.

It had crossed theirs, though. In a big way. But what she wanted to know now was if they'd uncovered her past all on their own, or if Cal had gone to them. Had he somehow found out about Aunt Blu entering them into the competition and reached out to the show? He and Aunt Blu used to be close. And Jill knew they stopped to chat any time they saw each other in town.

But if he *had* done that, then why? Did he hate her that much?

She hated *him* that much. But still . . . she had a right to that hate. Because *he'd been the one to leave!*

She fought the urge to growl again. She and Cal had both been too hotheaded back then, but he'd simply refused to see reason that morning. It had to be his way or no way. No delays. No consideration of her wants. What had made it even worse, though, was how he'd been unwilling to believe in her. Even for a second. No matter how much she'd begged.

He'd offered only ridicule—and then he'd walked away.

She'd wanted to kill him.

"We've got to at least go to the houses," Trenton said. Her eyes remained on the road, her hands at ten and two, while Heather had an arm wrapped around Jill's shoulders. Heather patted Jill's thigh as Trenton's eyes flicked from the road to the rearview mirror.

"I can't believe they brought your marriage into this," Heather said, attempting to soothe.

Heather was the comforter, but all three of them fully understood that it was so much more than bringing her marriage into this. None of them had openly stated as much, though. Yet. They'd simply driven. And fumed.

Heather patted Jill's leg again.

And Heather had soothed.

"It's Aunt Blu," Trenton said as her phone rang through the truck's speakers.

"Don't answer it." Trenton's phone had rung three times in the fifteen minutes since they'd driven away, all calls coming from Blu. No doubt someone had been dialing Blu's number at the same time as Jill had been exiting the café.

Trenton glanced in her rearview again. "Maybe we should just"— she cut a look at Jill—"they're still following us, Jilly."

"And likely recording us," Heather added softly.

Jill squeezed her eyes shut. "Fine," she forced out. "Just go. You're right. They're not going to stop, and I'm doing nothing but making us look like idiots. Let's just go and get it over with."

Only, she had no idea what she was supposed to do once they got there.

"We didn't say you were making us look like idiots," Heather argued half-heartedly.

Trenton said nothing.

Jill kept her eyes closed. She couldn't go through with the show now, could she? How could she possibly hold it together if she had to deal with Cal for the next six weeks?

Her chest ached. She'd truly been excited about doing this.

Heather's phone rang then, deep in the shoulder bag that had dropped to the floor of the truck, and Heather reached down for it at the same time that Trenton made a left and headed back toward Pear Street. Though they'd been driving since leaving the café, it had mostly been in a large loop. They weren't far away from the houses.

"Tell her we'll be there soon," Jill muttered. She hated letting Blu down.

Except, the look that flashed through Heather's eyes indicated that it wasn't their foster mother on the phone.

She answered anyway.

Jill couldn't hear the person on the other end, but Heather's eyes flicked to Jill as she listened. Her throat moved up and down with a swallow. Then she nodded, closed her eyes, and nodded again.

"Thank you," Heather whispered. "I'll let her know."

She hung up as Trenton hit Pear Street, and the first thing Jill saw was Cal's black four-wheel-drive truck.

"That was him on the phone." Jill didn't bother phrasing it as a question.

"Uh-huh."

Jill eyed the empty driver's seat of the truck before scanning the remaining vehicles and people milling about on the closed-off street. There was no sign of Cal. "What did he want?"

Heather didn't immediately answer.

Trenton pulled to a stop twenty yards behind Cal's truck, muttering under her breath about how she couldn't believe they'd done this to them, but Jill ignored her. Her only concern at the moment was what Heather had to say. But when Heather continued her silence, Jill turned to her, finding her foster sister's usually serene eyes riddled with anxiety.

"What did he want?" Jill repeated. She was hanging on by a mere thread.

"He wanted to . . ." Heather sounded as miserable as Jill felt. "He snuck off to call us. He wanted to make sure you understood that *he* is our competition—"

Jill grunted in disgust.

"And he said that he"—Heather swallowed—"feels bad for blindsiding you like that."

"Then why did he do it?" Trenton bit out. Her tone announced that her anger was a close second behind Jill's.

"He didn't say *why* he did it," Heather continued with a grimace, "but he said that once he got in the café and . . . saw your face . . . that he regretted it."

Hurt battled with anger. Jill had known he'd had to be involved.

"He apologized?" Heather made the sentence sound like a question.

Jill didn't bother pointing out that his apology wasn't accepted.

"He also offered to tell them that filming would have to be delayed." Heather licked her lips. "Whatever we need him to say, he'll do it. Whatever *you* need to happen so that you don't walk into the upcoming meet and greet mentally unprepared." She scrunched up her face and finished with reluctance. "After the way you left the diner, he's concerned that you might lose your . . . *shit*. On camera."

Jill's eyebrows shot up. "My shit?" The audacity of the man. "Cal is worried about *me*? After *he* set me up?" She didn't buy it for a second. "If he's that concerned, why do it to begin with? Why *go* to them with the idea?"

"But he didn't." Heather's voice came out with urgency, and Jill swore it also carried a positive lilt.

Jill just stared at her.

"He said *they* came after him," Heather explained. "That he didn't even apply to be on the show. He didn't even know anything about the competition until they sought him out."

Jill blinked. "And I'm supposed to believe that?"

Not that it would make it a lot better. He'd still agreed. He'd still kept it hidden from her.

Heather nodded, the light in her eyes now matching the positive spin still heavy in her voice. "That's what he said. And they made him sign a contract saying that he wouldn't tell anyone. That he wouldn't tell *you*."

"And you believe him?"

"I don't," Trenton grumbled from the other side of the truck.

"I . . ." Heather began, but when Jill glared at her, she let her words trail off.

Heather and Trenton had always had her back when it came to Cal leaving her the way he had. Or so they'd said. But Heather and her damned soft spot.

Jill never knew when it would rear its head at the wrong time.

"I'm just saying . . ." Heather tried again, but her words once again trickled to a stop.

"You're saying what?" Jill's voice was hard. Her anger ran deep. "That I shouldn't be mad about this? That since he supposedly didn't go to *them*—and because he's now apologized *so sincerely*—then I should just forgive him for being a part of it? Is that what you're telling me, Heather?" she continued, her words now coming out in a heated rush. "Well, hell. Maybe I should also swallow my pride and show how *excited* I am to be facing my lying jerk of an ex-husband. Would that make you happy, too?"

"I'm not saying any of those things," Heather argued.

"Then what *are* you saying?" Jill yelled.

"The cameras are still watching us." Trenton spoke in a rapid clip of words, and Jill whipped her gaze to her other foster sister. Heather's hand touched Jill's thigh once again, and as if doused with a bucket of ice water, Jill's fury flagged. Her hands trembled. She knew it wasn't fair to take her anger out on Heather.

She also knew that Heather truly did have her back. Always.

Even if she *might* believe that Cal wasn't entirely the brand of evil Jill knew him to be.

"What am I supposed to do?" Jill whispered to both of them. She covered her mouth as she spoke, just in case the cameras had zoomed in that far. She did *not* want to face Cal. Not in any sort of situation. She'd sworn to herself that she'd never so much as speak to him again, and she intended to keep that promise.

She also didn't want to be on the other end of competing with him, because truth be told, there had to be a reason he won all the decent jobs in town. Other than just *their* bad luck.

Maybe he really was that much better than they were. He had years more experience, and he'd already been incredibly skilled as a teen. Jill had seen it firsthand when he'd worked at the farm for Aunt Blu.

But it was just as possible that Bluebonnet Construction lost out on all those contracts because *they* weren't good enough. Or more likely, because everyone in town still worried about *her* and her "anger issues." That thought had been in the back of her mind since day one of opening their doors, even though neither she, Heather, nor Trenton had ever suggested it.

"They're looking for drama," Jill told her foster sisters now. She had to get herself under control. She'd been through worse than this. "It's what I'd do if I were creating the show. Drama makes for good TV."

Trenton swallowed. "So it'll up the ratings, right?" Her voice came out thin and tight as she tried to put a positive spin on things. "More viewers. More chances to build the business."

"But we don't have to give them what they're after," Heather insisted. She turned Jill's face to hers, and the determination in her eyes almost made it through to Jill. "We're very good at what we do," Heather said. "You know that. We all know that. And we *can* win this competition. We can also make it a great show, even without the drama they're looking for."

"And what if we aren't personable enough to pull it off *without* the drama?" Jill asked.

What if I can't control my temper when I'm around him? was what she really wanted to ask, but she couldn't bring herself to do it. She didn't want to let her foster sisters down.

"Then they'll flash the 'Reynolds charm' on camera enough to make sure they still capture the viewers," Trenton answered.

When Jill turned back to her, Trenton glanced down at her hands. She didn't have to voice her additional thoughts for Jill to follow along with them. The Reynolds charm would add more to the show than the three of them ever could. They were just orphans who'd had the unfortunate circumstances that allowed them to grow up together.

The viewers would fall in love with Cal well before the end of the first episode, and no one would even know who the Bluebonnets were.

"We're here for you," Heather said from the other side of the truck. "We'll do whatever you say. We'll walk if that's what you need us to do."

"Lawyers and legal contracts be damned," Trenton added under her breath.

Heather reached over and pinched Trenton on the ear.

"Ouch." Trenton smacked Heather's hand away. "Stop it."

"You stop it. We're supporting Jill in this."

"I didn't say we weren't supporting her." Trenton glared at Heather before turning a slightly softened gaze back to Jill. Her chin remained thrust forward. "Of course we're supporting you, Jilly. You know that. I'll walk, too. Me, you, and Heather. We're The Three. You just say the word." Her glare fired back to Heather. "But I was *just* pointing out the logistics of the situation."

The phone began ringing through Trenton's speakers again. Aunt Blu. No one answered it.

"We'll figure it out," Heather said calmly. She took a deep breath, and Jill could tell she was mentally steeling herself to go into battle.

Heather liked to pretend she was tough, but on the inside, she was as soft as they came.

Trenton's mouth opened again, but Jill interjected. "We're not walking."

Trenton slammed her mouth shut.

And at that precise moment, Cal Reynolds decided to enter the picture. He turned the corner of the sidewalk on the opposite end of the street, and his gaze landed on Trenton's truck. He stopped dead in his tracks.

"We're not walking." Jill forced the words out again.

Damned if she'd let her ex steal her one opportunity at proving herself. She dug deep into her acting skills, reminding herself that she absolutely could do this. It would just be a matter of being "Jessica Grant" for the next six weeks instead of Jill Sadler.

"And I won't be losing my shit for anyone," she added, her voice now a picture of calm. "Especially not for a man whose only purpose in the coming weeks is being a backdrop to showcase our skills."

This was not only their chance to prove themselves as a viable construction company, but also *her* opportunity to finally put Cal in his place. Time to show the man he was nothing to her.

She pasted a cheery smile on her face then, looking for all the world as if she had not one *care* in the world, and took in Trenton and Heather one by one. "Let's do this, ladies." She nodded toward Trenton's door handle. "We have a house to choose. And we have a house full of men to show who the better team is."

Trenton nodded cautiously, and as she reached for the driver's door, Heather spoke from Jill's other side. "Are we taking the dog's advice?"

Jill froze. "The dog?"

She turned back.

"Bonnie Beckman's dog," Heather explained. "He barked at the Cadillac House while out on their walk last week, remember? And he never barks."

Jill stared at the woman who sat on the seat next to her. Auburn hair swept up into the perfect sloppy bun, a trendy tunic sweater and leggings, and a wide belt that should be lethal the way it accentuated her curves.

Nothing about her indicated that she'd lost her mind.

"Do you *want* to take the advice of a dog?" Jill asked.

"I'm just saying . . . did you ever once hear him bark while we were over there building that retreat?"

"And Bonnie *has* made predictions in the past that came true," Trenton added.

Jill blinked. It was as if she'd fallen down a rabbit hole.

She slowly turned back to Trenton. Had they both lost their minds? "You're the sensible one," she told her youngest foster sister.

"I know. But you weren't paying attention when Bonnie told her story this morning. The dog went absolutely nuts in front of that house. And *only* in front of that house."

"Probably because he sensed a ghost!"

The Cadillac House had gotten its name due to Pastor Wainwright once driving his Cadillac through the front door. The story was that he'd returned early from a business trip to discover the silhouette of his wife and another man in the upstairs window. And they *hadn't* been up there talking. Though he'd denied to his death that he'd done it on purpose—or that there'd even been a man in the house with his wife—Mr. Wainwright had crashed through the front of the house in anger. In the ensuing chaos, the unnamed other man slipped out the back door and was never heard from again.

Some years later, Mrs. Wainwright died alone in that very room, and the rumor was that her spirit had never left. It remained to this day, waiting for her lover to come back to her.

Heather loved that story.

"I don't even know what to say to you two." Jill shook her head in confusion. "We talked about this already. We decided on the Bono House."

The Bono House had once been owned by a huge fan of Bono, of the '80s band U2, and the owner spent a fortune decorating it with U2 memorabilia. It had stayed like that through several years of rentals.

Though both houses had been built around the same time, and both were essentially the same style and size, Bono had been renovated several times over the years, while Cadillac had only gone through upgrades when the front of the house had needed to be reconstructed. Chances were good that Cadillac would have more hidden issues. No matter what some dog implied.

"Why would we change our minds now?" Jill asked.

Someone tapped on Trenton's window before either of them could answer, and Jill looked up to find Patrick smiling in at them. The redheaded cameraman stood to his left.

"Christ," she muttered.

"Time to put on our game faces," Heather said, and Trenton added, "But first we vote."

Jill had no time to object before the other two piped in, both saying "Cadillac" at the same time.

Jill just stared at them. She was *not* voting for the ghost house.

"Cadillac, it is," Trenton mumbled, dropping her gaze from Jill's.

The three of them climbed from the front seat of the truck then, all standing tall and not acting in the least as if they were walking straight into the firing line. But then Jill mentally faltered. Because she realized they were all still wearing their mics. And they'd all been hot the entire time.

Chapter Four

"Nothing worthwhile will come from screaming. At least not outwardly."

—Blu Johnson, life lesson #23

Cal stood at the red Formica countertop of the Cadillac House late Wednesday afternoon, sketching a small wine fridge onto the approved plans. Then he erased the lines and moved the fridge to another section of the soon-to-be-enlarged kitchen. He gave a quick nod. It would barely take away any usable space if put there.

He glanced up as Pete Logan entered the room. Pete had been working for him since Cal took over the business six years before, but they'd known each other long before that. They'd played on the high school basketball team together, and in the years since, their friendship had grown.

"You hear back on that final permit?" Cal asked.

Pete waved a piece of paper in the air. "Just came from the courthouse."

"Good deal." The city had come through, rushing all approvals as they'd promised.

Cal tossed a glance out the kitchen window, wondering if Jill had gotten hers, too. He had a direct line of sight into the Bono House living room, but there was no sign of her. He knew she was over there, though. Her pickup had been sitting in the driveway since he'd arrived early that morning, and every light in the house remained on.

Heather and Trenton were likely still on-site, as well. Like he and Pete, the three of them would have spent the last few days buried in details to ensure that demo could start first thing the following morning.

Along with lining up permits and inspections, and working out specifics for a very tight budget, he and Pete had also created a schedule for everyone on We Nail It's crew who wanted to be a part of the work at the house. Men would be rotated out on a weekly basis, and though it would add a layer of difficulty to keeping things running seamlessly, Cal knew his men could handle it. He had a good team.

That would be the tip of the iceberg with the craziness of the upcoming weeks, though. Because as Cal had discovered today, filming a show about a renovation job was way more than simply doing the renovation job. By the time Cal had arrived that morning, Patrick and his crew had already been on-site wiring cameras and lighting throughout both houses. Interview stations had been prepared, both inside the homes and out, catering had pitched a tent and filled it with food, and no less than three producers had spent time "coaching" him for when the cameras started rolling.

Then Bob and Debra Raines had arrived. And that's when the reality of filming a reality show had truly set in.

Cal hung his head in exhaustion, rubbing at the tight muscles in the back of his neck, and realized that Pete had left the room. He could hear footsteps coming from the second floor as Pete made a final sweep of the house, and Cal reminded himself to give his best foreman a hefty raise before the six weeks were up. Pete would be splitting his time between the Cadillac House and all the other jobs currently on their roster, and Cal knew the other man had to already be as bone tired as he was.

But then, Pete didn't have quite the same mental contortions going on as Cal.

He looked out the window again. Jill had been screwing with his mind since the second she, Heather, and Trenton had stepped out of the truck two days before. By sending him to the café, Patrick had set up Jill to arrive at the houses ready to blow a gasket. Cal had understood that. He'd gone along with it. And then he'd seen the look on Jill's face when she'd connected all the dots. He might be angry with her, but he *hadn't* wanted her to make a fool of herself on camera. So he'd called Heather.

There had been no return call requesting a delay in filming, though. There had been nothing from them. Just three confident women climbing from the cab of the truck, all walking tall and looking as if they planned to kick anyone's butt who got in their way.

Cal hadn't been able to take his eyes off Jill for a second. She'd surprised him with her calmness. With her control. Of course, she hadn't exactly followed Patrick's plans for a meet and greet in the middle of the street, either. Instead, she'd acknowledged to Patrick that she could see who her competition was, and that Bluebonnet Construction was *thrilled* to be going up against such a talented competitor. They couldn't wait to have their skills gauged against his.

Cal had overheard all of this from a safe distance, of course, due to the death stare she'd fired when he'd gotten within fifty feet of her.

Once Jill had finished laying out how *she'd* seen the day going, Patrick had struggled for an excuse to do any differently. He couldn't very well admit that the entire point of putting them face-to-face right off the bat had been to capture her losing her cool, so the man had conceded, and they'd gotten down to the business of choosing houses.

A coin toss had happened, Cal had won, and they'd finally scored their first glimpses of the houses' interiors. And against his better judgment, he'd ended up choosing the exact house that he *hadn't* wanted.

He sighed with frustration. He'd picked the home that nearby residents swore housed a ghost. The home hadn't been worked on in fifty years—therefore, he knew his contingency fund, as well as his timeline, would be on shaky ground—yet he'd chosen that house anyway. And he'd chosen it *only* to keep Jill from getting it. Because he'd seen the interest on her face.

That lapse in judgment had *not* set the tone of the competition the way he'd hoped. Nor had his inability to understand this "new" Jill. Since returning to Red Oak Falls, Jill had either changed course whenever she'd seen him, or turned her head as they passed. And if neither of those were options . . . she'd launched mental daggers via her eyes. She'd hid her hatred of him from no one.

Yet during the last three days—though never actually saying anything nonscripted directly to him—she'd been pleasant, cute, and downright funny every time they'd had to be in the same vicinity together. And damned if it hadn't been hot to watch. As hot as when she lost her temper. Which she hadn't done once since arriving on set.

Not during the multiple times Patrick had tried to trick her into sharing a camera with Cal, nor during the official meeting of the teams after Bob and Debra had arrived, the filmed walk-throughs, or the redoing of the coin toss. Throughout all of it, Jill had been nothing but charming. She'd even had Bob and Debra rolling with laughter on several occasions. All while practically glowing every single time a camera had turned her way.

It had all made Cal want to test her. To poke at her just to see if he could get her going.

Because, first . . . *he* was the one who was supposed to be charming on this set. He had it in his blood, after all. That was *his* role to play.

But also, if he wasn't positive that Jill still hated his guts, he'd almost swear she didn't. She'd been that convincing.

He returned his attention to the reno plans, trying his best to shove his ex from his mind. He'd spent far too much time thinking about Jill over the years, and it should have stopped a hell of a long time ago. He pulled out the kitchen design once more and lined it up with the drawings of the dining room and living space. They intended to knock down the interior walls running between the three rooms, so they'd need to get going on that first thing. Patrick's team would be back to film the demo tomorrow, and along with capturing the action on camera, they wanted to start one-on-ones with the talent.

Cal looked out the window again. He and Jill were part of that talent. And he found himself wondering how long she could keep up her charade. Or if he should do something to try to crack it.

He leaned forward to see more of the other house and finally caught sight of her coming in the back door. Her hair, as usual, was the first thing he noticed. He'd never crossed paths with another human being whose hair had the same inky blackness as Jill's.

He let his gaze scan over her body as she passed in front of the dining room windows. Not one thing about her had changed over the years.

"Need me to do anything else before I go?"

Cal jumped as if Pete had stabbed him. He hadn't heard Pete return from upstairs.

Then, when he realized that Pete stood at the back door instead of on the other side of the room, he glanced behind him to peer through the kitchen's opening, toward the front of the house. How had he missed Pete coming back downstairs?

"We're good." Cal returned his attention to his friend. Clearly, he's been too engrossed in thoughts of Jill to pay attention. He put his back to the window. "I plan to get out of here myself soon."

Pete nodded, then he angled his head toward the window behind Cal. "Do I need to cover that up? I can bring over a piece of cardboard."

Pete had been around when Cal returned alone from Vegas. He was the only one Cal had ever talked to about his and Jill's breakup, and the months that followed it had been pretty rough.

"No." Cal offered no other words.

"She's a cool one."

Cal lifted a shoulder. "I can be just as cool."

Pete's brows rose before he crossed to stand shoulder-to-shoulder with Cal. He peered through the glass that looked out over Jill's house, while Cal remained stoically facing the other direction.

"Not hard on the eyes, either," Pete mused. "Impressive the way she's been a full participant during filming so far . . . yet has managed to never once acknowledge your existence."

"Wouldn't expect anything different."

The truth was, though, that Cal had once expected a heck of a lot different. From both of them. And it pissed him the hell off the way she continued to ignore him after all this time.

Pete finally turned from the window, and as he mimicked Cal's stance by leaning against the sink, he shot Cal a hard look. "Five and a half more weeks. Keep your head in the game."

"My head's always in the game."

Pete nodded. "No need for me to be concerned, then." He walked out of the room, and as the front door closed on the opposite side of the house, Cal let out a ragged breath.

Then he turned, and once again looked out the kitchen window.

~

Music from an '80s hair band blasted from the portable speakers sitting in the front room, echoing throughout both floors of the house. Trenton had brought the speakers over earlier that day in preparation for demo the following morning, and Jill had located an '80s station on her phone and plugged it in. The music choice seemed fitting, given that they were working on the Bono House. She'd never been a big '80s music buff, but the almost incomprehensible screeching filling her head was exactly what she needed.

She'd convinced Heather and Trenton to leave about thirty minutes before, swearing she wouldn't be far behind them, then she'd checked to make sure the lights were off at the house next door. She was alone.

And there was one thing she had to do before she could go home.

She settled a pair of goggles over her eyes and twisted her hair up behind her head, then she picked up the sledgehammer she'd brought in from her truck. She tested the weight of the tool in the palm of her other hand as she eyed the first wall she intended to take down. It wasn't that she wanted to get a head start on Cal by staying late, she just had pent-up frustration she needed to shed. Frustration that came from spending the last three days acting.

Or, at least, acting like she didn't mind being around Cal.

She rolled her shoulders, loosening up her too-tight muscles, and angled her head from side to side to stretch out her neck. She could use a good massage. But more than that, what she really wanted was to rear back and treat the sledgehammer as if it were a baseball bat.

She dropped her gaze to the tool gripped in both hands. Cal had been the one to teach her this trick.

Then she grunted as she pulled back and swung. The head of the sledgehammer splintered slats between two studs, instantly showering the small kitchen with chaos, and she retracted her arms and swung again.

Damn man.

She brought the sledgehammer up over her shoulders and chopped down with a vertical strike. The section of wall she connected with shattered as if a small bomb had gone off inside it.

She didn't want to *think* about Cal. Or be *near* Cal.

The hammer sliced through the air once more, this time connecting with the side of the lower cabinets. They splintered, as well, and the case of bottled water that had been sitting on top dropped to the floor.

And she certainly didn't want to be thinking about the day that Cal Reynolds had first handed her a sledgehammer and told her to go to town.

She swiped loose strands of hair out of her eyes and jabbed forward with the head of the tool, pounding the weight of it over and over into another section of the wall until there was nothing left but studs.

Cal should *not* be in her life these days. He'd given up that right. And she should not have to worry about being caught on a stupid camera staring at him!

She took another swing at the cabinets.

Stupid cameras. She'd played the part they'd expected with Bob and Debra today, and she'd done an excellent job. She'd played the part for the last three days! And throughout it all, she'd been damn near perfect. However, every single time she'd so much as peeked next door—just to see if she could get a read on how things were going—she'd found at least one of the cameramen turned her way.

"They need to leave me alone!" she shouted as she wound up and took another swing. The redheaded cameraman's name was Len. She'd learned that not long after getting into the house Monday morning and discovering that it was his job to stay on *her*.

Trenton and Heather liked Len. They thought he was a big teddy bear.

"Len needs a new hobby!" She swung again. That time taking out the pantry door.

"And to trim his stupid beard!"

After slamming the head of the sledgehammer into the last unmarred surface scheduled to come down in the room, she left the tool wedged in the wall, and bent over at the waist. With hands on her knees, she fought to catch her breath, her panting so loud that it temporarily blocked the music coming from the front of the house. Who needed a gym when they could have a sledgehammer and a couple of walls to tear down?

She scrubbed the back of her hand at the sweat collecting along her hairline and hung her arms and head toward the floor. Gravity pulled at her muscles, stretching them out, and when she once again straightened, she discovered that the door leading out the back of the house now stood open.

And that Cal Reynolds stood just on the other side of it.

"I see you still remember how to swing a sledgehammer," he said.

Anger scorched her insides. "Get out of my house." She pointed to the backyard.

He only crossed his arms and leaned against the doorframe.

"I'm not kidding." She would have swung the sledgehammer again, but her shoulder muscles pleaded for a break.

"And it's good to see you actually speaking to me again."

She narrowed her eyes. "I am *not* speaking to you."

"Could have fooled me." He lifted one booted foot onto the half step leading into the house. "Just like you have everyone else around here fooled. They think your little temper tantrum at the diner Monday morning was a fluke. That you're nothing more than cute and charming little Jilly-Bean Sadler."

"Do not call me Jilly-Bean," she growled. She wanted to take the sledgehammer and pound it into his smug face, but since that would likely only get her thrown in jail, she grabbed it and went for one more swing instead. Only, in her disgruntled state, she connected with the wrong wall. She took out a chunk of an outer wall, punching a hole clear through to expose the pipe running the length of it—as well as the yard on the other side.

"Be careful there, Jilly-Bean. Wouldn't want you creating more work for yourself."

She whirled and jabbed a finger in Cal's direction. "You don't get to call me Jilly-Bean ever again. Or Jilly. Or Jill, for that matter. You don't get to call me at all."

She shoved her goggles to the top of her head as the music in the other room switched, the new song starting off with a heavy bass thumping in the background, and she worked to calm herself down. Nothing worthwhile would come from screaming at the man she hated most in the world. "This is not *me* speaking to *you*," she began in a strained, but much more sedate voice. "This is a contractor informing a trespasser that if he doesn't get out of the house she's renovating, then he'll be answering to the police."

She once again pointed to the backyard.

"Now leave."

He didn't leave, but he did slide his foot back down beside his other one. The laughter also disappeared from his eyes. He held up both palms. "I just came over to see if we could call a truce."

"I don't do truces."

"Come on, Jill." He tilted his head. "It's been almost twelve years. I'll admit that I handled things poorly back then. Very poorly. In fact, I've wanted to say that to you for a long time. I'm sorry about the way things went down."

"But you're not sorry that they went down to begin with?" she asked. Not that she expected him to be.

Or that she cared one way or the other.

"I'm sorry I didn't handle things in a more grown-up fashion," he clarified, and if she hadn't known better, she'd have thought he actually meant the words. "I know my actions hurt you, and for that I do apologize. Sincerely."

She didn't want his apology.

The man had ripped her apart by doing the only thing she'd ever asked that he not do. That he'd *sworn* he would never do. So no, she didn't want his apology. Not now. Not ever.

Not so long as she was drawing breath.

Yet as she stood there looking at him, for some reason, it felt as if a tiny portion of the anger she'd been so proudly hauling around for the last twelve years was trying its hardest to leak out. But not in a bad way. It was as if a pin had pricked her outer shell, and she could either plug it to keep her anger securely bottled tight . . . or she could allow the hole to be an escape hatch. Slowly releasing steam until there was nothing left. She wanted to ask if he'd told Heather the truth. Had he really not been the one to tell *Texas Dream Home* about them?

If not, he'd still jumped at the chance.

He didn't need this opportunity the way she did, and he knew it. He was doing this purely to hurt her. Because knowing she'd failed in Hollywood clearly wasn't enough.

She shook her head as if he'd asked *her* a question. The decisions he made were his alone. She neither wanted nor needed to know the reasons behind them. But she also found herself unable to immediately repeat her demand that he go. Instead, she dropped the sledgehammer to the floor and grabbed a bottle of water from where it had rolled across the room.

Unscrewing the cap, she drank the entire bottle, and when she finished she decided to say one thing to him before she kicked him out. Because it was important to her.

"You didn't have to make that offer."

When he only shot her a questioning look, she added, "In the truck Monday. To get them to delay filming."

She couldn't have him thinking his gesture had mattered.

"Oh." He gave a casual nod. "I guess not." Then some of his smugness returned. "Should have known you wouldn't need any help from me."

"I don't. But I also have more sense than to lose my shit on camera."

"Is that so?"

She braced herself, thinking he'd bring up the two chairs she'd sent flying across the linoleum as she'd left the café, but he surprised her by looking around at the damage she'd done tonight instead. At the dust particles floating through the air. The room looked like a war zone.

Then he brought his gaze back to hers. "Yet wouldn't you call what you've just done a hefty dose of that very thing?"

"And do you see any cameras following me around at this very moment?"

When his gaze lifted to the far corner of the room, Jill had the violent urge to throw up. She'd completely forgotten about the cameras that had been installed "for those moments when the crew wasn't around."

Son of a—

"What do you think, Jilly-Bean?" Cal taunted. He brought his dark gaze back to hers, laughter dancing in it. "Think they're recording right now?"

"It doesn't matter if they are."

He laughed out loud at her lie, and he laughed so loud and so long that his voice boomed right over the guitars shredding in the other room. As it continued, Jill found herself once again having the desire to pound the sledgehammer into his face. So much for that escape hatch.

"Tell me another one," Cal said when he finally got himself under control. "No need to stop now. You've been entertaining me all week with your 'acting' skills."

He air quoted the one word that he knew would get under her skin the most, and that was the final straw. Dammit, even after all this time, the man could slice her to the core. She marched across the room, stopping only when she got within two feet of him.

"My *shit* is fully intact, Calhoun Reynolds. Now and always. No need for you to worry." She motioned to the mess around her. "What you see here is simply Bluebonnet Construction getting a jump on the competition. A competitor they're going to grind into the ground. So you run along now." She waggled her fingers at him. "Go find someone else to play your games with, because sweetheart, it is *not* going to be me."

She slammed the glass-paneled door in his face, and when he didn't immediately turn away, she shot him the bird.

He only smiled. And danged if her pulse didn't try to flutter at that. The stupid man and his stupid charm.

"Go away," she mouthed, and in return he winked.

Then he blew her a kiss.

She gaped. But before she could pick her jaw up off the floor and figure out how to retaliate, he'd disappeared into the night.

Chapter Five

"Always tell the truth. But only if you tell anything at all."

—Blu Johnson, life lesson #75

"I seriously have to get back into lifting weights." Jill ground the words out as she hefted the blue ceramic sink above her shoulders and sent it sailing over the side of the metal dumpster. It clanged against the wall before being muffled in the pile of flooring that had already been tossed in. She, Heather, and Trenton were working hard on cleaning up the debris that had been removed from the house, determined to have a clean slate by the end of the day.

"I call uncle," Heather huffed out. Her usually stylish hair was a matted mess of sweat and dust, and her jeans and T-shirt were as grimy as Jill's and Trenton's.

"You're too soft," Trenton informed her. Trenton scooped up a pile of subway tiles and tossed them into the bin.

"Someone in this group has to be soft," Heather argued.

It wasn't that Heather wasn't into the physical-labor side of the job, but she was better suited for the beautification of it. She typically designed the interiors, as well as made final decisions with the landscapers. Those were the activities she enjoyed most.

"And someone has to get the job done," Trenton lobbed back. Another shovelful of tile clattered off the walls of the dumpster.

"I'm siding with Heather on this one." Jill glanced at her watch as she caught her breath. "We need a break. We've been going since before daylight."

"*And* we forgot to eat lunch," Heather added.

Trenton stopped midmotion, shovel angled down for another scoop, and put a hand to her stomach. It responded with a loud rumble. "How did we forget to eat lunch?"

Trenton had a healthy appetite, with a metabolism to match.

"We worked through while everyone else took a break, remember? No time to waste."

At the mention of the other ladies working with them, an interior door sailed from the hole on the second floor where the dormer window used to be. It landed in the middle of the dumpster, and Ashley Mayberry immediately poked her head out and looked down. She cringed when she saw them. "Sorry," she called out. "Sarah bet Josie that she couldn't score two points."

Sarah's and Josie's faces appeared beside Ashley's, and Heather muttered something about "not having time for this." She headed off to retrieve their lunches, while Trenton searched out a spot in the front yard to "get horizontal."

Jill shaded her eyes and looked up.

Bluebonnet Construction was a company that hired only females, mostly girls who'd spent time living with Aunt Blu and who needed a place to land after they turned eighteen. And thankfully, a lot of those women were either still around or already working for Bluebonnet. Jill had reached out to each of them, and pretty much everyone had been eager to be a part of this project. Which meant a full crew had been lined up for the remaining five weeks. However, also thanks to that same excitement, a few of that crew were *over*excited.

"We have a house to renovate first and foremost," Jill reminded them. "No horseplay, no one gets hurt."

"Yes, boss," the three of them recited.

But almost as soon as the words left their mouths, their gazes locked on something behind Jill and their postures straightened.

Jill turned—and then she groaned. "Seriously, Len. Don't you ever get tired of following me around?"

Len produced a broad grin. "I can think of worse ways to spend my time. Especially when I'm in the 'following' position."

If Jill hadn't been so exhausted, she would have laughed at the big man. Or punched him. Since pounding out some of her frustration on the kitchen walls a couple of nights ago, she'd been noticeably less worked up, and as part of that, she'd also begun to see her personal cameraman through her foster sisters' eyes. He really did seem to be a good guy.

Len was originally from Georgia and had lived in California when he'd started out in the business, but since holding a permanent position with *Texas Dream Home*, he'd bought a house in Waco, where he now spent most of his time.

He was kind of like a jolly Santa Claus, only with red hair—and a lascivious mind.

"You'll miss me one day." Len winked, and tired or not, Jill laughed.

"I will, Len. But not soon enough."

Len winked at her again—a man who could appreciate a good smart-ass comment—and Patrick made his way over to them. He had his trusty clipboard in hand and motioned toward the porch. "Can we get in a quick stand-up before you break for lunch? Then while you eat, Len can get shots of the interior now that it's down to the studs."

"Get some shots of us, too, Len," Ashley singsonged down from the second floor.

Jill looked up again to find a dormer full of smiling faces staring down at them, and she just shook her head. At least they were hard workers. Otherwise, with most of them trying to finagle their fifteen minutes of fame, the schedule would get out of hand in a hurry.

She also knew that Len most definitely *would* get shots of all of them. He'd at least check them out. Because from what she could tell, the man's libido could put a younger man's to shame.

Jill allowed Patrick to position her on the porch where he wanted her as Heather returned with a backpack cooler thrown over her shoulder. Heather had also managed some quick repair to her hair while she'd been gone, but instead of her and Trenton digging into the food, they sat together under a nearby tree and turned their focus on her. That had been the strategy they'd come up with. All three of them had pieces of their lives they'd rather the show not delve into deeply, so if anyone got pulled to the side, someone else would "stand guard"—ready to rescue, if need be. Thankfully, no rescues had been needed thus far.

Patrick walked Jill through a series of questions about the work that had been done over the past couple of days, as well as the next steps they'd take in the renovations, and Jill instantly relaxed into the role. She'd easily grown comfortable with the cameras.

"So, just one more thing." Patrick slid a photograph out from beneath the papers on his clipboard. "We came across this beauty the other day."

Jill stared down at the photo of her and Cal on their wedding day.

She'd gotten used to Patrick's attempts to get her to talk about Cal. Or to be on camera with Cal. In fact, she'd turned his attempts into a game, trying to predict and then outsmart the producer's next maneuver. But this one caught her off guard. She passed the picture back.

"We were cute, huh?" They'd looked amazingly happy. Especially for two people who would be divorced a short twenty-four hours later. "Don't we all wish we could still look the way we did at eighteen?"

At her question, Heather and Trenton rose to their feet.

"I understand the two of you went down different paths after that," Patrick pushed.

"That's right."

"Cal came back *home*." Patrick stressed the last word. "But you went to California. You had an LA address for a while."

"You're a thorough man, Mr. Whitaker." This bit of news didn't surprise her.

Trenton inched closer.

"Just doing my job, Ms. Sadler. So let's talk about LA, shall we? Why there?"

She gave a casual shrug. "Why anywhere?"

"What did you do?"

"A little of this, a little of that." She used the words as a stall tactic as she worked out how best to play this. She wasn't about to give him the reasoning she'd given her friends at the time. It was none of his business that her father was supposedly a big-name actor. And she sure as hell didn't plan to tell him she'd gone out there with big hopes and childish dreams.

But she could see she'd have to give him something. Otherwise, he'd keep digging.

So she decided it was time for a useful sound bite or two. The purpose of coming on the show *was* about winning new clients, after all, and she could totally provide a story in keeping with how the town had seen her at the time. It was bound to tug on hearts.

She glanced at her hands before looking back up. "Mostly, I tried to get lost." She said the words with heavy emotion, making sure to show the same on her face.

Everyone around them seemed to hold their breath.

"From Cal?" Patrick asked.

She shook her head. "I didn't need to hide from Cal. He wasn't looking for me. I was hiding from *myself*. Have you ever just not wanted to be *you*, Patrick? Ever had that bad of a day? A week?" She paused for dramatic effect and pressed her lips together as she swallowed. "Years?"

she whispered. "I wasn't hiding *from* someone. I was simply not being Jill Sadler for a while. That girl had a rough start to her life."

Patrick nodded—the wind had been knocked out of him. "I understand that she did." He glanced at Heather and Trenton, and legit concern seemed to fill his eyes. "Did you want to go ahead and talk a little about that now?"

The three of them had decided to tell the stories of how they'd come to be orphans by being interviewed together.

"Not now." She glanced up at the one-and-a-half-story house, at the now-missing porch roof, and pictured the open trusses they'd eventually add to create a more welcoming entry into the home. And she let herself go to a place she rarely visited. She thought about coming home to discover that her life was suddenly different. About how her mother had killed herself—without consideration for her only child.

She pictured her mother as she'd found her.

She thought about all the times she'd tried her best to be there for her mom. To give her mother something to live for.

And she thought about how she'd failed.

Jill allowed the hurt from those years to define her features, and other than noise from the work going on at the other house, no one made a sound.

Before the memories became too much, she forced her mind to the man next door. To the competition at hand. She hadn't lost the ability to show the cameras what she wanted them to see. She knew that now. Which meant that she had Cal beat when it came to winning viewers. He might have charm on his side, but she had skill. *And* she had a backstory.

She let a tear slip from her eye, then wiped it away and refocused on the job at hand. "I needed to escape." She faced the camera. "To find the real me. And when I did, I came home." She motioned toward Heather and Trenton and saw that another cameraman had repositioned on them. "The three of us started out together almost sixteen years ago . . .

and then we found each other again ten years later. I came *home* when it was time, Patrick. As did all of us. And I decided to make something of myself other than just being 'that poor little Sadler girl' from Red Oak Falls, Texas."

Trenton and Heather swiped at their eyes as she finished her monologue, and Jill knew she'd scored. Because her foster sisters cried as rarely as she did.

~

"I cannot *believe* all of that was fake." Trenton was horizontal in the grass again, all three of them under the massive oak that shaded both the front yard and the crumbling sidewalk, and none of them were currently wearing their mic packs.

Jill had declared a break from being recorded after finishing on the porch—also insisting that Len find someone else to harass for a while—and instead of simply muting their mics, they'd taken great pleasure in stripping them off each other. The tape and wires weren't the easiest things to get out of, and Patrick would be annoyed when he realized someone would have to redo it all. But after the wedding photo he'd sprung on her, Jill didn't care.

"I wasn't bad, was I?" Jill took a sandwich from Heather. "I even made you both cry."

"Only because we thought *you* were crying," Heather protested. She passed a bottle of juice and a sandwich to Trenton, and Trenton pushed to one elbow to eat.

Trenton made a face at the sight of the green juice. She wasn't nearly as health conscious as Heather—but she would also never reject anything with calories. She unscrewed the cap and looked up at Jill. "You were so believable that I'm beginning to think being around all those LA types for so long must have worn off on you. You shine on camera, *chica.*"

Jill grinned. She'd take that compliment.

"And I totally get why they wanted to center the show around you," Heather added. She unwrapped her own sandwich, though it was on a spinach wrap—and likely only contained veggies. "I had no idea you had that in you."

Jill chewed on her bottom lip as her foster sisters dug into their lunches. She couldn't eat thanks to the anticipation suddenly filling her. She wanted to tell them. The feeling of failure had always been so prevalent that she'd preferred not to think about those six years. About why she'd gone out there. But for the first time since coming home, she *wanted* to talk about it. She wanted her friends to know.

She plucked a blade of grass from beside her thigh and spoke while staring at the ground. "It might not come from being *around* those people, so much as from the years of *acting* classes I took."

Heather choked on her juice. While Trenton shot upright.

"The what?" Trenton screeched.

Heather coughed into her fist.

"The . . . *uhmmm* . . ." Jill gave them an apologetic grimace. "Acting. Classes."

"Since when?" Heather wheezed.

"Since . . . the whole time I was out there."

Heather and Trenton just stared at her. Several people had glanced their way after the initial commotion, but when nothing else happened, they returned their attention to their work.

"I thought you went out there to find your dad," Heather finally said. Her confusion drew a vertical line in the space between her eyes.

"I did go out there to find him," Jill hurried to assure them. "That wasn't a lie." She *had* wanted to go to Hollywood to find her father. From an early age she'd had fantasies of bringing him home so her mother would finally have someone who would love her enough. "Only, I . . ."

Only, her mother had died, and her wants had shifted.

"Only, you wanted to act, too," Trenton accused. She'd managed to sit up even straighter, so that she now looked down her nose at Jill. "You said you took classes the whole time you were out there. Does that mean you knew you wanted to act *before* you left?"

Jill nodded.

"And what?" Trenton continued. "It just never occurred to you to mention this to us? Neither before, *nor* in all the years since?"

"I'm sorry," Jill whispered. She felt horrible, but the reality of the situation was that she'd never truly expected to see them again. They'd been great friends, sure. Life wouldn't have been the same if she hadn't had them back then. And they'd all said they would keep in touch.

But words were easy. She'd learned that with her mom.

It was also far too easy to believe you meant more to others than you did.

Pain touched Trenton's eyes. "Did you think we wouldn't support you?"

"No," Jill protested. "That's not it. I just . . ."

She swallowed. She'd just needed a layer of protection around what she'd desired the most. And the fact was, they *had* lost contact for a few years.

"I'm sorry," she said again. "I think it was more that saying it out loud scared me too much. It scared me *more* than the thought of not going. And I really wanted to go. I used to watch the drama club at school." She could remember those days clearly. She'd be in the background as part of the stage crew, but at the same time, she'd keep an ear out for everything being said on stage. She'd never missed a rehearsal. And she'd memorized every line. "I so wanted to be in the plays," she admitted now.

Those words had never been uttered out loud.

"But I was too terrified to try out. Too afraid to fail."

"You should have told us," Heather said. She reached over and rested a hand on Jill's thigh.

"I know." Jill nodded. She put her hand over Heather's, and she glanced at Trenton. "I should have. But we all had our issues, right? I wanted to prove myself before sharing something like that."

She'd wanted to be the fourth person from Red Oak Falls to make it in the world.

After Cal left her in Vegas, she'd been too mortified to talk to anyone. About anything. She'd ignored her phone for weeks. Then she'd just been angry. That anger had fueled her stubbornness, and her visions of grandeur had grown. She'd worked her rear off trying to make it as an actress. Only, grandeur never came. And by the time she'd been on the bus heading back to Texas, she realized she was even more alone than she'd ever been. She hadn't spoken to either Heather or Trenton in years—they'd drifted apart as time passed—and she'd had no idea if Aunt Blu would so much as open her door for her.

She'd failed. No one had wanted her. And she'd had nowhere else to go but Red Oak Falls.

"So what happened?" Heather asked. She was more easily forgiving than Trenton.

"Nothing in the end," Jill answered. "I went out there and I was instantly overwhelmed with the talent I saw everywhere, so I enrolled in a class. I took every acting class I could find for the first few years, and after that, I mostly did improv. Stuff like that. I couldn't keep up with the cost of the classes all the time, but I kept trying. Because I really thought I had talent. That I could make a career of it."

"You *do*!" Heather flapped a hand toward the porch. "You *could*. We just saw it. And it wasn't only today, either. You were stellar when Bob and Debra were here. We just didn't say anything because we thought that was about putting on a face around Cal."

"Oh, it *was* about putting on a face around Cal. Don't think for a second that I'm not still angry at him. But there's no way I'll give him the pleasure of seeing it play out on screen."

Of course, he'd seen it in person Wednesday night.

"So you just beat the crap out of our kitchen instead?" Trenton said, and Jill gave a little nod.

"At least it was work that needed to be done," she offered.

Her foster sisters had commented on the kitchen's destruction the morning after, but neither had asked a pointed question about it until now. Jill had also kept secret the fact that Cal had come over while she'd been in the middle of it.

"That was a little concerning," Trenton told her. "Coming in and seeing that. You haven't lost your cool like that in a long time."

"I would maintain that I didn't lose my cool so much as have a controlled burn," Jill explained. "The first few days of this week were tough. I wasn't prepared for everything. You know"—she nodded toward the Cadillac House—"with *him*. I needed to work out a few kinks."

"And you're better now? You're okay with *him*?"

"You do *seem* better," Heather offered.

"I'm adjusting." Jill gave a little chuckle. "I'm also counting down the days."

Pete Logan came out of the house next door before they could get back to Jill's story, and captured their attention. The man was not bad looking at all. At least six foot, solidly built. And he currently had clumps of dust clinging to the black cotton of his T-shirt. It was strangely adorable. He glanced at them sitting under the tree, before turning back to speak with someone still inside the house. Then instead of going wherever he'd been headed, he disappeared back inside.

As they watched, Heather let out a mopey-sounding sigh, and Jill looked at her questioningly.

"I still wish we'd gotten that house," Heather explained.

"But we didn't," Trenton asserted. "And we're not talking about the house right now. We're talking about Hollywood. And Jill's rise to fame."

They'd actually been talking about her temper at that particular moment, but Jill didn't point out the distinction. "It was more like my *non*-rise to fame," she clarified instead. She then returned her attention to Heather. "And seriously, why would you still want that house? It has so much more potential for problems. Didn't you hear about their plumbing inspection? Even worse than we'd expected. And *much* worse than ours."

The report had reinforced the pleasure she'd taken in manipulating Cal into choosing the worst house. During their initial walk-through, she'd caught him studying the three of them. As if watching for a tell as to which house they preferred. So she'd given him the sign he'd been looking for.

She'd oohed and aahed over all the tucked-away spaces and the gorgeous trim work. She'd let her breathing pick up as she'd "visualized" what the main floor could one day become. Only, she'd done it all "secretly," while making sure Cal witnessed her trying to *not* let him see. Her acting skills had already been razor sharp on day one.

"But Bonnie Beckman is still going on about it," Heather told them. "She caught me at the grocery store last night. She's already calling Cal the winner. That could have been us."

"It can still be us," Trenton added, though her tone implied she couldn't care less about winning at the moment. "Now seriously. Hollywood. What happened? Did you get any parts?"

Jill pulled her thoughts back from screwing with Cal and answered the question. "No," she stated bluntly. "Nothing worth mentioning, anyway. I went by the stage name of Jessica Grant, so you wouldn't find my name on anything if you tried."

"And what made you finally come home?" Heather scooted around until she sat facing both of them. "Because at this point, I'm assuming it wasn't that you 'found yourself,' as you told Patrick."

Jill grinned. She did enjoy messing with Patrick.

She finally unwrapped her sandwich. "Correct. I did not find myself. In fact, I'm pretty sure I'm still looking." But she also wasn't sure she was ready to admit what had finally driven her out of California.

Not all of it, anyway.

"Mostly it was money," she told them. "I was out of it, and it costs a fortune to live there. I also discovered that I didn't like LA the way I'd always dreamed I would. It wasn't . . . *home*. You know?"

Heather nodded silently, while Trenton simply watched. As if understanding there was more to the story.

"And talk about demoralizing," Jill continued. She let her eyelids drift closed as she went back to those days. "No matter how hard I tried, I couldn't get anywhere. It ticked me off. But it also broke my spirit." She swallowed. "It beat at my confidence."

"That's why you don't watch TV."

Jill opened her eyes at Trenton's statement. "Right. My failure wouldn't crush me quite as much if I wasn't constantly reminded of what I failed to achieve. At least, that was the theory."

"And did it work?" Heather asked.

Jill only shrugged. She still didn't watch TV.

"Then tell us . . ." Heather motioned to one of the camera crews. "You're very good at acting. I can understand why you wanted it. So, is all of this making you miss it? Is it making you wish you could try again?"

"I'm not quitting our company," Jill assured her.

"That's not what I asked."

But that *was* what was most important, Jill thought. It had taken her too long to realize what these two women meant to her. Not to mention Aunt Blu. She wouldn't give that up now for anything. Or for any part.

However, with Heather's question hanging in the air—and with Trenton still eyeing her, as well—Jill forced herself to think about the situation. She'd been so focused on lining up the subs and getting work under way that she hadn't really given thought to how she felt about the rest of it. She put her back to the tree and worked on her sandwich as she stared at both houses.

"I don't know," she finally said. She *was* having fun. She could admit that. "I am enjoying it. More than I expected to. Especially considering that so much of my energy has to go toward avoiding Cal."

Trenton snorted. "I'd say your avoidance is adding to your fun."

Jill sat up straighter. "What do you mean by that?"

Trenton rolled her eyes at the defensive tone. "Don't get your panties in a twist. I'm just saying that you always did enjoy trying to one-up people. And Patrick is like a dog with a bone the way he tries to get you to talk about Cal. Or be caught in the same shot as Cal."

"That he is." Jill smiled. "And yes, I am enjoying it. A lot. I sense he doesn't appreciate my efforts as much as I do, though."

Trenton and Heather both laughed, and Trenton dropped back to the ground, her head now pillowed by the grass. She stared up at Jill. "So, do you think he'll stop?"

"Would you if you were producing the show?"

Trenton shook her head, and Jill did the same. It may be all a game to her, but the man had a show to put on, and she knew it. No way would Patrick give up trying to get his two stars on camera together. Especially when there was an ongoing feud between them.

Cal came out of the other house then, and though Jill hadn't once looked directly at him since he'd caught her with the sledgehammer, she couldn't stop herself from watching now. He was a solid six two, no extra fat anywhere, and he moved in a kind of slow roll. His shoulders swaggered a little, which alone could draw any woman's attention, but it was his thighs that had always reeled Jill in. They were thick and muscled, same as the rest of him, but they turned outward just the slightest amount. As if what lay nestled between needed that little bit of extra room.

Her throat went dry. She knew what lay nestled between.

Jill felt Heather's gaze on her as she watched Cal, then Heather turned her head, same as Jill's, and joined her in tuning in to the action next door. Trenton rolled to her side to participate, as well, and the three of them admired the view as Pete came out of the house next. Following him was the redhead who'd been working with Cal and his crew that week. The redhead wasn't an overly large man—and there was a softness to his features that made him look closer to twelve than whatever age he might possibly be—yet he moved with a strength not unlike Cal's.

They headed to Cal's truck, each hefting a couple of bags of leveling concrete out of the bed, and as their legs ate up the space back to the house, the redhead glanced toward the tree. His gaze landed on Jill and his footsteps slowed.

"That boy needs to get laid," Trenton muttered under her breath, and Jill promptly snorted, choking on a gulp of the juice she'd been drinking.

"I vote Heather do it," she croaked out. "Heather's the one who likes redheads."

"Oh, but sweetie. It isn't *me* that redhead has his eye on."

Jill lowered her gaze with embarrassment, because Heather was right. The guy's name was Doug Caldwell, and yes, he had his eye on her. He'd done some phenomenal tile work over at the Rusted Rooster when the owners had decided to class up the place the year before. Therefore, Jill was aware of who he was. But over the last two days, every single time the boy's eyes had turned her way, she'd sworn she felt steam radiate off him. And that didn't even include the heat filling his cheeks with every glance.

Poor little redhead.

"How old can he possibly be, anyway?" Jill looked up from her lap. "He can't be more than twenty, right?"

The men returned to the truck.

"Eighteen, maybe?" Trenton guessed. "At least that would be legal."

Jill once again snorted her juice.

Trenton snickered at Jill's choking, and Jill threw the almost-empty bottle at her. But Trenton caught it and fired it right back. It bounced off the side of Jill's head, splashing the final drops into her hair, and as she cackled with laughter, Little Red tripped over his own two feet.

Jill smiled at him then. Giving him a full-blown I'm-watching-you-watch-me grin.

Heather elbowed her in the ribs when Red smiled back. "You're evil," she whispered.

"I know." The boy's cheeks were darn-near red at that point.

But Jill was also aware that Cal had lingered at his truck while Little Red had been dawdling in the yard. *And* that Cal was looking at her, as well. That's where her true evil lay.

She stood then, fearing that if she didn't soon get out of there, she'd take another direct look.

"Break's over," she announced.

She swiped at her rear to dislodge whatever dirt might have accumulated while sitting on the ground, then helped to gather the mic packs and the remainder of their lunch—all while ignoring her ex-husband, Little Red, *and* Len—who was once again heading her way. And as they walked off to find Patrick, Jill conceded that though she might have managed *not* to take another look toward the Cadillac House, she was very much aware that Cal's gaze had remained affixed on her.

Only thirty-five more days to go. She had this.

Chapter Six

*"The facts may not always be what you want to hear. But
learn to listen."*

—Blu Johnson, life lesson #61

Cal unlocked the door to his grandmother's house Saturday evening and
pushed it open to a dark kitchen. He was almost too tired to cross the
threshold, and it was barely seven o'clock.

Blowing out an exhausted breath, he forced himself to move, flipping on lights as he went and dropping the box he'd picked up outside
onto the kitchen table. He then went straight to the fridge and pulled
out a Coke.

He eyed the empty case of beer sitting on the top shelf and slid
a glance around the room. A couple of empty beer bottles sat on the
countertop, as well as the ones he'd shoved in the garbage can the night
before. Muttering a curse, he tossed the two empties before grabbing
a can of cat food and dumping it into the ceramic bowl on the floor.

"Lily," he called out. The cat usually met him at the end of the day.

He leaned his head into the hallway and looked up the stairs when
she didn't appear, but there was no sign of her. He knew she was around,

though. And that she'd come out only when she felt like it. Because she, like everyone else in his life, did only as she pleased.

Grabbing a bag of chips, his soda, and the monthly guilt package off the table, he headed for the living room, turning on more lights as he went. He'd wanted to check out the other jobsites today instead of being stuck over on Pear Street, but they'd had one problem come up after another. To top it off, the plumber needed an extra day to replace all the lines, so Cal would be meeting him at the house first thing in the morning, just to keep from starting the week off behind schedule.

All of that meant he wouldn't make it out to his place that weekend at all. As well as no Sunday visit to see his granny. He hated when that happened.

Dropping to the couch, he propped his feet on the coffee table and eyed the hand-printed label attached to the box he'd brought in. Neither his dad nor his dad's flavor of the month would have been the one to address the package. Nor would they know what was in it. His phone beeped as he turned on the television, and he used that as an excuse to shove the box out of his lap. It was Marci wanting to know if she should come over or if he would be picking her up.

He frowned as he thumbed out a reply.

Can we reschedule? I'm seriously tired tonight. And grumpy.

And he simply wasn't in the mood. He and Marci had been going out for a couple of months, and though she was fun, he was finding that most days she was a bit too much. She was so damned cheerful all the time.

Occasionally, he didn't feel like being charming Cal. He just wanted to sit and stew.

Marci also always wanted to be going out or being seen. Or she wanted to talk things to death. Whereas he often preferred to relax, eat a good steak, and just "be" with the other person in the room. Silently. Or better yet, go out to the farm and work. By himself.

Which wasn't fair, he knew. If he ever wanted a relationship to last, he'd have to give more than that. But at the same time, he had yet to find a relationship he wanted to give more to. They simply didn't seem to be worth it.

I don't mind, Marci replied. I could rub your tired muscles.

He dropped his head to the back of the couch and stared at the ceiling. Marci was already frustrated with him because he'd cut their date short the night before, but she was still trying. That's more than he could say for himself. But after a week of the stress of keeping the Cadillac project on schedule, along with cameras in his face every time he turned around, he was too tired to even fake it tonight. And too frustrated.

And too damned mad at his ex-wife.

That sledgehammer episode . . .

He groaned at the thought. What the hell had he been thinking by going over there? The majority of his stress that week had been due to having witnessed that.

He'd seen her through the windows when he'd come back to the house. He'd *known* what she was about to do the instant he'd caught sight of the tool in her hand. And he'd remembered—*with clarity*—how much anger she could hold.

He'd also recalled how she'd once been likely to express that anger.

He blew out a breath. She'd been fifteen the day she'd climbed that ladder behind him at Blu's house. Furious over something that had happened at school. He'd looked over his shoulder to ask what she thought she was doing coming up behind him like that, and she'd had a look on her face similar to what he'd witnessed the other night. She'd ignored his demand to get off the ladder, reaching out a hand to him instead, and demanded he give her a hammer. So she could pound on something.

He'd given her a sledgehammer instead.

After she'd beaten a rotting tree trunk to a pulp, he'd suggested another way she could work off some steam. Because he was an ass.

And because he'd heard the rumors about her.

Yet despite him being an ass, she'd been all for his suggestion.

He dragged a hand down over his face as he futilely attempted to stop the memories. He hadn't touched her for two years after that. Not one hand anywhere on her body. And though he shouldn't have let his little head dictate his big head that day, he could still remember every detail from that afternoon. And he still loved those details.

Therefore, why in hell's name had he taken one look through that kitchen window the other night, and let his feet walk him straight to her door?

Because he was an idiot. Obviously.

And because he apparently still got a kick out of pissing her off.

He sent Marci a reply.

Really sorry, but no. Going to bed early. Working tomorrow, too.

She would be ticked at the cancellation, but there was no way he could be around her right now. He shouldn't have gone out with her the night before, either. Not when his ex-wife wouldn't get the fuck out of his head.

Then maybe I'll be busy next weekend . . .

He stared down at the reply. Yep. Ticked. He tossed his phone to the couch and turned on the TV, then he pulled a knife from his jeans pocket and cut through the tape on the box. Ever since his dad had moved out of town, he'd sent a monthly guilt package. Neil Reynolds knew Cal visited his grandmother on a regular basis—therefore, the shipment came to him.

Cal sorted through it now.

Lotions, a new toothbrush and toothpaste, a gown and robe set.

There was also a new bedside radio and a shoebox full of yarn and knitting needles.

She didn't need any of this stuff, but he'd take it to her anyway. And she'd be thrilled to get it. To know that Neil was thinking of her. Not that her oldest son bothered to visit her enough to count. He put in twice-a-year trips—with whomever he happened to be shacked up with at the time—to the home where he'd stuck her, and he sent monthly packages of junk. No calls. No other concerns.

She'd been in the home for seventeen years now. She'd started going blind before Papaw had died, and only two years later—because of one stupid accident with the kitchen stove—Cal's father had shoved her into a twelve-by-fourteen-foot room that was forty-five minutes from everything she'd ever known. After that, he'd basically written her off.

Cal pulled out a smaller box that had his name written on the top and tossed it into the kitchen, aiming for the trash can. The box clattered with the empty beer bottles, tumbling everything to the floor, and the cat, who'd finally made her way to her food bowl, shot back out of the room.

Cal sighed. "Sorry, Lily!"

The cat didn't care.

The kitchen door opened, and his uncle appeared, and upon spotting Cal on the couch, a smile broke out on Rodney's face.

"There he is." Rodney headed to the living room. "Big celebrity."

"Hey, Uncle Rodney." Cal patted the couch cushion. "Have a seat. Missed you at the set yesterday."

"Yeah. Uh . . . Something came up." Rodney grimaced with the words. "I'll get out there, though. Wouldn't miss it."

"Sure." Cal focused on the TV instead of his uncle. A game show was on.

Rodney had been scheduled to be filmed helping with the demo, but he'd been a no-show. Cal hadn't seen anything of him at all the day before, and likely wouldn't have known where he'd ended the evening if not for the 2:00 a.m. text from a bartender buddy over at Joe's. Joe's was a little dive on the outskirts of town that catered to loose women who liked cheap beer, and Cal's buddy tried to help out when he could. He'd text if things looked like they might get out of hand, and Cal would climb out of bed to go and retrieve his uncle.

He and Rodney never talked about it the next day, nor did Cal ever know how his uncle got his truck back after he sobered up. These things just had a way of working themselves out.

"How about you stay in tonight?" Cal suggested. He flipped to the local news. "Just me and you. I've got a couple of steaks I could thaw. I'll toss them on the grill."

His uncle looked toward the fridge. "I'll think about it."

There was no beer in the fridge. They both knew Rodney would be going out.

"You don't have a date with Marci?"

Cal shook his head. "Too tired."

"Too tired for a woman?" Rodney grunted. "Some days I'm not sure you're deserving of the Reynolds name."

Cal shrugged. It wasn't a concept his uncle was familiar with, but Cal had grown tired of chasing skirts some time ago. He'd put his years in and he'd done a fine job of it. And if the women around town were to be asked today, they'd likely say that he was still chasing. But that was only because every relationship he tried ended before it really took off. The women were the ones to dump him, though, so at least they couldn't claim he was a player. It was their choice to end things. They just *blamed* him for them having to make that choice.

The local news came on, and Rodney muttered something about forgetting to pick up something while he'd been out. He headed for the kitchen. "I won't be long," he called before the door slammed behind him.

Cal went back to watching the news. They both knew Rodney wouldn't be back soon.

After the top news story finished airing, Cal's and Jill's pictures splashed on the screen. He put his feet on the floor and sat up.

"Local companies We Nail It Contractors and Bluebonnet Construction are making Red Oak Falls proud this week, with exes Cal Reynolds and Jill Sadler leading the charge."

The picture cut to the houses as the story continued, showing Jill, Heather, and Trenton standing on the other side of a camera while one of the producers fed them questions. Cal had managed to eavesdrop on that interview when he'd been doing a preliminary walk of the yard with his landscaper, but he hadn't noticed the news van there at the same time.

The camera panned to him, hovering at the corner of the house. He'd been standing with his lawn guy, but neither of them had been talking. They'd both been watching the women.

The reporter commented on that fact, chuckling at what she called a tongue-hanging-out moment for "the boys," and he scowled at the TV. His tongue had been securely inside his mouth the whole time.

The clip cut to the interior of the Bono House then, and as the reporter spoke to Heather, Cal tuned her out. He watched for glimpses of Jill instead. The three of them were good at what they did. He remembered their budding skills when they'd first started working with him out at Blu's, but he'd also seen some of the retreats they'd built. They knew what they were doing, and he'd best not forget it or he might find the Bluebonnets giving him and Pete a virtual ass-kicking on national television.

Jill stepped into the house behind Heather, and the instant she saw the camera, she put on her "face." That's what he'd been watching for.

They brought her into the conversation, and Cal had to acknowledge that she had full control in front of the camera. She was personable in a way that he knew was both her true self and also not. It was acting, he admitted. She had the ability to highlight the traits that would win her the most favor, and she even seemed to have a knack for comedic timing with the one-liners. She was damned mesmerizing to watch, actually, and he found himself wondering how much of that was natural and how much had been learned during her stint in Hollywood.

How much had he missed when he'd been dating her?

He eyed his phone where it lay on the couch. He still had her number. It was the same one she'd had as a kid. Maybe he should call and apologize for the crack he'd made about her acting skills Wednesday night. He'd just been trying to get under her skin.

And maybe he could cut off his balls and hand them over while he was at it?

Because that's how she'd take it. Him conceding her win. Giving in.

Him begging her to quit ignoring him on set and to once again speak to him.

He shoved his ex-wife from his head for the umpteenth time that week and reached for his phone. He'd call his granny instead. That would be a conversation worth having.

They talked for twenty minutes, him telling her about the first week of filming, and her sharing details of her week. He also let her know that he wouldn't be able to make it the following day. He'd try to see her during the week, though. He routinely made a trip or two during the weekdays.

She asked about Rodney, as well, and as was standard, Cal lied. Cal told her that her youngest son was doing great. Because he *couldn't* tell her the truth. He wasn't about to be the one to inform his grandmother that though she'd already lost one son to drinking and driving when he'd been only sixteen . . . her youngest had been heading down that very same path for a number of years.

At least her oldest wasn't an addict. She had that going for her.

But then, Neil Reynolds also had nothing to do with her.

They said their good-byes soon after, and Cal decided to use the evening to do something useful. Like figuring out a way to rile up his ex enough to get her to acknowledge his existence.

~

Jill stood in the outdoor interview spot with her foster sisters and fought to keep her nerves from showing. The day had come for them to talk about their pasts. Patrick had pulled them aside that morning to go over the discussion points for telling their story, and she was equally as nervous for Heather and Trenton as she was for herself. None of them liked talking about how they'd come to be at Bluebonnet Farms, but they were as ready as they'd ever be.

She waved at the people standing behind the rope on the other side of the road. The crowd had been growing daily, and some of them even had signs with either "We Nail It" or "Bluebonnet" printed across the front. And surprisingly, a lot of them boasted "Bluebonnet." So much for the Reynolds charm.

"We have fans," Trenton whispered at her side.

It was a giddy feeling.

"It's crazy," added Heather. She smiled, her dimples flashing, as someone from the crowd called out her name. Their lives would certainly be different after this, no matter the outcome. They had several new clients lined up now, as the phones continued to ring. People were anxious to get on their radar before their schedule filled.

"Let's start with Jill," Patrick said, looking up from his clipboard.

Heather and Trenton squeezed her hands as all three of them turned their attention to the camera.

"I understand you showed up at Bluebonnet Farms first," Patrick started.

"I actually only got there one day before Heather."

She wouldn't have gotten there that soon if Aunt Blu hadn't overheard the police reporting a 10-56 at the apartment where Jill and her mother lived. Since Janet Sadler had worked for Big Gerry, Blu had known Jill long before her mother committed suicide. Therefore, she'd dropped everything when the call went out.

That would be the extent of her talking about the day of, though. On camera or off. Only one person knew the entire story.

The three of them answered questions for the next forty-five minutes, recounting many good memories of their years together, several of which overshadowed some of the worst ones, and as they talked, Jill noticed that Cal spent more time outside the house he was supposed to be working on than in it.

He was eavesdropping again. She'd caught him doing that several times over the past few days, and if not eavesdropping, he would occasionally just . . . be there. She'd come out of the house and practically trip over him supposedly retrieving something the wind had blown her way, or she'd go to her truck, only to discover him heading to his own truck. Which would be parked directly behind hers.

His continual encroachment into her space had even caused her to give up the battle of making no direct eye contact, and she'd switched to scathing looks instead. But that hadn't gotten her far, either. He didn't give a hoot about her go-jump-off-a-cliff glares.

So this time, when his gaze landed on hers, she screwed up her face and crossed her eyes. Maybe that would clue him in that he needed to back off.

He only laughed.

Len pulled away from his camera and looked in Cal's direction at the same time that Cal laughed at her, and Jill realized she'd forgotten for a second that she was being recorded.

Oops. They'd have to edit that one out.

She stopped herself before making another face when Cal continued to watch. She still hadn't talked to him since the night of the sledgehammer, and she'd perfected her sidestepping abilities when it came to Patrick trying to get the two of them together. But she'd swear that Cal had joined in on Patrick's cause.

Nothing in her contract said she *had* to be on camera with their competition, though. Therefore, Patrick would have to up his game if he expected anything different.

"And that should do it," Patrick announced, and she realized she'd missed the last few minutes of filming. Hopefully she hadn't looked too ridiculous by not paying attention.

The three of them got back to work, and it was several minutes later before it occurred to Jill that it was *only* the three of them in the house. Not even Len. She looked up from the budget she'd been reviewing. Heather sat on an overturned five-gallon bucket at a makeshift desk of two two-by-twelves resting across a pair of sawhorses.

"Where is everyone?" Jill asked.

Heather glanced around. "I don't know." She had her cell phone in hand and was tapping on the screen.

"Trenton?" Jill yelled out. She knew Trenton had come back in with them.

"Up here."

Jill tilted her head to look up at the exposed rafters. "You seen our trades anywhere?"

"Not since we got back in."

Laughter trickled in from the open windows. *Female* laughter.

"That sounds like our women." Heather held her hand over her phone as she spoke, and at the sound of additional giggles, Jill moved to the living room windows to look out. And sure enough, there they were.

All seven of their female workers scheduled for the day were currently in the competing yard, all facing Cal as he held court on his front porch. Len stood off to the side, recording it all.

"You've got to be kidding me," Jill muttered.

She ignored her flickering anger long enough to study Cal. What was he doing?

His words weren't loud enough to decipher, but the familiar rumble managed to reach her ears. Whatever story he told, he did it with the type of smile that any woman would be hard pressed to ignore. His arms were open, extending out from his chest, while his hands and fingers remained in constant motion. The women alternated their gazes from his mouth to his hands as if mesmerized, but it was the casual sexiness of his stance that got to Jill. Because she'd bet money that stance wasn't *casual* at all. The man knew exactly what he was doing.

And what he was doing was being up to no good.

But two could play at that game. She hadn't taken all those acting classes to walk away with nothing. She was halfway out the front door, ready to march across the yard and entice all *his* men over to *her* house, before it occurred to her that this might be a ploy.

She paused. Was she walking into a trap?

She slowly brought her foot back inside and glanced back at Heather. "Will you go get them? They seem to have forgotten which house they're working on."

Heather once again covered the phone with her hand. "I've just gotten someone on the line." She pointed to the glass tile sample she'd chosen as the backsplash. "I need to make sure the tile will be here on time."

Jill looked up, but before she could ask, Trenton called down, "You go, Jilly. You're in charge of the trades. Plus, you can't . . ."

At Trenton's pause, Jill cocked her head. "I can't what?"

Trenton stopped whatever she was doing and finally looked down. Her legs were spread wide, each foot on a crossbeam, while her hands matched that position, only gripping rafters at shoulder level. She stared at Jill, the look on her face a mix of both conviction and contrition. "Plus," she said, more slowly that time, "you can't keep avoiding him forever. You have to know that."

Jill barked out a laugh. "Watch me."

"But the thing is"—Trenton glanced at Heather, who'd turned her back to both of them—"it would make for a better show if you *did* talk to him. Which is what we want, right?"

Jill's brows arched. "And how do you figure that?"

Trenton winced. "Surely you see what we see?"

"I have no idea what you see."

When Trenton didn't expound on whatever point she was trying to make, Jill looked back over at Heather—who continued ignoring them.

"What *exactly* do you see?" Jill asked, her words slowing as her breathing threatened to pick up.

And again, Trenton winced. She then pursed her lips as if trying to find the right words—or maybe considering not answering at all—but Jill held her ground. Whatever her foster sisters thought they were witnessing, she needed to know about it.

She never took her eyes off Trenton, yet she instinctively knew when Heather turned back to them. Trenton seemed to sense the same, as she flicked a glance toward the other woman before giving an almost imperceptible shrug.

"I see two people," Trenton finally began, the words seeming to pain her, "who, were they to get into a room together, would go off like a bottle rocket."

"In T minus ten seconds," Heather added softly.

"And we *don't* just mean your anger."

Jill's mouth dropped open. "Then what do you mean?"

Trenton released the rafters, now balancing herself with only her legs, and touched her fingertips together in front of her. She mouthed the word "poof" as she slowly pulled her hands apart. She followed the action with a shudder and a look on her face that could only be indicative of pleasure.

Jill gaped. "You mean sex?" Heat crawled up her neck. "Sex with Cal? *Me* and Cal?"

Trenton repeated her "poof" move, and Heather giggled into her hand.

"I would *not*!" Jill denied. She pointed a finger up at Trenton. "Putting him and me in the same room together would *not* end up with us naked. I *hate* him. Have you forgotten that?"

But hadn't that been her biggest worry going into this? That she'd fall back into old habits?

"Some people have sex without getting naked," Trenton offered. "That could possibly even make it better."

Jill gasped. "Stop it."

Trenton shrugged. "I'm just saying."

"And you know how much he hurt me. You shouldn't—"

"We know, Jilly." Heather got to her feet. She'd put the phone down. "She's just messing with you."

"But you think it, too?" Jill asked.

Heather grimaced and Jill sighed.

"Really?" She looked out the window to where she could still see Cal on his porch.

"You two have just always been so . . . combustible," Heather explained, apology in her voice.

Trenton "poofed" once again from up above, and if Jill had been close enough, she'd have punched her right off the crossbeams.

"I don't want to be combustible!" she yelled.

Trenton stared down at her, her brown eyes reminding Jill all too much of the man she'd once loved. "But our wants and our actions don't always make complete sense, do they?"

Jill scowled at her foster sister. She couldn't believe either of them were even thinking these things, much less saying them. "I will *not* be acting on any perceived *wants*," she announced.

"Good." Trenton nodded. She gripped the rafters again. "Because I'd hate to have to kick his ass again."

"What do you m—"

Raucous, high-pitched laughter filled the air, and Jill gritted her teeth. She had to go get their women.

She pointed at Trenton again. "We're not finished talking about this."

"I suspect we're not."

Irritation at her foster sisters had Jill tossing down the papers she'd been holding and stomping out the door. Before she made it beyond their yard, though, she was stopped by someone calling out her name, and when she turned she saw Little Red waving her down. Doug jogged her way, and even though she was still ticked, Jill couldn't help but smile. He was just so darned cute.

And he'd kill them if he knew they called him Little Red.

"I've been trying to catch you for a few days," Doug said when he finally reached her side. His cheeks were pink, but she couldn't tell if that was from exertion or the thought of finally talking to her.

"And what have you been trying to catch me doing?"

Doug chuckled. "You're cute." He held out a hand. "First of all, I wanted to properly introduce myself."

She shook his hand. "I know who you are, Doug."

"Do you, now?" His cheeks turned a deeper shade of pink.

"I've seen your work at the Rusted Rooster. And as a matter of fact, if you had the right parts, I would have taken you away from that one a long time ago."

She nodded Cal's way, and they both turned to look at him as he continued entertaining the ladies surrounding him. She noticed that Doug took a step closer to her at about the same time that she recognized an irrational flare of jealousy when Cal put a hand on Bridget Mason's shoulder. Bridget was gorgeous, single, and would have her MBA from Baylor in a matter of months. She'd be running her own company someday, and she likely wouldn't have to go on TV just to build her business.

But if she did, the cameras would certainly adore her.

"He's got a talent, that's for sure." Doug nodded toward Cal. "I've been watching them for the last few minutes. It's almost as if he's emitted some sort of siren's call, and they're incapable of looking away."

Jill checked Doug out a little more. "You into Greek mythology, Doug?"

He grinned. "It was a hobby of mine in high school."

"And *when*, exactly, was high school?"

"Come on," he blustered. "I'm not that young."

She bumped her shoulder against his. "Are you sure about that? Because you *look* that young."

"I'm twenty-five."

Though shocked that he was even in his twenties, she gave an over-exaggerated cringe at the number. "That's still almost a baby."

He stepped in front of her then, his shoulders broader than she'd realized and now fully blocking her view of Cal, and suddenly the look in young Doug's face was no longer that of an innocent boy. "Go out with me Friday night. Wherever you want. I'll show you I'm not too young."

Now it was her turn to blush. He was quite forward. "Don't you think that might be a conflict of interest?" she suggested. "You work for my competition."

"I'm not a conflict." He jerked a thumb over his shoulder at Cal, who—Jill noted—was now sliding *them* a look. "I'm easy compared to that one."

"Then it's a good thing I'm not interested in that one, isn't it?" Before Doug could risk making the situation more uncomfortable, Jill angled her head toward her workers. "I really do have to get those ladies back to work, and something tells me Cal would want you to do the same."

He shrugged, keeping up his bravado. "We get breaks."

"Yeah, well, my ladies have been on theirs for too long."

"I suppose they have." Doug flicked a quick look over her, and dang if the heat that flared in his eyes didn't try to warm her right up.

Something told her she'd be hearing more from Little Red before the six weeks were over, and she couldn't find it in herself to be insulted in the least. It had been a long time since she'd had someone so brazenly come on to her.

He tossed out one more grin. "I'll let you know if he steals them again."

As Doug walked away, Jill ignored the camera now pointed at her. Len had shifted focus during her and Doug's exchange, and had likely caught the entire thing. She also didn't worry about the second camera crew, whose lens was on Cal. Instead, she put her fingers to her mouth, and with a quick burst of air, a sharp whistle ripped through the air.

Cal stopped talking midsentence, and one by one, the ladies turned her way. Once she had their attention, she motioned to the house, and without a word, the women filed across the yard. She couldn't really blame them for getting caught up in Cal's web, though. He was a heck of a good-looking man, and he'd been putting everything he had into that little show.

When the last woman edged past her, Jill turned a bored look Cal's way.

He responded by blowing a kiss, same as he'd done the week before, and as had happened with Doug, she couldn't find it in herself to be properly offended.

What was up with that?

He turned to go back inside, and a half second before he completely disappeared, she realized she was staring at the curve of his butt. Because damn. His smile wasn't the only thing that could captivate a woman.

She forced her gaze away and marched back to her own house. What the heck was wrong with her, anyway? Had her libido fired to life from a multiyear hibernation, and now anyone was fair game? She heard a soft snicker coming from behind the camera now following her, and without looking back, she flipped Len the bird. At least she wasn't undressing *him* with her eyes.

As she stepped up onto the porch, still focused on getting away from Cal, she literally bounced off Patrick's chest.

"Whoa." He steadied her. "Sorry about that. But I'm glad I caught you." He gave her a wide smile. "Can we have a few more minutes?" He motioned for Len. "We forgot a couple things before."

When Jill didn't immediately follow him to the interview station, Patrick turned back.

"It won't take but a few minutes," he assured her.

She glanced at the door. She'd really rather Heather or Trenton go with her.

But Patrick stood waiting, and when a quick peek next door indicated that Cal didn't seem to be involved, Jill gave up and decided this wasn't a setup. She trudged across the lawn behind the two men, and hoped it really wouldn't take more than a few minutes. She had far too much left to do today. Len slowed to align his steps with hers, and by the time they got her positioned with the best lighting, she'd already relaxed and was ready to go. And that's when Patrick attacked.

"We just have a quick question about the day your mom died."

Every hair on Jill's body stood on end.

"I have down that you were the one who found her body," Patrick continued. "That you'd left the apartment early that afternoon, but when you came back—"

"Where did you get your information?"

Patrick jerked his gaze to Jill's. No one knew the details of that day, except . . .

Jill looked toward the Cadillac House. Her breathing picked up. What had he done?

"Is that not right?" Patrick asked. He flipped to another sheet on his clipboard. "It says that around six thirty—"

"I'm fully aware of what happened that day."

She stared straight ahead, seeing nothing, though Len leaned out from behind his camera to peer at her. If she'd been in a better frame of mind, she would have appreciated the concern written in the larger man's eyes, but as it was, she only wanted to lash out.

"And I will *not* talk about that day on camera." Her voice rose. She forced herself to face Patrick. "We discussed that beforehand. It isn't open for negotiation."

"I'm not asking for specifics," he countered. "More about the aftermath. We know that sometimes the people who are left behind . . ."

Blood roared in her ears.

"Sometimes there's 'survivor's guilt,'" Patrick continued.

Cal stepped around the corner of his house then, and as she fired a glare in his direction, he stopped as if sensing her anger. With boxes balanced on both shoulders, he rotated to face her, and she didn't even think. She couldn't have if she'd wanted to.

She simply screamed.

Chapter Seven

"Protect what matters to you. Always."

—Papaw Reynolds

"Whoa!" Cal dropped the boxes of pipe fittings at the sight of Jill running toward him, fists raised, and took an automatic step back. Rage contorted her face.

"You son of a—"

Without thought, he stooped as she closed in, and rammed his shoulder into her stomach. Jill's upper body pitched forward with an *ompf*, allowing him to pick her up fireman-style, and he immediately turned for his truck. She thrashed against him as he ate up the space, screaming curse words with each bounce of his steps and pounding her fists into his back.

He ignored all of it. There were at least four cameras on them, and though he didn't have a clue what had happened to set her off, he knew enough to get her out of there.

He tossed her across the front seat of his truck and had the vehicle in motion before she clued in that she could have escaped out the opposite door. As he pulled away, he looked in his rearview mirror. The cameras were still positioned on the truck, and it seemed as if everyone who'd previously been inside the houses had poured out. Heather and Trenton stood off by themselves, worry clear in their body language, as their glances alternated between him and the crowd behind the rope. There was no way anyone had missed any of that.

"Stop this truck and let me out," Jill yelled. "Right this minute!"

He slammed his fist on the "Door Lock" button and returned her fervor. "Not on your life."

"I'm warning you."

She reached for her door handle, and he pressed down on the gas pedal, shooting them away from the last of the watching eyes and tossing her against the back of the seat. "And I'm saving your ass," he growled out. "So sit there and shut up."

Surprisingly, she shut up.

And thankfully, she didn't open her door and go careening out.

He turned onto the main highway and sped down the road, his focus on getting them as far away as he could, as quickly as possible, and it was several minutes before he realized that Jill wasn't the only one in the truck who was breathing hard. They were both worked up and angry, and he didn't even have the pleasure of understanding why.

But he—like *her*—wanted to yell about it.

"That was quite impressive back there," he snarled out. "Way to shine, Jill."

He took a turn too sharp, flinging her against him.

"At least I didn't kidnap someone." She scrambled to the other side of the seat and strapped herself in, then seared him with a holier-than-thou look. "And don't even think I'm going to have sex with you!"

He damn near missed the next curve. "What the hell are you talking about?" he shouted. "Of course we're not having sex. Have you lost your mind?"

His tires squealed as he slammed on the brakes—he'd forgotten there was a one-lane bridge on this road—then the truck bumped, still going too fast, over the rickety bridge.

"Good Lord. Don't kill us." She gripped the loop hanging from the ceiling of the truck and once again turned a glare in his direction. "What are you doing, anyway?"

"I don't know what I'm doing!" This woman could drive him insane. "I'm getting you out of there, that's what. What were *you* doing? Why did you run screaming at me like that?"

"Because you—"

She bit off her words, and Cal glanced at her as he made another turn, this time at a more reasonable speed. She'd lost some of the steam, but pain was carved deep over her face.

What had happened?

"I can't believe what you did." Her voice cracked as she spoke. She stared out through the front window, no longer looking at him, and he wracked his brain trying to figure out what he could possibly have done. He hadn't even spoken to her in days.

"Jill." He forced his breathing to slow. One of them had to be rational. "You're going to need to give me more to go on here. I don't have a clue what you're talking about."

"How could you?" she whispered. She still wasn't looking at him, and Cal decided to let up on the gas. They were in the middle of nowhere, and there wasn't another car in sight.

"Tell me," he said. "Because I can't help if I don't know."

She let out a sad laugh. "You've already helped enough."

She glanced at him then, her eyes seeming too deep in their sockets, her gaze masked with both hurt and loss, and he thought about the afternoon when she'd been only fifteen. After they'd had sex, she'd cried in his arms for twenty minutes. Her eyes had looked exactly the same that day.

"Jill . . ."

"You told them about me," she said softly. "About my mother."

He reared back. No words could have surprised him more. "What?"

She'd looked away again, her head now seeming to hang from her shoulders, and Cal stopped the truck in the middle of the road. He shifted on his seat so that he faced her, and reached for her hands. They were icy.

"Jill." She still didn't look at him. "Jilly. Honey. I told them nothing about that day." He squeezed her fingers. "You know I wouldn't do that."

"But you did." She peeked at him. "They asked me about it. They know."

How could they possibly know?

He tilted his head, trying to figure it out. He didn't want to suggest the thought that crossed his mind, but . . . "Heather or Trenton?" he asked, his voice as unsteady as hers. "Could they have mentioned—"

"No."

"I don't mean now. In the past. A friend, maybe. Not the producers."

She just stared at him.

"That's possible, right? They likely don't even remember talking about it."

"It's *not* possible. I only told *you* about that day. And you know that. I told you that back then."

"But I thought . . ." He pressed his lips together. She'd really only told him?

"Not even Aunt Blu," she whispered. "Not that part."

"And Patrick knew about that part?"

At her pause, he finally began to breathe again, and when she dropped her gaze to the seat, he bent down and got in her face. "Listen to me, Jilly. Whatever they know, it wasn't me. You know I wouldn't tell those kinds of secrets. To anyone. I'll admit I've messed up plenty of times in my life, but this one—*I swear to you*—I didn't do." He could see the mixture of wanting to believe in him, but at the same time having learned personally that she couldn't, in her eyes, and he once again squeezed her hands. "Tell me what they said. Exactly."

"They said they knew I'd found her."

He nodded for her to continue. That part was public knowledge, though Blu had threatened every police officer in town that they weren't to breathe a word of it. No one had needed to know that Jill walked in on her mother's lifeless body. That she'd fallen in the blood as she'd tried to get to her.

She'd had enough on her shoulders at fourteen without the whole town looking at her with even more pity. Knowing they wanted to ask how she'd dealt with it. What it had been like.

People could be horrid with their curiosity.

"They knew that I wasn't home that afternoon," Jill continued. She closed her eyes as if seeing a different day and a different place, and Cal wanted to pull her to him. "That I'd left her there alone. He said that he knew I'd come home at six thirty . . . that some people have survivor's guilt . . ."

Cal waited, but she didn't say anything more.

"And?" he finally asked. "What else?"

She shook her head, and her eyelids fluttered open. It was the middle of the day, but in the cab of his truck, out on Caterpillar Road, there seemed to be no light filtering in on them. "I don't know," she said, so softly he almost didn't hear.

"What do you mean you don't know?"

"I got mad and I ran." She swallowed. "To you."

"And that's all he said? That you were out that afternoon, and that you found her?"

She nodded. "And survivor's guilt."

"Okay. Then we can deal with that. That's not so bad."

"How do you know?"

"Jilly, they could have gotten that from the police report, or by talking to anyone who'd been on the scene that day. But if that's all they said to you—"

"I ran before he could say any more."

"But you never told anyone else, right?"

She shook her head, her eyes a mix of blue and green as she stared back at him.

"And I've never told a soul," he repeated. He let go of her hands and cupped her chin. "And I *won't*. I promise."

"But you once made other promises . . ."

He let his own head hang then. And dropped his hold on her. "I did. And I regret them." He forced himself to meet her eyes. "I should never have said half the things I did back then. I meant them at the time. I swear. And it never crossed my mind for a second that my promises—that what we were to each other—wouldn't so much as enter my consciousness when put to the test. But the truth is, Jilly . . . a twenty-year-old guy isn't the smartest kid in the classroom. At least I wasn't. And I'm sorry about that."

"So would you do it differently if you had to do it again?"

His lungs felt as if all the air were being sucked out of it. "You mean *how* I left?" He nodded. "Yes. I'd do that differently in a heart-beat. But leaving in general?" It hurt to even look at her. It was as if they were eighteen and twenty all over again. He slowly shook his head. "I don't think so. I'd still leave. I had to come home." His granny had needed him.

"I suggested she go with us," Jill reminded him, even though he didn't voice his thought, and finally, her voice began to refill. She no longer sounded like a lost little girl who'd come home to find her mother's wrists slit.

"And we would have supported her how?" he asked gently. "I had a job here. I was going to buy into the business."

But when he sensed the age-old anger firing back to life in her, he held up his hands.

"Don't," he said. "Just stop. It's over and done. Not worth fighting about again."

"*We're* over and done."

"Yes. We can't go back, Jilly. Even if we wanted to."

"Not that you'd want to." Her sarcasm was heavy.

"Would *you*?" He studied her after he asked the question. She was suddenly brewing for a fight, but he knew fighting was her armor. And he didn't want to fight with her anymore. He didn't want to fight with her ever again. "Would you seriously change how anything happened?" he repeated. "Even the fact that we got together to begin with? We had each other for a while, and it was really good. I think we both needed that. But you had to go, right? Just like *I* had to stay? That's what you said."

"Yet I still failed."

He pulled in a controlled breath. He'd been wondering that for years. "On all of it?"

She looked away. "I never found my dad, if that's what you're asking."

That's what he'd been asking. "And the acting?"

He didn't know how else to even phrase that question. Clearly she hadn't made it big. She was here fighting an uphill battle in what was traditionally a man's world. Not in Hollywood schmoozing with the A-listers. And as far as he knew, she'd never even been in anything. He'd watched for her for years.

She put several inches between them. "How does it look like it went?"

And that was the end of the congenial conversation. She'd shut back down.

Cal didn't immediately return to his side of the truck, though, because something about the look on her face kept him from retreating.

It was more than just anger hiding in there. Or at least, more than anger at *him*.

But what else was she upset about?

"Did you ever come close?" he asked. Had he misread her desire to act back then? He'd laughed at her impassioned plea as she'd tried to convince him to go with her. He'd even accused her of trying out her so-called acting skills on him. But he'd known her leaving hadn't been about building a career. LA had been her opportunity to run as far away as she could. Her wanting to be anything but her mother's daughter.

The look on her face now struck him hard, though, and he couldn't help but wonder if something else might have happened other than her *not* making it as an actress.

When he finally accepted that she had no intention of saying another word on the subject, he turned back to the wheel. "Mind if we drive around a bit before going back?" He needed a moment to reorient himself. Being this close to Jill shifted his equilibrium.

Plus, he simply wasn't ready to return to the reality of reality TV.

"Whatever," Jill tossed out. There was zero emotion in the word. "But don't think this means we're friends again."

He chuckled without humor. "I'd never think a single conversation with you would equate to us being friends again." He checked to make sure no vehicles were heading their way and put the truck into gear. "You don't even have to talk while we drive," he added, tossing his own sarcasm into the mix. "In fact, I'd prefer you didn't. Let's just . . . *be*."

She nodded at that—still not looking at him—and he drove them around the back roads of the town where they'd both grown up. It was a beautiful time of year for central Texas. The bluebonnets were beginning to die out, but there was enough color left to make for a gorgeous backdrop on a middle-of-the-week drive with two people who'd once cared for each other. It was a shame, actually, that that's all this was. He remembered his grandparents taking these kinds of drives on a regular basis. Papaw would have his arm thrown over the back of the car seat, and Granny would be scooted in next to him.

He smiled slightly at the memory. They'd take him and Rodney, and they'd pick out a tree along the river for a picnic. Or maybe one of the many bridges around the area. Red Oak River wound its way throughout the county, and there was never a lack of beautiful scenery.

He made a right turn, still thinking about his grandparents, until his thoughts were interrupted by Jill.

"You should have told me about being on the show."

He glanced across the front seat. Her eyes remained on the road. "And how would I have done that?" he questioned. "You don't talk to me, remember?"

"I would have talked to you about that."

"Really?" He signaled and turned left. "If I'd just called you up one day? Or stopped you in town? *Hey, Jill*"—he mimicked himself—*"guess what I signed up to do? And I heard you're doing it, too! Won't this be fun?"* His bark of laughter rang harsh in the enclosed space. "You wouldn't have let me get past your name, and you know it."

She looked out the side window, her chin jutting forward. "Did you do it just to hurt me?"

Her question shouldn't have surprised him, because she'd never been one to beat around the bush. Yet it packed a wallop. *No.* He hadn't done it because he'd *wanted* to hurt her.

But at the same time, he'd known it would.

His papaw would have been disappointed in him.

"It's great exposure," he finally answered.

She huffed. "Heather said the same thing. And you're avoiding the question."

"I am," he acknowledged. And he also knew he'd taken perverse pleasure in agreeing to be on the show in the first place. He supposed that meant he hadn't left all his childish ways back in Vegas twelve years before. But he could take solace in knowing that he'd changed his mind. The hurt he'd witnessed on Jill's face in the café Monday morning had stung. She'd deserved to know what she was walking into. To not be ambushed.

The truth was, she probably deserved for him to have said *no* to the offer.

"I signed up because of you," he admitted. "But I didn't really think it through."

She said nothing in reply, and a few seconds later, he once again flipped on his turn signal and slowed to make a turn. Then he jolted when he realized he was two seconds from pulling into his own farm. He straightened the wheel, intending to drive on past, his heart suddenly racing. But he changed his mind at the last second, and without looking at Jill, he turned onto the rutted gravel driveway and kept the truck moving steadily forward.

Jill sat up, one hand going to the dashboard, and her gaze darting around. "Where are you going?"

He didn't answer. Just focused on the ruts.

Once he got through the line of trees, though, where the openness of his land could be seen, he struggled to pull in a breath. He still couldn't say anything to the woman sitting next him, but he wanted to know what she thought.

"Cal." She looked out the back window. "We're trespassing. We just passed a 'No Trespassing' sign."

When he still said nothing, she finally turned to him. He didn't look at her.

"Do you *know* whose property this is?"

"We're not trespassing." He still couldn't pull in a complete breath.

"Then hopefully that means no one will start taking shots at us. We are in Texas, you know."

"No one's going to shoot us." He kept driving, the gravel no longer as rutted as it had been out by the highway, and didn't slow until he topped a slight ridge. As he crested the hill, the twenty-five-hundred-square-foot log cabin he'd been renovating for the last year could be seen in the distance. It sat on another rise, its wraparound porch like wide arms hugging what was inside, while rolling hills and trees reaching high into the sky spread out as far as the eye could see.

The sky was a clear blue today, and he couldn't have set the scene any better.

"Whose house is this?" She asked the question more softly, as if the serenity of the land had overtaken her.

"It's mine," he said simply.

He'd put the truck into park, and Jill turned in her seat, this time being the one to face him. His breaths remained short, his nerves tight, but he forced himself to look over at her.

"This is *yours*?" Her blue-green eyes lost the pain that had been so clear before. She shifted in her seat, peering out through all four windows, and after taking in a full 360-degree view, she once again faced him. "How much land is here?"

"Three hundred acres."

Her mouth hung open. "What are you going to do with it?"

He gave a little shrug. "I don't know."

Jill shifted in the seat to face the front window, and all Cal could hear for the next several minutes were the breaths she took. She looked both right and left once again, as well as straight ahead at the house, and she even leaned forward and stared up at the sky. Once she'd gotten another good look, she dropped back to the seat.

"It's gorgeous," she said. "Both the house and the land. And this view is one in a million."

"No one knows I bought it," he admitted. He had no idea why he'd told her that.

She slid him a glance. "No one?"

He shook his head. He hadn't even told his grandmother. He would eventually, though. He'd bring her out to see it.

"Marci thinks she's going to be the one to finally 'snag' you," Jill told him, and he understood where she was going with her comment. He'd heard that Marci had been claiming as much, yet he'd never had the urge to bring his supposed "girlfriend" to his home.

"Marci doesn't know," he told her. "She thinks if she manages to 'snag' me, as you put it, that she can talk me into moving into the house her father bought her." Which was huge and came with every feature a person could possibly want. But it was totally not his style. It was all straight lines and sleek polishes.

"Those were her words," Jill pointed out. "Not mine."

Cal shrugged again. "She hasn't said them to me."

He didn't want to talk about Marci.

He didn't even want to think about Marci.

He nodded toward his house. "It was built in the '50s. I'm renovating it in my spare time."

"I'm doing the same to the house I bought last year." She bit her lip on a laugh. "Mine is a tad smaller, though." She stared at the home he'd someday live in. "And nothing at all like this."

He tried to look at it through her eyes. "This one is too big for me."

"But it's so perfect." She said the words wistfully, and Cal found himself watching her again. He'd once sworn to build her a house like this. He'd forgotten that until now. They'd planned to fill it with kids.

He pictured inky-black-haired kids running around the yard. Then Jill stepping out on the front porch with a baby to her breast.

Damn. He still had feelings for her. He'd thought he'd gotten over that.

"Maybe I'll buy some cows," he said. He had to get his mind on something other than Jill. And cows *were* an option.

"Or horses." She pointed to an open field. "Can't you imagine horses running through that pasture? A barn tucked up next to those back trees."

"There's a pond in that area, too. You can't see it from here, though." He pointed out another section of land. "But there's also one back there. In that dip just before the hill. You can see that one from the back of the house."

That wistful sound hit his ear again. "Ponds are nice."

He nodded, but he said nothing else. They just sat there, enjoying the moment, while he tried his best to keep his mind on cows and horses.

After several minutes, he knew it was time to go. He had to get out of there. Otherwise, he'd be tempted to head down the hill instead of away from it. And if he got her down there, he wasn't sure whether he'd want to show her the workshop he'd fixed up for himself, whether he'd point out the pond he'd mentioned could be seen from the house . . . or if he'd lead her *through* his home and try to talk her into testing out the springs in his new king-sized mattress.

He glanced over at her. He had issues. "You ready to head back?"

She nodded.

Allowing himself to consider no other options, he circled the truck around and headed back the way he'd come.

"They're going to be watching for us," she pointed out. "Cameras will probably be trained on the truck the second we roll back into town."

"I imagine they will be." He watched his land in his rearview. He had to get his mind on something else. "This is going to be a hell of an interesting show by the time they air it. They're so in our faces all the time. Do they do this to all competitors?"

"I have no idea. I've never seen an episode."

He laughed lightly. "Me neither. Though Marci has tried her best to talk me into a *Texas Dream Home* marathon ever since she found out I was doing the show."

They fell silent again as he circumvented the ruts, and when he made it back to the highway, he decided to share one more piece of info with her. It felt important. "Marci didn't find out about me being on the show until last Monday, either."

Jill nodded. "And I haven't watched *any* television since I moved back home."

Cal turned to her, but she was looking out her window again.

"I don't even own a TV," she said softly.

He got the significance. "I take it that's a personal choice? Not one dictated by finances?"

"Personal choice," she acknowledged.

He wanted to reach over and squeeze her hand again, but he wasn't sure she'd accept the action as she had earlier. "I'm sorry LA didn't turn out the way you'd hoped."

She merely shrugged.

He pulled out on the highway, and they rode for several miles with neither feeling the need to speak, and when he turned onto Main Street, he caught sight of Loretta sitting in her car at the gas station. The second her gaze landed on them, she lifted her phone to her ear. Their return was being reported at that very moment.

Cal looked over at Jill, not quite ready to get back to "reality," but knowing they had no choice. But he found himself wanting to stir the pot just a bit more before they returned. He wanted to be a bug in her ear, just as he knew she would be one in his. "You know," he started. "We couldn't have had sex, anyway."

Surprise rounded her eyes. "What are you talking about?"

"When we drove away before. You started yelling at me that I shouldn't think we were going to have sex. But I wouldn't have ever thought that, because the rule is that we can't have sex while either is still angry with the other, right? No sex until the anger passes."

He could see her processing his words, but he didn't have a clue what she might be thinking. Nor did he know if she even remembered the rule. They'd come up with it together.

She finally nodded. "Right. No sex until the anger passes. And the anger *isn't* passing."

He nodded, as well. "Good thing we're not planning on having sex, then."

Chapter Eight

*"Sometimes a man can come in handy. But then . . . you
also have fingers for that."*

—Blu Johnson, life lesson #89

Good thing we're not planning on having sex, then.

Jill stared at the cards in her hand, but as had been the case with
every round they'd played during the last two hours, she couldn't
concentrate.

Good thing we're not planning on having sex.

Why had he brought that up? But then, why had she?

Because the only thing she'd now thought about for days was having sex with Cal.

"Rummy!" Heather slapped her cards on the table, fanning them
out, then held her arms up as if she'd just kicked a field goal. "Boom.
In your face."

Jill and Trenton both leaned forward to scrutinize the winning
hand, while Aunt Blu tossed down a shot of whiskey.

"I swear, you girls want to play rummy just to see me get drunk,"
Aunt Blu said, her words slightly slurred. "Father Kibby is going to give
me the evil eye tomorrow morning."

"Father Kibby will only give you the evil eye because you didn't invite him over to share." Trenton eyed the bottle of Jim Beam while Heather poured.

"Bottoms up, ladies."

Jill and Trenton downed their shots.

"Good Josephine, Heather." Trenton coughed. "Give us a break with this stuff."

"No one breaks until—"

"I call uncle." Jill raised her hand. "You know whiskey isn't my thing."

In fact, drinking was rarely her thing. Mostly just when they had Saturday-night game nights, and only then if Aunt Blu had no girls. Seeing as there were currently no foster girls in the house, she and Trenton would both be staying the night with Heather. Assuming they could even make it down to her place in the dark.

"I double her uncle," Aunt Blu announced with one finger raised in the air and her eyes half-shut. She pushed back from the table, but didn't go anywhere. She just sat there blinking, as if trying to bring the room into focus. "How many hands did I lose?"

"All of them," Heather snickered.

"And Jill and I only won one each," Trenton added. She licked a drop of whiskey off the side of her thumb.

Other than Heather, they were all about half a gust of wind from falling face-first on the floor, and calling uncle admitted it. And all of them hated calling uncle.

"Trenton?" Heather prodded.

Trenton groaned. *"Uncle."*

Heather stood and did her victory dance. Which looked very similar to a chicken dance.

"So how's the house coming?" Aunt Blu asked. She stared a little too hard at Heather, likely directing the question at her simply because Heather was the one who sat directly across from her.

"The house is coming along great," Heather answered. "We got most of the drywall up already, the wiring and plumbing finished this morning, and we start mudding and putting the windows in next week."

"We also have these cool beams ordered for the living room ceiling," Jill added. "Totally perfect for Texas. You should come out and see it."

Aunt Blu had been to the house before they'd started demo, but she hadn't wanted to be in the way after that. She preferred doing the whole "before and after" thing if she could stay away until the work was done. "I'll get out there eventually." She had her eyes closed again. "That little fella called me today. Wants to interview me in a couple a weeks."

Jill smiled. Aunt Blu called Patrick "that little fella," and Jill thought it fit.

"I'll prolly wait until then to come out." Aunt Blu nodded, then she swayed in her chair.

Trenton and Jill reached out to steady her.

"Want us to help you to bed?" Jill asked.

She was rewarded with a hazy gray-eyed glare. "I am not ready for bed, and when I am, I'll see myself to gettin' there." She turned to Trenton. "Everyone in town is talking about you running off with Cal the other day. What was that about?"

Trenton pointed to Jill, and Aunt Blu swung her gaze back to the other side of the table.

"They said you were gone a long time." Blu now spoke to Jill.

"I was," Jill admitted. "That little fella ticked me off, and I needed to cool down."

"So you went on a drive with *Cal*?"

Jill really didn't want to go into the specifics. Heather and Trenton had grilled her over it when she'd returned, of course, and she'd told them about Patrick pushing for details concerning the day of. She hadn't explained in depth what she'd truly flipped out about, or why she'd gone after Cal when she had, but given that Cal had been playing into

Patrick's games to get them on screen together, she'd let them believe she'd thought Cal had a part in it.

She'd spoken to Patrick upon returning, as well, and as Cal had guessed, the only specifics the show had were what had come from the police report. She'd made it clear once again that the day of was off limits, and that if they didn't adhere to that deal, then she would be done. They could sue her for the rest of her life if they wanted, but she'd walk. And Heather and Jill would go with her.

They'd agreed.

"I went on a drive with Cal because I thought he'd set me up," Jill told Aunt Blu now. "He shoved me in his truck to keep me from beating the crap out of him in front of everyone, and we were heading down the road before I realized what was going on."

"Good for him." Blu turned her shot glass upside down on the table and leaned in to peer through the bottom part of the glass. "That boy always did care about you."

No one said anything for a moment, and Jill reached out to scoop up the cards. She didn't intend to deal another round, but shuffling them would keep her hands busy. At the same time, Trenton reached over and stole a chocolate-covered raisin from Aunt Blu's bowl. Blu smacked Trenton's hand.

"They also say you've been more mellow since that ride," Aunt Blu continued.

Jill frowned. No one had seen her be anything *but* mellow until she'd flown into a rage and run across the yard. In fact, they'd seen nothing remotely similar to that in twelve years—the chair incident at the café notwithstanding. But memories were long in their town, and one mistake could bring it all back. "I am more mellow," she assured her foster mother. "It wasn't my best look that day, so I refuse to go off like that again."

"Good. I always hated getting that call."

"That call" would be the two times Jill got picked up by the police for fighting. She'd not been the easiest teenager to take in.

Aunt Blu scrunched her nose then and peered down toward her mouth. She'd apparently moved beyond talking about that week's episode at the house and was now trying to see her own nose. Jill kept a straight face because Blu hated when they got her drunk and laughed at her, but Heather wasn't so chivalrous. She flat-out chortled.

"Your nose is still there, Aunt Blu."

Blu slapped her hand on the table and looked at Heather. "I reckon I know there's a nose there. I was just trying to see if it's *my* nose or someone else's."

Jill and Trenton joined in on the laughter, and as Blu tried to shoot them both her evil glare, they reached out to once again steady her. "It's *your* nose, Aunt Blu," Jill assured her. "No one switched it out when you weren't looking."

"Good. Because you know people do that."

Jill nodded. "I know." She inched her bottle of water closer to her foster mother, but didn't suggest she drink it. Blu didn't take the hint. Jill went back to shuffling the cards as Aunt Blu tried again to see her nose, and Heather rose to get more water for everyone. Trenton muttered something about peeing on herself if she didn't get to the bathroom and left the room, stumbling only slightly when she got up too fast.

Jill stayed where she was. And she thought about Cal.

And that drive.

And the fact that Cal had a three-hundred-acre farm that no one but *she* knew about.

She'd run those facts through her head multiple times over the last few days. Never would she have pictured that kind of acreage for Cal. Not that it was hard to come by in their part of Texas, but just that it seemed so . . . *settled.*

Yes, they'd gotten married, and yes, leading up to that marriage, they'd talked of building their own home someday. *And* filling it with kids. But she'd always imagined their home would be much less rustic and in a much more populated area. With maybe a quarter acre of land.

Yet the pride that had washed over Cal while looking out over his property had been unmistakable. He was in love with the spot he was carving out for himself, and she could see why. She just couldn't figure out his reasoning for being so secretive about it.

She kind of liked knowing she was the only person he'd told, though.

"What do you think, Jilly?"

Jill pulled her attention back from Cal and realized that Trenton had returned to the table. She'd brought the basket of leftover rolls from dinner, and she passed them around. Jill took one, needing to soak up some of the whiskey swilling around inside her. Aunt Blu did *not*.

"What do I think about what?" Jill asked.

Trenton nodded to Heather. "About Heather fixing you up with Little Red."

"Who's Little Red?" Aunt Blu squawked out.

Jill just stared. What had she missed?

"He works for Cal," Heather explained to Aunt Blu. "He's this sweetheart of a man who looks like he shouldn't even be old enough to drive, much less date, but he's totally got the hots for our Jill."

"He doesn't have the hots," Jill protested.

Heather smiled innocently. "Yet look at you. You're blushing just like Little Red does when he looks at you."

Jill made a face at Heather. She *was* blushing and she knew it. But only because it was so endearing the way Doug's cheeks heated every time he saw her.

"And for the record," Heather continued, "the whole thing wasn't my idea, but I do think you should do it. He stopped me yesterday, asking about you. Said he wouldn't be back at the house for a couple of weeks, but he was 'surely hoping' to see you before then." She waggled her brows at Jill. "He practically begged me to set something up."

"I hope you told him no."

"I told him I'd do my best."

"*Heather.* You know I don't date."

"Well, I think you *should* date," Aunt Blu announced. Her words came out a little too loud, and she reached over and patted Jill's hand. "You haven't been out with a man since you came home."

Jill put a hand over Blu's. "I haven't been out because I don't want to, Aunt Blu. And that hasn't changed."

"But it *could* change." The look in the other woman's face was earnest, if a little glazed. "A woman needs a man once in a while."

Jill knew the words weren't meant to hurt, yet they stabbed anyway. The statement was eerily reminiscent of what her mother used to say.

Janet Sadler would follow up her words by pointing out that Jill was more like her than she realized, and that she'd someday understand. All women needed a good man in their life. It's what made them whole.

But Jill didn't understand. She was fine just as she was.

She'd convinced herself she did one time, though. That her mother had been right.

Jill had been trying her entire life not to be needy. Not to be like her mom. But then she'd met Cal, and he'd simply gotten her. Even when they'd been fighting—and they'd fought a lot—they'd connected in a way she'd never expected to find with another person. So she'd given in. She *was* just like her mom, and she'd finally understood the need for a good man.

Only, turned out he hadn't been so good, after all. He'd left her in the exact fashion as her mother's last "good man" had done.

"I really *don't* need one," Jill said again. "And honestly, the only thing I can think a man would be even the slightest bit useful for would be sex. And . . . well . . ." Jill held up her hands, palms up, and Aunt Blu nodded solemnly.

"Right," Aunt Blu said. "You've got fingers for that."

Trenton and Heather both dunked their heads at Blu's words. The woman was a trip when she was drinking, and she'd been right. They liked to talk her into playing rummy just to get her drunk. She never won at the card game, and it was one of the few times Jill and the others ever felt they had the upper hand around Blu.

"Sure we can't put you to bed?" Jill asked.

Blu held up one hand and waggled her fingers in the air. "Because you think *I* don't need a man, either?"

"Aunt Blu!" Heather huffed out. "Behave yourself. What would Father Kibby think?"

"He'd probably think that I *do* need a man." She squinted in concentration. "And he might be right."

"He's not right." Jill put the water bottle directly into Blu's hand that time.

"Well, I stand by my statement," Heather continued. "Jill should go out with Little Red, if for no other reason than to have some fun."

"And you know that if I did go out with him, it would end up on camera for all to see. Heck, Len would probably *follow* us on our date."

"Len is *Big* Red," Heather explained to Aunt Blu. "He's Jilly's personal cameraman."

"He's a pain in my ass," Jill grumbled.

"I think you should go out with him *because* it'll end up on camera," Trenton told her. "That would take some of the focus off you and Cal."

Aunt Blu's water bottle dropped from the table and rolled across the floor. "Vote," she announced, ignoring the escaping water. Then she raised her hand.

Heather and Trenton followed suit.

"We are *not* voting on whether I'm going out with Little Red or not."

"Three to one," Blu announced. She slapped her hand on the table. "Done!"

~

The driver of the car behind Cal laid on his horn as he pulled out into the other lane, and passed Cal doing no more than the speed limit. Cal looked down at his odometer. No wonder the other driver had gotten ticked off. They were out on the open highway, and the needle on Cal's truck pointed to forty.

He pressed the gas pedal, nudging his speed higher, but didn't force it all that much. He was enjoying his Sunday-afternoon drive, and no one would rush him through it. He'd just spent the last few hours with his grandmother, and though anxious to get back to his farm—to work on the table he'd decided to build for the Cadillac House—he was equally excited to do exactly what he was doing at the moment. Which was driving. And thinking about Jill.

He hit the button to lower the driver's window as he hung a right onto the road leading to his property, and a waft of good ole Texas air passed over him. There was nothing quite like his home state. Just as there was no *one* quite like his ex.

He'd had Jill in his truck the other day. *And* she'd actually talked to him.

Granted, she hadn't freely climbed inside, nor had their conversation been what anyone would ever term as cordial. At least, not at first. But then it had slipped beyond that, and he'd seen parts of the girl he'd once fallen in love with. Jill was still Jill. Angry, passionate, bold. And stubborn. Always so stubborn.

But also soft.

He thought about the look on her face when she'd been picturing his land with life on it—she'd even picked out a spot to build a barn—and he let out a wry chuckle. All this time, he'd thought her silence had merely been an annoyance to him. That he'd simply wanted to "win"—therefore, he'd sought to break her down and make her speak to him. Yet when he'd had her in his truck . . .

He stared blankly at the road in front of him. When he'd had her in his truck, he'd wanted to keep her there. He'd *wanted* her naked. In his bed. In the very spot she'd pictured horses running.

Up against the tree that shaded the front of his house.

He held back the groan the thought provoked. What the hell had that been about? He'd truly had no idea he had any remaining feelings for her. Not those kind of feelings, anyway.

He blinked as another car whipped around him, and he realized that he'd once again let off the gas pedal. He then forced himself to pick up speed. Maybe he *could* be rushed that afternoon, after all. Otherwise his daydreaming would likely get him *and* others into an accident.

And the thing was, he shouldn't be daydreaming at all. At least, not about Jill.

His phone rang as he passed a tractor and closed in on his driveway, and though he suspected the call to be from the woman he was dating—who was the only one he *should* be daydreaming about—he found himself hesitant to answer. Marci had gone to Dallas for the weekend to "punish" him for canceling on her the Saturday before, and he kind of didn't want his punishment to end.

But that was just him being a jerk. It was also the type of thinking that always precipitated the ending of his relationships.

He pulled out his phone. Marci was a good woman. She didn't deserve his attitude.

But the number on the screen was Pete's.

"Hey, man." Cal turned into his driveway. "Everything okay?" Instead of checking in on any of the worksites the day before, he'd decided to push through Pete's raise. Things were running smoothly with his foreman at the helm, so Cal had taken a small breather from the Cadillac project and had spent the day at his farm. Right after he'd bought the place, he'd converted an old barn into a workshop. The place had become his go-to for de-stressing, but it had been weeks since he'd had any time to spend there.

"Right as rain." Pete gave a quick rundown on a couple of the newer jobs they'd started work on, then segued into their weekly basketball game at the rec center. "We going to see you today?"

"Wouldn't miss it." They met up with several guys at the rec center every Sunday night.

He crested the ridge of his property and headed down the hill. The feeling of being home rolled through him.

"Want to a grab a bite first?" Pete asked. "Or are you with Marci today?"

Cal eyed the grill he'd purchased the day before, where it sat on his front porch, waiting to be assembled. Then he shifted his gaze to the basketball hoop he'd erected on the other side of his workshop. He had plenty of space here. He *could* invite the whole group out.

But then, concrete hadn't been poured for the basketball court yet. And he'd have to run to the store if he offered to grill steaks.

"Not with Marci," he finally answered. He put the truck into park. "I'll just meet you at the rec center, though. Got too much going on this afternoon."

He and Pete disconnected, but Cal didn't get out of his truck. Because he was thinking about Jill again. About how he'd brought her out here when he'd yet to tell anyone else about the place.

Why had he done that?

And did it even matter? They'd been driving, taking in the sights. It only made sense he'd naturally head this way.

Only, it hadn't made sense that he'd turn into his drive.

And it sure as hell hadn't made sense to picture her in his house. Or to put her there naked.

He let out a growl when that very vision once again popped to mind, and stepped from the vehicle. The wise thing would be to forget all thoughts of Jill, bare breasted or otherwise. Maybe to call up his girlfriend and offer an apology. Take *her* to dinner tonight instead of playing ball with the boys.

However, he'd proven time and again that he wasn't always so wise. And something told him this time would be no different.

Chapter Nine

"Believe in everything. Marvel at everything discovered."

—Blu Johnson, life lesson #24

Jill glanced at her watch Monday morning as work buzzed throughout the house . . . then she used the excuse of checking one of the new light switches while at the same time attempting to unobtrusively peek next door. Cal and his team hadn't worked over the weekend, and that fact had been bugging her since Saturday. The project was only two weeks in, but given the potential state of the house, she'd been hoping Cal would be behind by this point. If We Nail It didn't finish their renovations on time, Bluebonnet would be the automatic winner.

Not that she wanted to win by default. She'd rather best Cal in true skill—and then grind it in his face. Of course, she *would* take a win against him in any form it presented itself.

Heather strolled through the front door, and Jill brought her gaze back from next door and breathed a sigh of relief. They could get to work now. And *she* could quit thinking about Cal. "You're late," Jill informed her. She rummaged through the tools to find a level.

"And you'll survive," Heather answered. She then handed over one of her business cards, back side up, and Jill looked down to find a phone number scribbled across it.

"What's this?"

"Your date."

Jill jerked her gaze up. "My what?"

"Date," Heather repeated. "We discussed this Saturday night, remember?" She nodded at the card. "Friday night at seven. The Buffalo Nickel."

"I told you, I'm not going out with Little Red."

"We voted on it. You have to. Plus," Heather continued when Jill tried to interrupt her, "I'm going with you. A double date with me and Len. You and I will meet the two of them there."

Jill's eyes went wide. "You and Big Red?"

Heather shrugged. "Don't make a deal about it. It's just a date."

Jill stared at her foster sister. Though Heather was the romantic in the group, she rarely went on dates herself. Not anymore. She had a bad habit of falling hard, so she'd found it best to simply avoid.

Was Heather *wanting* to date again? "Len isn't the type of man to—"

"Just a date," Heather said once more. "He's too old for me, anyway. But he overheard me talking with Doug last week, and he suggested the four of us could go out together. It's been forever since I've had any fun, so I decided what the heck. I stopped him outside a few minutes ago, and it's done. Friday night at seven. The four of us. Be prepared for dancing."

Jill still didn't want to go on a date.

At the same time, it wasn't as if she'd risk getting serious about a twenty-five-year-old who looked to be about twelve, either. Which made him a *safe* date. Kind of the way Len would be for Heather.

Then something else occurred to her, and she pointed an accusing finger at her foster sister. "No cameras. That isn't why Len wants to go, is it? I'm not going on a date and having it filmed."

Heather held her hands up. "No cameras. I promise. It's just a date. Come on, Jilly," she pleaded, even batting her big blue eyes as if she thought that would win Jill over. "You know you need some fun," Heather wheedled.

"What I need is for us to win this competition." She motioned toward the window. "Any idea what's going on over there? How were they able to take the whole weekend off?"

Heather didn't answer. She just stared at Jill, silently calling her out on her attempt to change the subject.

But Jill wouldn't be so easily thwarted. "Don't you even care about winning?"

"Or course I care," Heather answered. "But we're not talking about work right now."

"Well, we should be." At Heather's continued stare, Jill finally conceded. "Fine." She sighed dramatically. "I'll go on the date. But you owe me."

"Sure. I owe you." She grabbed the level from Jill's hand. "Now let's get to it. I have other things I need to get done today."

"I'm the one who's been waiting on you," Jill mumbled. She handed over a pair of gloves. "We're starting upstairs."

They had a full crew that morning, with some of the women slapping mud on the drywall in the finished rooms, others tackling the final cutouts where the electricians had run the updated wiring, and two women on scaffolding in the oversized kitchen. Those two were finishing up the new vaulted ceiling. Which left Jill and Heather to get the windows on the upper floor installed.

Trenton had already left to pick up the windows, so there was limited time to get everything prepped.

As they made their way up the temporary risers of the U-shaped stairs, Jill looked out over the newly opened space and noted a handful of items scattered throughout. A couple of *Texas Dream Home* interns had shown up before the camera crews that morning, carting in tubs, and had distributed advertisers' products in places where they'd receive good visibility on camera. Something about the out-of-place items left a bad taste in Jill's mouth. The project was suddenly more about the television show than renovating two old homes.

Len came into the house then, spotted her and Heather, and followed them to the second floor, and thirty minutes later, Trenton pulled into the drive. After calling down for a couple of the women to go out and help, Jill pocketed a handful of shims that would be used for squaring up the windows. But the footsteps that soon made their way up the stairs were too heavy to be anyone working for *her*. And everyone downstairs had gone silent.

Jill sighed. What now?

She came out of the front room to find Cal single-handedly hauling their largest window, and he had the thing hoisted above his head. As if announcing his masculine prowess for all to see. And of course, every female on the first floor was *seeing*.

"What are you doing?" Jill crossed her arms over her chest.

"Helping." Cal grinned.

"We don't need your help."

She tossed around a quick glance to check Len's whereabouts, finding his camera pointing her way. The last thing she wanted was for anyone to think the all-female crew needed the big strong men to carry in the heavy stuff for them, and she certainly didn't want it recorded for television. So she held out her arms.

"Give it to me," she said to Cal.

He just laughed. He nodded to the opening in the room behind her. "Is it going in there?"

"I'm serious, Cal. I don't need your help. Why are you even here?"

He moved her way, not stopping as he neared, and she found herself being backed into the room. Heather hadn't followed her out, so now it was the three of them in the single room together. Plus Len.

Cal leaned over to set the window at her feet, and as he stood, he covered her mic with the palm of his hand. "I wanted to see what you know about ghosts," he murmured.

That was the last thing she'd expected to hear.

She pushed his hand away and covered her mic herself. "Did you say 'ghosts'?"

Heather perked up. "Have you seen her?" She sucked in a breath and sidled in beside them. "Can I come over and see her?"

When Heather realized Jill was attempting to muffle their conversation by covering her mic, she turned Jill around and hit the "Mute" button. Jill did the same for Heather, then all three of them stepped in closer. Cal's back faced Len, which blocked the other man from being able to see their mouths as they spoke, and when Len cleared his throat to get their attention, they ignored him.

"I think I've *heard* her," Cal told them. He kept his voice low.

He pointed to the matching dormer in the other house, and Heather turned with the motion. She poked her head out the window opening. Jill silently watched. It wasn't that she didn't believe in ghosts. But at the same time, she couldn't say she *did*, either.

And she wasn't sure she wanted to.

"What did you hear?" she finally asked. She suspected this was more a ploy than anything, and she craned her neck, assuming she'd catch Patrick loitering nearby. But there was no Patrick.

"A few random noises," Cal shared. "Footsteps. Something sliding across the floor a couple of times. Then this morning, some of our tools were moved."

"I think she was over there last night," Heather told him.

Cal nodded in agreement. "I do, too. What did you see?"

"Wait." Jill held up a hand to stop the words. She looked at Heather. "When were you even here to see anything?" They hadn't worked the day before, either.

"I'd left that phone number here Friday." Heather motioned to the pocket where Jill had shoved the business card. "I had to stop by and get it so I could set up your—" She cut off her words, as if realizing it was none of Cal's business that Jill had a date, then she peeked around Cal's chest to see if Len was listening in. Len had left the room. "It doesn't matter *why* I was here," she told Cal, "but I was. And *while* I was, the light in that upstairs bedroom was on."

Cal flicked a glance toward the Cadillac House. "And no one was over there?"

"No cars. I thought I saw someone in the room for a second, though. Just a shadow, really." Heather leaned in and whispered, "Did you know the story is that she and her lover used to make love in that very bedroom? It wasn't that she didn't want to be in her marital bed with another man, but that she didn't want *him* to have to be there. She even bought a new bedroom suite for 'their' room. Just for—"

"Heather," Jill interrupted. She shot a pointed look at her foster sister. "Get back to what you saw last night."

"Right." Heather made a face indicating that Jill was a stickler for "the facts," and Cal chuckled in solidarity. It made Jill want to stomp on both their toes.

She was still mad at the man, darn it. He shouldn't even be here!

Yet there they were, all whispering about a supposed ghost.

"So I thought I saw a shadow," Heather said, picking her story back up. "Just a flicker of movement behind the window, and I went out into the yard hoping for a better view. I was thinking about Mr. Wainwright coming home that night and seeing them up there, you know? Wondering if I could see what he'd seen."

Jill cleared her throat, and Heather shot her a scowl.

"I watched for several more minutes, but then . . . nothing." Heather shrugged. "So I left."

"Was the light still on when you left?"

She nodded. "Was it on when you got there this morning?"

"No."

"You two do know that interns went through both houses," Jill said.

Cal and Heather both stared at her as if she made no sense.

"This *morning*," she stressed. "They could have turned off the lights. They could have moved the tools."

She pointed out the can of primer sitting in the corner that had been one of the many items pulled from the totes. "They went through every room."

"It wasn't the interns," Cal told her.

"How do you know?"

"Because she was over there," Heather whispered again. "I saw her."

Jill fought against rolling her eyes. "No, you didn't."

She turned to the window, picturing being at the house late at night and seeing a light on next door. Thinking she'd seen a shadow in the room.

It couldn't have been a ghost. Why would a woman hang around an old house for years, just waiting on some man? Especially when she'd already had one? The whole story sounded as ridiculous as something her mother would do. No one needed a man *that* badly.

A movement from below caught her eye, and she ignored the idea of ghosts and "good men" and women too desperate to move on with their lives—or afterlives—and looked down. Where she found Marci peering up. Marci's cream pants and top were chic and stylish, but they were no match for a construction jobsite.

Jill's stomach soured. "Your girlfriend is here, Calhoun."

She nodded to the ground below them, and Cal stepped up beside her to look out.

"What's she doing here?"

"Didn't get enough of you this weekend, I'd imagine," Jill grumbled.

He shot her an odd look before leaving the room, and once he was gone, Jill reached behind her to unmute her mic. They had to get back to work, and she didn't have time to be worrying about ghosts, girlfriends, or the rumors that Cal and Marci had both been AWOL for the last two days.

She'd wondered if their absence meant that Cal had finally taken Marci out to his place. Had they spent the entire weekend holed up on his farm?

It didn't matter. Cal could do whatever with whoever he wanted.

She and Heather got back to installing the windows, but it wasn't long before they were interrupted yet again. This time, by Marci.

"Hey, girls," Marci called out as she navigated the unstable stairs.

Jill eyed the four-inch heels on the other woman.

"Hi, Marci," Heather said.

Trenton came out of the back room, and when she saw the photographer, she broke into a wide grin. "*Amazing* photos," Trenton told her. "I know I replied to your e-mail and said that already, but seriously. Amazing."

Marci beamed. "Thank you."

Marci had e-mailed the proofs for the calendar the weekend before last and had offered her suggestions on which ones should make the cut. Jill had wanted to hate them all the second she'd seen the e-mail in her in-box, but Trenton was right. Amazing.

"I'll print you each a copy of the one with all of you," Marci told them. "Blu was right. That last setup was the way to go. It's a special photo in a way that had nothing at all to do with my skill."

Jill appreciated the honesty. "Thank you. So what can we do for you today?"

Marci tilted her head and studied Jill, her eyes never leaving Jill's, yet seeming to take in every potential imperfection, whether obvious or only imagined. Then she tossed a quick glance at the other two. "Could you and I talk privately for a moment?"

Jill's eyes widened when Marci's gaze returned to her. "Me?"

"If you have a minute."

"Sure." Jill drew the word out. Why would Marci want to talk to *her*?

"Maybe outside? Away from all the cameras?"

Jill glanced out the newly installed window and saw Cal now back over at his place, his attention turned up toward them. He wore the same kind of perplexed expression that Jill assumed covered her face.

She led the way downstairs and out of the house, circumventing the newly collected debris—this time scraps of new material instead of demo of the old—and she didn't stop moving until she made it to the oak tree in the front yard. In a moment of petty rebellion, she didn't mute her mic. This conversation would be private only if the producers decided to keep it that way.

She turned to face the other woman, and as she did, Cal's uncle pulled up at the far end of the street. Jill smiled at the sight of his truck. She'd been hoping Rodney would stop by. They'd once been close, since Cal had lived with his uncle while the two of them were dating. She and Rodney had bumped into each other over the years, but she hadn't seen him in a long while.

"What can I do for you?" Jill asked, still smiling at the thought of chatting with Rodney.

Marci pushed a lock of hair behind her ear. "Could you stay away from Cal?"

The smile fell from Jill's face. "Excuse me?"

"He's been different since you came back in his life. And not in a good way."

"I'm not *in* his life." Jill glanced across the yard and noted that Cal continued to keep an eye on them.

Marci followed Jill's line of sight. "But still . . . you *are*, aren't you?"

Jill began to protest again, but then she thought about her and Cal's drive the week before. She didn't want to believe she was "in" his life, but she could admit she'd felt a kind of contentment while sitting beside him in his truck. Or the better word might be a calmness. The kind she hadn't felt since well before her mother had died.

But still, that didn't mean she was *in* his life.

Nor did him telling her about his ranch—while *not* telling his girlfriend—mean anything. That had just been a spur-of-the-moment thing. Similar to her sharing that she hadn't watched any TV since she'd moved back home. Something neither of them had intended to reveal. It had just happened.

But who the hell did Marci think she was, making this request? Because the fact was, if Jill wanted to be around Cal, then she darned well *would be* around Cal.

She turned her bubbling anger to sweetness, though, refusing to let anyone else have a glimpse at the thoughts inside her head, and when she next spoke, her words came out practically coated with a layer of sugar. "And if I were in his life?" She smiled from ear to ear. "Why would I choose to stay away from him?"

Marci looked her up and down then, and her top lip curled in the way that only people with money seemed to be capable of doing. And there was *nothing* sugary about it.

"Because he can do better than a two-bit orphan."

Jill gaped at Marci's back as she walked away, unable to believe the woman had just said that to her, and watched the overexaggerated sway of the other woman's hips. What a bitch.

No wonder Jill had never liked her.

Before she could turn back to the house, a hand touched the middle of her back, and Rodney leaned in close. "Whoo-wee. Looking good all dusty and dirty like that, Jilly-Bean."

Jill laughed and pulled the man in for a tight hug. He and Cal had been the only ones to ever call her that. She smelled beer on Rodney's breath as she pulled away. "Don't even think of turning that charm on me, Mr. Reynolds. You know it won't work."

"And why's that, Ms. Sadler? Because I'm the wrong Reynolds?"

Jill's smile faltered, and she suddenly wished she'd muted her mic. That would teach her to be petty. But she recovered quickly enough. "Because you're the wrong *decade*." She played it off with a laugh.

She turned her back at the sight of Marci, who was now primping for the cameras.

"What brings you by here, Rodney? Wanting to get your hands dirty with some real work again?"

Aunt Blu had hired We Nail It to do the addition at the house before Jill graduated high school, and she, Heather, and Trenton had helped. That's when they'd learned the majority of what they knew about construction. Cal had been working for Rodney by that point, so he'd been out there with Rodney every day, instead of only the couple of afternoons after school he usually spent there.

She had good memories of that time—with both the Reynolds men.

Rodney scrubbed his palms down over his shirt front now, as if straightening some imaginary lapel, and puffed out his chest. "Got me an interview for the show," he told her.

"Is that right? That why you're wearing your lucky boots?"

He looked down, and when he did, he weaved a little. "How do you know about my lucky boots?"

"Small town, Rodney. Everybody knows about your boots."

"Hmmm. I might have to rethink them then. Maybe that's why they ain't been working so good lately."

Patrick laid eyes on the older Reynolds not long after that and made a beeline for them, and as the two men walked away, Jill pulled out her cell and sent Cal a text.

Might want to keep an eye on your uncle.

He was still standing with Marci, while Marci talked a mile a minute, but Jill saw him look down at his phone.

Then he looked at her.

Marci turned her way, too—though her look could be classified more as scathing than Cal's questioning one—and when Cal refocused

on his cell, Jill directed an intentional look at him before slowly bringing her gaze back to Marci's. She sent the other woman a smug purse
of her lips.

Marci bristled. Which only made Jill laugh.

Why?

Rodney was in the interview hot seat now, and Jill tapped out a
quick reply.

Because he smells like beer.

When Cal immediately left Marci's side, she fired a hate-filled glare
at Jill. Jill returned the look with an innocent-looking finger-waggling
wave—then added one more smile for good measure.

Tired of playing with Marci, she headed back to the house. She had
work to do. But as she neared the porch, she realized that both of her
foster sisters had been standing just inside the door and had witnessed
her exchange with the other woman. Her favorite cameraman had also
been zeroed in on her.

Instead of letting any of it bother her, though, Jill simply stuck
her tongue out as she passed Len, and Len responded with a quick
thumbs-up.

Chapter Ten

*"Be there for others when they call. You might be the next
one picking up the phone."*

—Blu Johnson, life lesson #39

Cal rose from his kneeling position in the living room where he'd been
putting down new subflooring and grunted at the ache in his knees.
He lifted his arms above his head, stretching out his back, then bent
over and unclipped his kneepads. He'd been at it for too long without
stretching, but a setback with the stability of the underlying floor support had meant he'd needed to stay late to catch up.

In fact, several setbacks had kept him late on numerous occasions.

As he worked the kinks out of his neck, a door closed with a
soft click above him, and he smiled to himself. Mrs. Wainwright had
decided a couple of days ago that she wanted some attention, and she'd
been playing with him ever since. It seemed to happen most often when
he was there alone.

He glanced at his watch as he moved through the downstairs,
double-checking that all the flooring issues had been resolved, then
glanced outside to see if anyone was still around. It wasn't quite dark

yet, but he'd cut his crew loose a while ago, with Pete following not far behind. It looked as if the crowd across the street had packed up for the day, too.

No production crews remained, and he caught sight of a lone pair of taillights as a dark-brown SUV drove down the quiet street. Heather was heading home. And he'd seen Trenton pull out some time ago.

He ducked his head so he could make out the house next door from where he stood in the living room, and saw only a navy-blue pickup remaining in the driveway. That made him smile. Jill was still there.

When footsteps shuffled in the room upstairs, he pulled out his phone and sent a text.

Any way you could help me out for a minute? Come over?

He held his breath as he waited for a reply. The tension between him and Jill had definitely lessened over the last week, and although he hadn't spoken directly to her since she'd warned him about his uncle two days before, they'd passed in the yard several times.

She continued avoiding Patrick's attempts to interview them together, and Cal had even backed off helping the producer with his plight. But every time Jill thwarted an attempt, instead of seeing anger or smugness written on her face, Cal now usually caught a smile. She was enjoying herself.

A soft knock sounded at the back door, and he made his way to the kitchen to find an *unsmiling* face peering in at him. He opened the door, but instead of saying anything, Jill shot a look at the upper corner of his kitchen.

"I know, right?" Cal said. "What'll they think? Cavorting with the enemy."

She narrowed her eyes at him. *"Competition."*

"No longer the enemy?"

She sighed. "You were never my enemy, Cal. Just my ex. Whom I'm still angry at," she added quickly.

He nodded with contrition. "And whom you don't speak to."

"Right."

He held the door open wide and invited her in with a nod, and as he did, he didn't take his eyes off hers for one second. When she smirked, acknowledging his smart-ass comment about her still not speaking to him, a grin spread slowly across his face.

"Stop it," she grumbled. But she came into his house.

"I'm not doing anything."

She smelled like sawdust and Sheetrock mud, and he found it strangely arousing.

"You were thinking something, so stop it."

He was thinking a lot of things. "Fine. I'll stop it. For now."

She checked out every inch of the kitchen and new dining space as she walked in a small loop, and after her initial curiosity was met, she returned to the newly installed kitchen island. Where she crossed her arms and cocked out a hip. "So, what did you bring me over for?"

He pointed to the ceiling. "Listen."

She stood motionless and listened, even closing her eyes to hear better, and Cal could tell by her face when the soft music playing in the upstairs bedroom had made it to her ears. She opened her eyes. "What? You left a radio on?"

He shook his head.

"Then what is it?"

"Mrs. Wainwright."

Her gaze shot toward the staircase. "No, it's not."

The music changed to a jazz number, and Jill's eyes stayed locked in the direction of the upper room.

"I told you," he said.

"Pete has to be up there."

"Pete went home an hour ago. Want to go up with me and see for yourself?"

The music changed once again, this time to an '80s hair band, and Cal almost laughed out loud. Mrs. Wainwright had a sense of humor.

"I don't think I do," Jill answered.

"Scared?"

"Heather's the one into ghosts. Call her next time." She inched around to the other side of the unpainted island. The side that was closest to the door.

"I don't want to call Heather."

Blue-green eyes locked on his. "Then call your girlfriend."

"I don't want to call her, either."

He took a step closer, putting him at the island as well, only standing on the opposite side as her, and was pleased when she didn't turn and run. He'd wanted to talk to her again since Monday. Not about anything specific. Just to talk.

Just to see her.

It thrilled him that his text had brought her over.

"Thank you for letting me know about my uncle the other day," he said, and at his comment, her gaze moved to his collar. When she didn't see what she was looking for, her eyes inched lower. "Mic pack is off," he told her. The camera crew had unwired him before they'd left. "Yours?"

"Gone." She looked at the upper corner of the room again.

"The cameras in the house don't pick up sound."

"Really?" Relief washed over her. "I'd been afraid to ask."

His brows shot skyward. "What have you been saying over there that you don't want heard?"

"Nothing." She laughed softly. "Not really. Just some stuff about Len's beard that first night. You know, the night I lost my shit on the cabinets?"

His entire body relaxed with her joking reference to the evening he'd gone over to her house, and at the same time that his comfort level rose, Jill's feet went into motion. Cal stayed where he was, but turned in place to watch as she scoured the area. He feared getting any closer. If he did, he might find an excuse to touch her. And that would send her running the other way.

She stood on tiptoe and peered into the topmost cabinets. He'd taken the storage to the ceiling, though the doors were yet to be hung. They would get painted white before going up.

Next she peeked into the space where a six-burner cooktop would eventually be hooked up, and when she finally spoke, she returned to the topic of his uncle. "I was a little surprised when I smelled beer on him. It wasn't even noon yet. But even then, I wasn't going to say anything. Maybe he'd had one with his lunch, you know?" She checked out the pantry, and gave a little nod. "But then"—she looked over her shoulder at him—"he weaved. Not a lot, but I thought I should . . ." She stopped talking long enough to give him a little shrug. She might not have known what she *should* do, but she'd done the right thing. "Is he okay, Cal? I've heard some things . . ."

"He's fine." He didn't ask what she'd heard, nor did he attempt to finish her sentence for her. "He was celebrating his TV debut. Just got ahead of himself."

She nodded, but didn't say anything else, and the music above them changed yet again. This time to an instrumental. It also increased in volume. Not loud, but just enough to pull at them.

Cal wanted to take Jill's hand.

"Please tell me there's at *least* a radio up there?" She moved out of the kitchen to peer up the stairs.

"There is." Cal followed her. "I put it in there myself. For her."

Jill turned, and almost bumped into him. "You what?"

He stayed where he was. "I did some asking around after Heather got me interested the other day, and I managed to locate one of Mrs. Wainwright's nieces. She doesn't live too far away, and she told me that Mrs. Wainwright used to sit in that room and listen to music until the day she died." He let the back of his fingers touch Jill's. "That was her favorite room in the house. Her niece has a theory that the man who'd been here that night might have been a musician."

Jill looked toward the stairs again. "That could be." She closed her eyes, her head tilted slightly back, as if picturing a long-ago woman, unhappy in her marriage, and the man who *did* make her happy. "Or maybe they just liked to dance," she said softly.

"That could be it, too." He couldn't take his eyes off her.

She opened her eyes and moved away from him, roaming through the front of the house. She trailed her fingers over the custom trim work they'd repaired on the built-in shelving, and as she continued to check out the area, she began to sway. Her hips shifted in time with the music, but her focus remained so intent on the work that had been done to the rooms that he suspected she had no clue she was dancing.

"Whatever the man might have been," he said, "Mrs. Wainwright has good taste in music."

Jill's feet went still with his words, and she quickly looked down at herself. She tossed a casual glance back at him, as if to determine if Cal had been aware of her movements or not, and being the nongentleman that he was, he offered a wolfish grin.

She rolled her eyes at him, but he only grinned wider.

"You didn't see that," she muttered.

She crossed back to the staircase and looked up as the music switched once more, this time to a lonely piano tune.

He'd heard that one played before.

"I can't believe you're so comfortable with this," she muttered. She eyed the landing on the second floor, then leaned to her right as if trying to see inside the open door of the upstairs bedroom. She continued speaking, almost too softly to hear. "It's so weird. I wouldn't have believed any of—"

Her words snapped off and she whirled to face him.

"You really are just messing with me, aren't you?" She groaned in disgust and headed up the stairs. "There has to be someone here. I can't believe I fell for . . ."

Her words trailed off as Cal followed her into the empty bedroom. The small radio sat on the bare subfloor in the corner of the space, and with the closet doors currently propped against the wall instead of closing off the smaller area, it was clear that no other living soul shared the space with them.

"Want to dance?" he asked her. The volume lowered to a more reasonable level.

She shook her head, but her eyes remained on the radio. It was as if Mrs. Wainwright had brought them to where she wanted them to be. Cal wondered if Jill had picked up on that, too.

"Bring Marci up here if you want to dance," she told him.

"I don't want to dance with Marci."

Ever again, he added silently. He didn't share that he and Marci were no more.

"What did she want with you the other day?" he asked. "When she came over to talk to you?"

Marci had been close lipped about her conversation with Jill when she'd returned, but she *had* talked about other things. Such as the many specifics she—*as a Hammery*—required in a man.

Jill didn't answer his question. Instead, she walked to the window, and looked out over the darkening sky. She stood completely still as she took in the scene. Something was definitely running through the woman's head, though. Cal had no doubt. But he also hadn't the first clue what it might be.

When she finally did speak again, the subject change caught him off guard. "Did you take Marci to your farm last weekend?"

"No." He moved to her side. "I didn't even see her last weekend."

He didn't offer up that *he'd* been out there, though. Nor did he tell her about the table he was making. He'd started building it thinking it would be a nice gift for whoever eventually moved into the place, but after getting to know Mrs. Wainwright, he now hoped the piece would be special enough to entice her into leaving this room. There was sadness in this space, and though he'd never been a big believer in the supernatural before this project, he couldn't deny that this room felt different than the others.

"Why would you think I took Marci out there?" He had no clue where she'd gotten the idea, nor why it would matter.

And then he realized it was more than that she'd *thought* it. She'd been upset about it. That's why she'd made that dig about Marci not getting enough of him the other day. She'd been jealous.

He grinned at that thought, no more able to control the smile growing on his face than he was the urge to be closer to Jill.

"Stop it." She watched his reflection in the glass.

"I'm not doing anything."

"You're thinking things again."

He chuckled. God, he'd missed her. "I am thinking things. Want to hear what they are?"

"No."

"Ah, Jilly. You're such a chicken these days." He turned to her, eager to see her face instead of a reflection, and he allowed himself to do what he'd been wanting to do since she'd walked in. He took her hands in his. "When did that happen?"

Her fingers wiggled inside his. "It's not that I'm a chicken. I'm simply more mature these days. I don't jump quite as fast. It's saved me a few falls."

"Yet sometimes falling is good for you." He studied her. "You ever go out on dates, Jill?"

Her brows knotted. "Where did that come from?"

He wasn't sure himself. "I never see you out anywhere. Not with a man."

And, fair or not, this had pleased him immensely.

"I stay pretty busy," she answered.

She pulled her hands from his and left the room, stopping only when she got to the open loft. Her fingers closed around the unfinished railing, and she peered out over the space below.

Cal watched her as she stood there, trying to imagine seeing the upgrades through her eyes. The designs for the two houses weren't identical, but they had similarities. Both with an open concept below and a vaulted ceiling in the back half of the house. And both with a sitting nook in the space where they stood now.

But he'd seen her plans. They would be installing wooden beams and keeping the tone more rustic, whereas he'd decided to go with a more contemporary edge. Not too much, but a hint of sleek and modern. More airy than the look she was going for.

Jill put her back to the railing then and looked at him, and the intensity of her face made him realize that she hadn't been taking in the design below her at all. She'd been in her head. "Why don't *you* get angry anymore?" she asked him. "You used to be as bad as me."

"I was never as bad as you."

"*Fine.* But you were close. That's why we . . ."

She pressed her lips together instead of finishing her sentence, so he finished it for her.

"Why we connected?"

She nodded. That's what had drawn them to one another to begin with, and how it had remained strong for so long. They'd both needed the type of person who understood them.

"I still get angry," he told her. No one in his life knew that about him. He hid it well.

"But you don't show it. And it's so unfair. Both then and now." She laughed drily and looked beyond him. "Everyone watches me with an eagle eye, just waiting for me to blow. And back then, *I* was the one who had to go to anger-management classes." She brought her gaze back to his. "And you know you should have been right there with me."

He gave her a smart-ass smirk. "You shouldn't have gotten tossed in jail."

"I didn't!"

"*Almost* gotten tossed, then." He smiled at her again, and for the first time since he'd been a teenager, he felt an honest connection with another human being. "Thank goodness for Blu, huh?"

"Every day," she said softly.

Blu had saved him, too. He didn't know if she'd been aware of what she was doing at the time, but without her hiring him at sixteen, giving him a steadying after-school job, he suspected he'd have turned out much differently than he had.

Jill pushed away from the railing and prowled through the other rooms on the floor. There was a converted attic space not large enough for a bedroom, which he planned to turn into a small library, as well as an even smaller bathroom. The bath was large enough for a claw-foot tub and pedestal sink, both original to the house, and other than the toilet, that was it.

When she resurfaced from the bathroom, she stopped in the doorway and propped herself against the frame. "So how do you do it? If you still carry around that anger, then how do you never let it show? You're always so . . . *charming*." She made a face with the word, and he chuckled. "Always laughing." She pointed at him. "Like now. You seem so happy. So . . . content," she finished on a whisper.

He went silent. Because he wasn't content. He'd merely learned how to pretend better than she had. He wasn't willing to show that much of himself, though. Letting her see his place was one thing. But see him?

Best to get back to joking.

"How do you know I'm so *charming*?" he teased. "You been watching me, Sadler?"

She huffed in disgust. "Not watching so much as *hearing*. The whole damned town loves you. Every time we lose out on a bid, we get told how *that nice Reynolds boy just seemed like the better option*." She fired off a knowing look. "You go after our bids on purpose, don't you?"

Cal found himself nodding. He'd gone after them for years.

"Why?"

"I wanted to win," he said. Because it had infuriated him that she'd come home and refused to speak to him. As if she'd been the only wronged party in their breakup. Blocking her company from winning bids had been his only way to fight back.

"Same way as you want to win this competition?" she asked. "You said you agreed to do it because of me. But you didn't actually say *why*."

"I agreed because I wanted to make you speak to me again."

Shock colored her features for a moment, then she angled her head in acceptance. "And you did. I'll give you that one. You got me to speak to you." Then she did a quick one-eighty on the subject. "So since we're talking again, tell me how you forgave him. Because there's no way you still hold as much anger as you once did."

Cal stared at her, unblinking. She didn't have to say who "him" was. She meant his dad.

And whether she realized it or not, she was talking about her mother, as well. Because he suspected she'd never figured out how to forgive her mom, either.

He didn't immediately give her an answer. His dad was high profile in banking, both when he'd lived in Red Oak Falls and even more so now. And that was pretty much all he cared about. Cal had always compared his father to his uncle, which had only made the divide between the two of them wider. Neil and Rodney Reynolds had both lost a brother early in life. Tragically. They both had the same parents, both came from identical circumstances.

Yet Rodney had turned out normal. He could care about people.

He *wanted* to care about people.

But Cal's dad . . .

Cal ground his teeth together. He'd never understand why the man couldn't love his only son. Even when they were all the other had.

Jill kept her gaze on his, unwilling to look away even though Cal knew the message he was sending made it clear that he didn't want to talk about this. She simply stared. Demanding he provide an answer. And damned if he didn't feel locked into her gaze. As if he physically couldn't look away.

Eventually he sighed. He'd give her something, and hopefully she'd back off.

"I *didn't* forgive him," he admitted. "But I also don't let that anger run my life. I've learned that two grown men can be cordial when need be. He sees Granny twice a year and sends a care package once a month. That's enough to make me cordial."

"And how often do *you* see him?"

He looked away from her. "Twice a year." The man had never once come back to the house he'd grown up in. Didn't visit his only son.

And Cal had never done anything but try to love him.

"Then why does no one see your anger?" Jill asked again. The anger that he knew she could see resurfacing now.

"Because I don't want them to," he snarled out before he could stop himself.

He stomped down the stairs then, not looking to see if she would follow, and slammed out the front door.

~

Jill remained rooted at the top of the stairs as the echo of the slamming door reverberated through her ears, and the second Cal's footsteps disappeared from the porch, the music in the other room stopped. She eyed the bedroom, now cast in shadows, and she swore she could feel the other woman in there urging her down the stairs.

"What?" Jill asked. "I suppose you want me to follow him?"

The piano music started again.

"Fine," she ground out. She couldn't believe she was listening to a ghost.

She hurried down the steps and out the front door, slamming it as Cal had, hoping he'd hear her and slow his strides. But he kept plowing ahead. She'd been pushing at him back there. Intentionally. Because every time she'd looked his way over the last five years, he seemed to have pulled himself together with no lingering effects from his own childhood. While she bumped into metaphorical walls at practically every turn.

Yet the last few minutes had shown her that all was not as it seemed. Cal *did* have unresolved issues with his father. And that should *not* make her feel better about herself.

She jogged along the sidewalk and crossed the road, heading for the path that ran parallel to the stream. Cal hit the head of the path, and she picked up speed, but she also noticed that he finally slowed. By the time she caught up with him, his feet were barely moving.

They walked in silence while she caught her breath, the lampposts that lined the walkway casting light on them every thirty feet, and once they reached the footbridge that led into the city park, Cal stopped walking altogether. She moved to his side as they both faced the railing and stared at the water beyond. There were still a handful of people in the park, and kids' squeals and laughter could be heard, as well as the lower tones of their parents trying to round them up. A couple of vendors that were routinely in the area were likely still there, as well, no doubt closing up shop. The hot dog cart made a repetitive squeaking noise as it rolled, and after a few minutes of standing on the bridge, Jill picked out its squeak heading their way.

"You okay?" she finally asked.

Cal nodded. "Told you I still get angry."

"That was nothing compared to me."

He looked at her then, a wry smile on his lips, and motioned toward the entrance to the park. "Let's walk."

Together they turned to pass under the double rows of elm trees, whose canopies were so wide and overlapping, they blocked what was on the other side. She and Cal were greeted by a lone biker and several harried mothers on their way out, and then they found themselves on the other side of the trees, where a quieter, more private space awaited them. The acreage for the park had been donated to the city over three decades ago, and along with the traditional playground equipment, picnic tables, and walking paths, it also backed up to Red Oak Lake. That's where the beauty came alive.

Without either suggesting it, they headed for a bench overlooking the lake, which also overlooked the sunset. Though the sun had officially dipped beneath the horizon, pink-and-purple-hued clouds remained stretched flat across the sky.

They met the hot dog vendor heading in the opposite direction, and Cal lifted a hand.

"Hot dogs?" the vendor asked. He opened a cover to show that he still had several available, and Cal glanced her way.

"You haven't had dinner, right?"

She shook her head. She couldn't remember the last time she'd had a hot dog in the park.

"I'm starved, actually," she told him.

Cal paid the man for four hot dogs and two drinks, then passed half of everything over to her. They each added mustard and relish, before

Cal handed the vendor a large tip, and with food in hand, they made it to the bench offering the best view of the lake. As they ate, the remaining colors in the sky faded away.

Jill stretched her legs out in front of her and propped her elbows on the back of the bench. "Want to talk about it?"

Cal shook his head, so she let it drop. It was enough to know the two of them weren't so different from each other, after all.

They began to talk then. About everything, but about nothing at all. Each told funny stories from different jobsites over the years, a tale or two about something goofy one of their friends had done, but neither ventured anywhere close to forbidden territory. As they swapped stories, Jill ended up shifted on the bench so that she could steal glances of him as he spoke. Cal had always had a way of capturing her attention, whether it was with his quick wit, his charm, or simply the strength in how he carried himself, and she found that nothing about that had changed. He had her attention now, whether he wanted it or not, and though she knew she shouldn't be enjoying the moment as much as she was, she also couldn't stop herself.

He cut a quick look down at her during a break in a story, and caught her watching him, and she grinned with guilt. *Busted.*

"Want to tell me what you're thinking?" he asked.

She shook her head.

"Probably just as well." He picked something out of her hair. "You're likely plotting revenge on me for tricking you into following me to the park tonight, anyway."

"Probably." She chuckled. But she knew he hadn't tricked her. He'd been legitimately upset, and she'd authentically wanted to help. Even if her brand of helping only meant being with him.

She shifted so she couldn't watch him anymore, elbows once again on the back of the bench, and tilted her face to the night sky. It was beautiful out there.

Water lapped gently near their feet. "Ever seen Aunt Blu drunk?" she asked.

She thought Cal might fall off the bench the way he jerked in his seat. "I can't *imagine* Blu drinking, much less being drunk." He turned to her. "How did you get her drunk? And *when?*"

Jill grinned, but kept her eyes on the sky. "We make her play whiskey rummy. She has game night at the house at least once a month. When there are no girls around, one of us often calls rummy before Aunt Blu can choose another game. She's horrible at cards."

"And the whiskey?"

Jill chuckled softly. "When someone gets rummy, everyone else takes a shot."

"That's brutal."

"It's fun." She closed her eyes and felt the falling dampness whisper across her cheeks. "And it's one of the things in my life that I most look forward to. Not because of the drinking, but the fact that Aunt Blu quits worrying about teaching us or taking care of us for a while. On those nights, she's just *one* of us."

She could sense Cal nodding in understanding. "I was happy to hear the three of you had come back," he told her. "She missed you."

Jill was certain she had. Though she, Heather, and Trenton had only been foster daughters, Jill now understood that in a way they'd taken the place of Blu's own children. They'd filled her need to be a mom. Their ages had been similar to Blu's girls' when the girls had died, and they'd always picked at each other—same as any other sisters would do.

And then they'd all left her.

"We missed her, too." Jill blew out a breath. "Though I had no idea how much until I came home." She cracked open her eyelids and peeked at Cal. His dark gaze was on her. "She misses you, too."

His brows lifted.

"You were always around," Jill continued. "Always a part of the family she'd replaced."

Blu had a nephew who'd been sent to prison not long after she'd opened her home to others. He'd been found guilty of killing a man. It had broken Blu's heart when Trey had been locked up. He'd been like a son to her. To Gerry, too, before Big Gerry's death.

"When I finally came home," Jill began, and then she cut off her words and intentionally broke eye contact. When she'd come home, though she'd been unaware of it at the time, she'd severed the relationship between Blu and Cal.

It had never occurred to her the two of them had stayed close during her absence, but then she'd run across Aunt Blu's box of hand-carved saints. After getting hired to work at Bluebonnet Farms, Cal would carve out a different saint of the Catholic Church for Blu every Christmas. From a young age, he'd liked to make things with his hands. Both furniture as well as carvings, and he'd been good at it. There had been only four statues when Jill moved away, but they'd been displayed with pride in the corner of Blu's china cabinet. Jill hadn't thought about those figurines when she'd come home, but earlier this year, she'd been helping with spring cleaning, and she'd unearthed the box of them. Only, there had been sixteen saints in pristine condition, all tucked safely away in tissue paper.

Jill had questioned Aunt Blu about them, and while Blu admitted she and Cal continued exchanging gifts every year, she also kept the carvings put away so they wouldn't upset Jill. Additionally, Blu had confessed that Cal used to visit her at least once a month. Until Jill had come back home.

"You should visit her," she said now. "I know you used to. You didn't have to stop."

"I felt like she was *yours*," he explained. "Like I shouldn't get in the way of that."

Jill nodded. She understood that, just as she'd gotten why Aunt Blu had kept her prized gifts from Cal hidden away. But Jill shouldn't have allowed that to continue after she'd discovered them. She needed to rectify that. "Go see her," she told him. "I know she's always meant a lot to you."

He didn't respond at first, but finally he nodded, his eyes registering his gratitude. "Thank you for that. And I will."

He motioned with his head. "Should we head back?"

"Probably."

Jill got to her feet, and they strolled side by side the way they'd come in. No one else remained in the park, and singing insects, along with the water trickling over the rocks in the stream, made for a peaceful way to end the day. When Cal's fingers brushed against hers, she thought about that moment earlier at the house when he'd taken her hands in his. It hadn't even occurred to her, at first, to pull away.

He glanced down at her now. "Thank you for following me out here."

She nodded in reply. He hadn't asked her to come with him, but at the same time, she'd understood that he'd hoped she would.

"And for setting your anger aside long enough for us to take a walk." He winked with his words. "This was nice."

She smiled. "Yes, it was. And thank you for the hot dogs." She bowed her head in a tiny curtsy, but then she shot him a crooked grin. "But don't worry. I'll find my anger again tomorrow."

Both laughing, they made the turn toward the bridge as one, and as they walked under the trees that would empty them out of the park, she held her breath in a manner similar to when she'd been a child and her mother would drive over railroad tracks. She didn't make a wish as she would have done back then, but she did appreciate the too-short moment of seclusion they'd had inside the park.

The second they cleared the trees, however . . . there was Len. Capturing the moment.

Neither of them broke stride or so much as glanced at the man—or the sound guy following them with a boom mic. They made a right on the other side of the bridge and headed for the houses, and as soon as they were out of earshot, Jill stepped in a little closer. "We totally should have asked for more money to do this show," she whispered. "I had no idea how popular we would be."

Cal tossed his head back and laughed, and they finished out their walk, both of them with smiles on their faces.

Chapter Eleven

"Let go of anger, and see what life can bring you."

—Blu Johnson, life lesson #66

"I call that one."

Cal glanced toward the door of the Buffalo Nickel, eyeing the woman his buddy Travis had just indicated was *his*, and silently acknowledged that Trav could do worse. The woman looked to be in her early twenties and wore a skintight red minidress with a zipper running the length of the front, oversized gold hoops, and fuck-me heels. Chances were, she didn't intend to go home alone that night. Might as well go with Travis.

"That one's already taken," Pete added from beside Cal.

"And how do you know that?" Travis asked, and Pete pushed back from the table.

"Because *I'm* taking her."

Laughter followed Pete as he went after the woman, the tableful of men both ribbing Travis and encouraging Pete. The group of them had decided to take the Friday night to wind down. They all either worked directly for Cal or subcontracted for We Nail It from time to time, and each of them had been on the Cadillac project at some point over the last three weeks. It was straight down the middle of the road to the finish line, and they could all do with letting loose for one night. Cal included.

It had taken exactly two steps into the bar, however, for Cal to realize that he wouldn't be relaxing at all that evening. Because his gaze had landed on a head of inky-black hair . . . that had been far too close to Doug Caldwell.

Cal took a drink of his water and cast a glance toward the back booth.

Yep. Still there. Still smiling.

Still making him want to show her that Doug wasn't the man for her.

No wonder the twenty-five-year-old had declined Cal's invite for the night out. Doug already had plans.

"Another round, boys?" their server asked. She smiled at Cal as she stopped at his elbow. It was Cinco de Mayo, and the bar was in full swing, but given that his wallet was open wide, their table had yet to find themselves wanting for alcohol.

"Make it a double." A couple of the men raised their voices to be heard over the crowd.

Cal acknowledged the order with a nod of his head. Nothing for him, but he'd spring for another round for the table.

The server disappeared, and Cal watched as Doug talked Jill onto the dance floor for the third time. Heather and Len went out with them—they'd been occupying the other side of the booth with Jill—and as the music in the bar thumped out a popular pop hit, Cal thought about the night Jill had come over to the Cadillac House. There'd been music playing then, too. *And* she'd danced.

Nothing like the gyrations she had going on at the moment, though.

His back teeth ground together when Doug's hands landed on the top curves of Jill's hips. Doug didn't pull her in close, though. Or maybe it was Jill who didn't allow it. Either way, the touch was too much. Cal looked away. He couldn't watch Jill with another man, no matter what he'd told himself for the last decade. And he certainly didn't need to be present the night she finally decided the time had come to "get out there" again.

He'd asked her about dating the other day, but even though she'd avoided his question, he'd known the answer. She'd dated no one for the last five years. Or if she had, the guy hadn't lived in Red Oak Falls. He'd watched for it. For a long time. It had been none of his business, and he'd been well aware of that fact. But that hadn't kept him from keeping an eye out for her. Or wondering who filled her bed at night.

Yet in all that time, he'd never once seen her with another man. And though he'd had no right to care—the thought had pleased him way the hell too much.

The server showed back up with a tray of drinks, and after distributing them to the waiting hands, she also put a shot glass down for Pete. Pete hadn't made it back to the table, though, and Cal spotted him in one of the darker corners of the bar. With the pool table at his back, Cal's friend worked like the champ that he was, no doubt trying to talk the woman in the fuck-me heels into kicking those heels off under his bed tonight.

He'd likely succeed, too. The ladies were big fans of Pete's.

Cal's eyes landed on Jill once more, and he wondered how Doug was doing with his mission. Cal hoped he crashed and burned.

"What's on tap for next week, boss?" Jacob asked as he changed seats and squeezed in next to Cal. Jacob was an eager twenty-two-year-old who would one day turn out to be a heck of an employee. He just needed to quit being such a suck-up first.

"You really want to talk work tonight, Jacob?" Cal motioned to the growing crowd. "Ask a woman to dance, why don't you? Buy one a drink. Heck"—he motioned to the shot of tequila sitting next to him—"take Pete's and hand it out. He's not going to need it."

The younger man seemed to sense Cal's mood and backed off—quickly returning to his original seat—and Cal found himself eyeing the shot of tequila himself. Maybe *he* should down it.

If his father were there, he would. Just because he could.

His irritation swelled to full bloom then. His father had shown up in his head more times in that week alone than he had in the last year, and Cal had the woman on the dance floor, currently dancing with a man who was barely more than a *boy*, to thank for that.

He shoved Jill from his thoughts yet again and slid the shot of amber liquid over in front of him. Tequila had been his liquor of choice the night his dad had gotten the call to pick up his only son at the hospital. Friends had dropped Cal off, passed out drunk, at the emergency room, before hightailing it out of the parking lot. Thankfully, after the hospital staff had dragged his inebriated ass inside, they'd chosen to call Cal's father instead of the police.

Cal had been fifteen that night, and the conversation the following morning had *not* been a pretty one. It had also only encouraged Cal to drink more. *Why not?* he'd thought. His dad didn't give a shit about him, anyway. Neil Reynolds had been more worried about "what people would think" than about why Cal had been drowning himself in a bottle in the first place.

Hell, if Cal were to drown today—bottle or not—his father would likely still be more concerned about people's perceptions.

Someone stumbled on the dance floor, a whoop going up as several others were taken down with the offender, and Cal slowly turned his gaze to follow the action. It wasn't the same area where he'd last seen Jill—but he knew who he'd find there.

Rodney Reynolds got tugged back to his feet as Cal watched, blowing the ordeal off as he always did. "No big deal. I just tripped. Let me buy another round."

Everyone returned to their partying ways, accepting the free drink from their favorite supplier, and Cal pushed the shot of tequila back over to Pete's seat. Cal hadn't had a drop of anything since the first night *he'd* had to go rescue Rodney. It worried him, how much his uncle drank. It had worried him for years. But Rodney seemed to be heading for a really bad place these days, and the speed at which he was getting there was only accelerating.

Cal had no idea what else he could do for the man, other than continue to try to hide the problem. He took note of how many pairs of eyes were currently turned on his uncle, though, and accepted that Rodney's issues hadn't been hidden in a long time.

He also had the thought that Rodney wasn't quite as different from his brother as Cal had always imagined. Neil Reynolds cared about himself, work . . . and *anything* more than Cal. But then, Rodney would sell his only nephew up the river for a pint of Wild Turkey.

It made Cal wonder how different *he* was from the two of them.

He looked at Jill again. He'd certainly dumped her in a fast hurry when a choice had to be made.

Pete and the woman wove their way back through the crowd, stopping at the table long enough for Pete to hand over the shot of tequila to the brunette. As she tossed it back, Pete leaned in toward Cal. "You okay if I get out of here?"

Cal shot him a confused look. "Of course. Have a good time."

Pete nodded. "But I'm not asking if I can leave, so much as if I need to stay."

Cal had no clue what he was talking about, and then Pete shifted his gaze until it locked on Jill.

Ah. Pete had been watching Cal watch Jill.

"I'm good," Cal assured the other man. He nodded toward Pete's date. "You go."

Pete's gaze flicked to the woman, who was currently undressing him with her eyes, and when she caught Pete looking, her lips began to curve. They continued their upward tilt, her gaze heating at the same degree that her red lips teased, until all conversation at the table came to a halt. And even though Pete paused in thought along with the rest of the men, he eventually pulled himself together enough to turn back to Cal.

Cal watched as his friend reset his mind from no-strings-hot-sex to worry-about-my-friend, and he appreciated the effort he knew had gone into it.

"I don't want to get a call from the sheriff." Pete kept his voice low.

"And I guarantee that you won't."

There'd been a handful of teenage fights Pete had to pull him out of back in the day, but through all of it, the sheriff had never once been involved. He wouldn't be called tonight, either. No matter how much Cal might want to pummel the redhead's face.

Pete finally gave a nod of acceptance, then tossed a two-fingered salute to the rest of the table, and as he and the woman exited through the front door, Cal returned his attention to the back booth. The sheriff wouldn't have to get involved tonight, because Cal had another weapon at his disposal. If Doug Caldwell so much as thought about crossing the line with Jill, Cal would simply fire his ass.

~

"Another turn on the dance floor?"

Jill blatantly eavesdropped on the other side of the booth as Len tried to wheedle Heather back onto her feet. Len was a dancer. And a charmer. And if Jill didn't know how difficult it was to get Heather to play, she might think the big man stood a chance tonight, whether he had fifteen years on her or not.

But as it was, the night was quickly rolling to a close.

"A few more minutes to recover?" Heather begged. "You're too much man for me, Big Red."

Len growled with the nickname, while at the same time, he caught Jill listening in and graced her with a wink. She ducked her head and smiled. Len might be her temporary pain in the butt, but their almost constant closeness had caused them to form a budding friendship.

"If I were to guess," Jill added, once again looking at Len, "I'd say you're too much man for most women."

Len's teeth flashed white. "That so? How about we test your limits, then? What do you say, should we give Little Red a rest with Heather, and you and I take a spin?"

Doug groaned before Jill could reply, and everyone at the table laughed.

"Just stop it," Doug begged. "You know I hate that name."

Heather had accidentally given away their secret earlier in the evening, and as suspected, Doug hadn't been pleased. It was also apparently not the first time he'd been called that. Nor had Len fallen on the side of empathetic with the man. Instead, he'd spent a large portion of the evening egging it on.

"No to your offer, *Len*. Thank you very much." Jill turned back to Doug. "And how about if *everyone* at the table"—she shot Len a hard look—"stops calling you that, and in return, *you* don't try to talk me back out into the middle of that chaos." Jill nodded to the dance floor. The four of them had spent a lot of time out there tonight, and though Jill had just "gone with it" as Heather had coached her to before they'd shown up, she'd had her fill.

"Not even one more?" Doug angled his puppy dog eyes at her, and she couldn't help but laugh. The boy was cute.

"You're a troublemaker, Doug Caldwell."

"But I'm worth it." He waggled his brows at her.

She supposed he might be for some women, but though he was fun and she was actually having a good time, he wasn't exactly her cup of tea. First, he really *was* too young for her—she suspected he'd also figured that out. But also . . .

She pulled her glass of diet soda closer and cut a glance to the man who *was* her cup of tea. And as had been the case for most of the night, Cal's gaze was on her.

His mouth shifted, and she thought he was about to mouth something to her across the crowded bar, but Loretta from the diner landed in his lap before Jill could find out what he might have to say.

Jill looked away.

However, a few minutes later, she found herself seeking him out again, and this time when their gazes connected, he made a quick motion with his head. He was asking her to meet him by the restrooms.

Loretta was nowhere to be found. Nor was Marci. Or any other woman.

But that didn't mean she should step away with him just because he asked.

She gave an equally quick negative response, and he volleyed with a pleading look.

She shook her head again, but this time his lips curved, and she felt that charm his family was so proud of being directed her way. Then he motioned with his head once more.

Damn him. She wanted to go.

Glancing at her date, she listened as Doug recounted a story about "the good ole days" with a buddy of his. His friend had shown up a few minutes earlier, dragging a chair over to Doug's end of the booth, and he and Doug had been engrossed in conversation since. Heather and Len were still involved in the conversation they'd been having for the last few minutes, as well, and Jill found herself once again turning to Cal. And once more, he grinned. He knew he had her.

And she knew he was right.

"Excuse me," she said before she changed her mind. She stood, and Heather quickly looked up.

"Want me to go, too?" She set her drink on the table.

"No," Jill answered, the single word stopping Heather in midscoot across the bench, and without intending to, Jill flicked a glance to the other side of the bar. Where Cal's seat was now empty.

Her foster sister caught on fast, and straightened on the seat. She also asked a question without speaking.

Really?

Jill lifted one shoulder, almost apologetically. Heather and Trenton had picked up on Jill's modified attitude around Cal over the last few days, but Jill had produced little explanation for it. She hadn't told them about the walk to the park, nor about the conversation concerning Cal's dad. That one was something just between the two of them, anyway. It always had been.

But she *had* told them about going over and listening to music with Mrs. Wainwright.

Heather had been seriously jealous.

"I won't be long," Jill told her.

Heather nodded, her brow just the tiniest bit furrowed. "Let me know if you need me."

Len speared Jill with a look before she could turn away, and she could read in his eyes that he, too, understood where she was headed. He'd been there when she and Cal had come out of the park together, after all. And though he'd told neither Heather nor Trenton about that evening—nor had he commented on the shift in Jill's behavior toward Cal—she'd been aware that he'd picked up on it, as well. It was hard to spend that much time in such close proximity to another person and not start to think along the same wavelength.

"Why do women always need other women to go to the bathroom with them?" he teased now, proving himself an even better guy than Jill had thought. "What do they do in there, anyway?"

Jill chuckled under her breath and sent the man a look of thanks for not pointing out her traitorous behavior. "All *kinds* of things, Len. But don't worry, I won't take your date away from you. I can handle it all by myself tonight."

Doug glanced up from his conversation before she walked away, tossing Jill a quick smile, and she almost felt bad for slipping off. He was an attentive date, even if he had already figured out that what he'd hoped would happen tonight would *not* be happening.

She made it to the hallway where the restrooms were located, expecting to find Cal waiting there, but the hallway was empty.

Turning to look back the way she'd come, she saw only the packed crowd on the dance floor and servers weaving their way through with more drinks. No Cal. She frowned and stood on tiptoe, then she lost her balance when warm fingers wrapped around her wrist from behind and tugged. She stumbled through the open outside door, almost landing against Cal, but caught herself just short of being plastered to the man.

The door closed with a thud behind them, and they were alone.

"Cal." She narrowed her eyes at him.

"Jill," he mocked. Then he grinned at her, and she forgot whatever she'd been intending to say. The man could ooze charm without a single word.

She sighed. "Why did you just pull me outside?"

"Because it's too damned loud in there to be heard."

"And what is it that you wanted to make sure I heard?"

She thought she might be flirting with him, but she wasn't sure. She pretended she wasn't, though. Just to be safe. Because that likely wouldn't be wise.

Also, because he had a girlfriend.

"I wanted to know if you're still mad at me," he told her.

"About what?"

His eyes grew darker, and the corners of his mouth turned up. "So there's no more anger?"

No more . . .

What was he talking about?

And then she got it, and she blushed as hot as her date was prone to do. They couldn't have sex if they were still angry with one another. That had been their long-ago rule. She stared over his shoulder, her gaze locking onto a twenty-year-old two-tone Ford sitting in the back parking lot, and silently commanded her mouth to produce a frown. "Of course I'm still angry."

He leaned to his left and put his face in front of hers. "Are you sure about that?"

She didn't know what to think *or* what to say. Because she'd completely forgotten to be mad at him tonight. She'd forgotten for a few days now. Even though she'd assured him while they'd been in the park that she'd bring it back out.

Refusing to give in to his teasing, she propped her hands on her hips and cocked her head at him. "You did see that I'm on a date tonight, right?"

"Oh, I saw that."

She didn't ask why *he* wasn't on one. "Then you can understand why I need to get back."

"Nope. Because you *shouldn't* be on a date."

She wasn't sure what he meant by that.

"You're fraternizing with the competition," he explained. "I haven't decided if you're trying to get info out of my *boy*, or if I should give him a raise for trying to get info out of you."

She caught the way he stressed the word "boy" and suspected the man's ego was at play.

Was he jealous at seeing her out with another man?

And if he *was* jealous, what did *she* think about that?

She decided to delve into that question later, and returned to the conversation at hand. She smirked. "No info is exchanging hands."

He leaned in and put his mouth next to her ear. "Maybe *nothing* should be exchanged."

A tiny trickle raced down the back of her neck.

"Plus . . ." He retreated before she could get used to the warmth of his breath. Then his dark eyes flashed a fast up-and-down over the front of her. "He's too young for you."

She got offended as quickly as she'd almost been turned on. "And how old is Marci? And come to think of it, *where* is Marci?"

Cal gave no hint as to where his girlfriend might be, so she put her hands to his chest and shoved. He needed to take his charming self back inside with the boys. But he didn't budge. "I *do* need to get back to my *date*," she told him. "He's quite the charmer." She then gave him a matching up-and-down, same as he'd done to her. "I suspect he's pretty good at other things, too. What with so much *youth* and all."

Without waiting for a reply, she opened the door and left Cal standing outside alone.

Chapter Twelve

*"Occasionally wine should flow free. But make sure you're
with trustworthy friends when it does."*

—Blu Johnson, life lesson #81

Jill rolled to her back and wiped at the gunk in the corners of her eyes,
but she refused to actually open them. She could tell the sun had come
up, without needing to look for verification, and she'd decided sometime during the night that she didn't intend to adult today.

She and Heather had left their dates at the bar the night before,
and when Jill had brought Heather home, instead of simply dropping
her off, she'd come inside. The next thing she'd known, they'd been two
glasses deep into their third bottle of wine, and neither of them had
been looking for a way out. They'd touched on several topics before
stumbling to their beds, but the one to leave the sharpest sting had
been Jill's mother.

For some reason, Jill had claimed to understand her mother.

Yet Jill had *never* understood her mother. The woman had been
focused on one thing, and one thing only, her whole life. And that had
been to have a man. She'd think she'd have one, swear he was the man
of her dreams . . . and then something would happen and he'd leave her.

And Jill knew why it happened. Even back then. Her mother had been too needy.

But last night, in a very inebriated state, Jill had confessed to Heather that she finally understood what having that kind of need was like. Because apparently, she'd felt needy herself.

The very idea terrified her.

She also remembered admitting to being lonely, and to hoping that Doug would have turned out to be her type. As if she had a type. Yet there she'd sat, spouting out things to one of her best friends in the world that she'd had no clue she'd been thinking. And with each confession, she'd become a little more unclear about who she even was.

She didn't want to date, did she?

And lonely? Since when?

But she *was* tired of being angry. She'd tossed that nugget out, too. And she didn't regret saying that one. It was time to find a way beyond the anger.

She rolled back to her side and decided that if she stayed in bed long enough, Heather would leave for her yoga class, and then she could sneak out without having to face her foster sister just yet. Some days were better spent alone.

Only, the sheets rustled at her feet.

So much for avoidance. She kept her eyes firmly closed and her nose buried in the covers. Heather was *always* perky early in the morning, too much wine or not. She probably thought she could talk Jill into going to yoga with her.

"Go away," Jill grumped. "I'm still asleep."

Heather didn't answer.

"I mean it, Heather." She'd pried her eyelids open. "I don't want to—"

That wasn't her foster sister staring back at her. It was Cal!

In the next instant, Jill pushed up toward the headboard. But the second she was fully upright, she yelped and crumpled back to the mattress. She clamped both hands over her head. *"Oooohhhh,"* she moaned. *"Crap.* Why did I do that?"

"What did you do, exactly?" Cal's deep baritone seemed to rattle inside her skull.

"Close the blinds." She flapped a hand toward the window behind him while keeping the fingers of her other hand firmly clasped over her eyes. "And don't talk so loud."

The room dimmed into shadows . . . and then the bed dipped. Right beside her hip.

"Get out," she growled. "Why are you here?"

Cal captured her free hand and placed something in her palm, and after snatching her hand away from him, Jill peeked out of one eye to see what it was. Ibuprofen. Four of them.

"Drink up," he told her. He held a glass of water out to her.

She didn't want to *get* up, much less drink up. But she hated wine headaches worse than she valued maintaining illogical stubbornness, so she grudgingly accepted the water. And though she slowly pushed herself back into a sitting position, she kept her eyes closed. She also turned her face away from him, as if doing so would negate the fact that the man was in her bed.

Once the pills were down, she blindly held out the glass, and when it disappeared from her hand, she reattacked the gunk in the corners of her eyes. Her head got stopped up anytime she drank too much wine, and aside from clogging her sinuses, her eyes also oozed grossness.

Why she *ever* did this to herself, she had no idea.

When she'd finished clearing the worst of it, she finally opened her eyes all the way, but she kept her chin tilted down.

"Better?" Cal asked.

"No." She scowled up at him. "Why are you here? And how did you *get* in here?"

His stupid massive shoulders shrugged. "Heather let me in."

She was going to kill her foster sister.

"And?" she asked.

"And what?"

"And why are you here? *Why* did she let you in?"

"She let me in because I asked her to."

Jill groaned. The man could be as hardheaded as she was.

He put a hand to the bed and leaned in then, dipping the mattress even more, and Jill barely kept from tumbling into his lap. "And I'm here because I wanted to know something."

His tone had softened, and Jill slowly blinked. "And what was that?"

"If you went home alone last night."

It took a second for his words to register, but when they did, her anger spiked.

Seriously?

She pulled back, putting a couple of inches between them, then shot him her snottiest smirk. "In case you missed it, I didn't even *go* home."

Why in the world would Heather have let him into the house, much less into the bedroom? This was the very room where the two of them had first—

She snapped off her thoughts and adjusted her look to a glare.

Heather was fully aware of what had once happened in this room. Her foster sister was as good as dead.

Then Cal lowered his gaze, and it traveled along the rumpled sheets before lingering on the pillows. Jill held her breath, wondering if he remembered what had once gone on in there, too. The house had been deserted at the time, and the covers had been dusty from not being used for a while. But that hadn't stopped them.

He brought his gaze back to hers. "So, did you?"

She couldn't believe he had the nerve. "Do you see anyone in here with me?"

He lifted the covers and ducked his head to look under.

"Stop it." She smacked his hands.

"Well, how would I know for sure if I don't look?"

"Get out, Cal." She thrust her arm toward the door, but the quick motion sent a sharp stab of pain through her skull, and she once again grabbed for her head. "As you can see," she gritted out, "no one is in here but me. Now leave."

He didn't leave. "I didn't like watching you with another man last night."

"Are you kidding me?" She gaped at him, eyes burning from the trickle of daylight making its way through the blinds. "I've watched you with other women for years."

"I know. But I never have, and I didn't like it."

"I don't *care*."

"Did you go anywhere else before coming here? Was anyone here before you went to bed?"

"I cannot believe—"

His fingers snagged her chin and brought her face to his, and that's when she finally saw the anger simmering just below the surface. "You didn't show up at the house this morning."

"That's because I'm taking the day off." She slid her gaze to the clock beside the bed, and realized that the sun had been up for hours. "And I *was* sleeping in," she finished in a grumble.

Then it occurred to her that she probably looked just as bad as she felt and that her breath was no doubt atrocious.

And Cal still held her face right up next to his.

She jerked out of his grasp. "Nothing happened last night, okay? Or every other night of my life, if you're so hard up to know." She made a face at him. "And speaking of going home alone, I'm sure Marci wouldn't appreciate knowing that you're currently in *my* bed."

"Marci broke up with me."

That caught her off guard. "Really?" She wouldn't have expected that.

But then she remembered Loretta sitting in Cal's lap the night before. Loretta must have been aware of the breakup. Therefore, she was back and looking for action. And given her and Cal's history . . .

"Did *you* go home with Loretta, then?"

He shook his head. "I went home alone. And I thought about you."

"Stop it."

"I'm just stating the facts."

"You shouldn't be thinking of me."

"I can't help it."

"Is that why Marci broke up with you?" Marci *had* claimed that Cal had been different lately.

"Marci broke up with me because it was time. Every woman I date eventually breaks up with me."

She blinked to focus better. "Every one? Why?"

And why was he in there telling her this?

How had he even *known* to find her there?

He broke eye contact then, dropping his gaze to the bed once more. But he didn't seem to be looking at it this time, so much as he was lost in his own thoughts. When he finally lifted his gaze, his eyes gave nothing away, and Jill once again found herself holding her breath.

"They claim I don't care enough," Cal told her, his words as expressionless as his dark eyes.

Jill swallowed. "And, do you?"

"I want to."

The three words together didn't say a lot, but at the same time, it felt to Jill as if they *should* be telling her more. In her disheveled state, though—and with her head still pounding out a rhythm any drum soloist could be proud of—she couldn't clue in to whatever the big revelation might be.

Cal picked up the empty bottle of wine from the floor and studied it, and she remembered bringing the last of the bottle to bed with her. Heather hadn't been able to down another ounce, but Jill had still been busy bemoaning the fact that her libido had reawakened and that it seemed to be pointed in only one direction.

She'd managed to keep that tidbit from Heather, however. Though given the way her mouth had been running, she had no idea how. But as Cal sat there beside her, she found that she couldn't deny it. She wanted him.

And she wanted *only* him.

"How's Rodney?" she asked. She had to get her mind on something else.

At the question, Cal brought his gaze back to hers. Cal had quit drinking years ago because his uncle drank enough for both of them. He'd never shared his reasoning, yet she'd known.

"He's fine," he replied. *Subject closed.*

Jill showed her disdain for his easy dismissal with a shortened version of a smirk.

He set the bottle on the bedside table and refocused on her. "How about your anger?" he asked. "You didn't get angry about anything before you left last night, did you?"

"*Cal.*"

Her frustration grew. Was he serious? She hadn't been that person in over a decade.

"Stop it. You're just being ridiculous now. Nothing happened last night. I didn't *want* anything to happen. And you of all people know that if I *had* gotten angry, even less would have happened."

"Less?" His eyes burned into hers. "So something *did* happen?"

He'd never once been this jealous when they'd dated.

But then, she'd also never looked at another guy after her first experience with that sledgehammer.

She couldn't resist teasing. "He did give me a kiss good night."

Cal's eyes narrowed.

"A *very* hot kiss," she added, though nothing more than a hug had actually been exchanged. "Little Red certainly knows what he's doing."

She grimaced at the name. She hadn't meant to say that out loud. It totally took away from the point she'd been hoping to make.

"No more dates with *Little* Red," he told her.

"Fine. I'll find someone else to date. Now, thank you for checking in on me, but as you can see, I'm fine. I might look like something the cat dragged in, but in reality, I've never been better."

When he didn't move, she looked at the door.

"My cue to go?" he asked.

"You've kind of overstayed your welcome. Plus, I need to get up. I may not be working today, but I can't sleep the day away, either."

Even if she really did want to.

Cal grudgingly stood and moved to the door, but before stepping through it, he fired a look over his shoulder. "For the record"—his gaze skipped to the T-shirt she'd borrowed from Heather, which had a faded stegosaurus in the middle of it—"you look far better than anything *my* cat has ever dragged in."

He disappeared without another word, and one thought passed through Jill's head.

Cal had a cat?

After the door closed at the front of the house, Heather poked her head into the room, with Trenton's face appearing just above Heather's shoulder.

Jill jabbed a finger at Heather. "You are in so much trouble."

"What was I supposed to do?"

"Not let him in!" She shoved the covers off. She was suddenly far too hot.

"But he had a look about him," Heather protested. "I'm not sure *not* letting him in was an option."

"And then, what? You called Trenton so she could witness my humiliation, too?"

"I was up at the house," Trenton informed her. "So you can retract your claws. Aunt Blu's getting a new girl tomorrow, and I was helping get the room ready. I saw Cal's truck when he pulled in."

"I don't even know why he was here," Jill told them both. "Or how he knew that I was here."

What had happened between them when she hadn't been looking? One encounter with a ghost, and she forgot to be angry?

"He was here because he's practically green with jealousy," Heather told her. She looked at Trenton. "That was *not* a happy man watching her out with Little Red last night."

"But he has no right to be jealous. He's dated other women for years. Not to mention, he and I are *not* together."

"That doesn't seem to matter." Heather sat on the bed with Jill, and Trenton circled to the other side. "Especially since he went to so much trouble to seek you out this morning. He apparently went to your house first. And then to Little Red's."

Jill's jaw dropped. "He went to Doug's house?"

"Don't worry," Heather assured her. "Doug was at work already, on another jobsite. I called him while Cal was in here with you. But before I let Cal in, he told me that he'd gone by there before thinking to check here."

"But . . ." Jill looked from Heather to Trenton. "Why go to all that trouble to begin with?"

She understood jealousy. She'd even felt a little of it last night. Cal may not like watching her dating another man, but the thing was, watching him with other women didn't do anything for her, either.

"Honey." Heather leaned in and put a hand on Jill's knee. "Don't you get it? He obviously still has feelings for you. And I think you . . ." She looked at Trenton as if seeking out help, but she didn't have to say more. Jill understood loud and clear.

"No." Jill shook her head. "I don't. We covered this already, remember? I don't feel anything for him. Not like that."

"But we *know* you," Trenton told her. "And something *is* going on with you. You've been different around him lately."

"I've simply *been* around him. That's all. You haven't seen that since I was a teenager. But nothing is going on with me. I promise you. I'm exactly the same as I've always been."

"Well, something is definitely going on with Cal," Heather stated emphatically. "Though I wonder if it ever stopped. We were still here when he came back from Vegas, remember? That was one messed-up man."

"You mean when he *left* me in Vegas?"

"Yeah. But I'm just saying it wasn't easy on him, either. He had strong feelings for you."

"Well, it sure as hell wasn't *hard* for him."

She and Cal had had a fight the morning after their quickie wedding, and she'd gone out to burn off some steam. When she'd returned—granted, it had been hours later—he'd been gone. And in his place had been matching quickie divorce papers.

"Not even twenty-four hours of marriage, remember?" She shook her head, unbelieving that only last night she'd been having thoughts of jealousy concerning the women he dated. How ridiculous could she be? "No," she said again. "I do not feel anything for him. Nothing at all."

Heather patted her leg. "Okay."

Jill didn't believe the sentiment for one minute, so she jerked her leg out of reach.

"Just let us know if Trenton needs to kick his ass again."

Jill almost smiled at that as she recalled the comment Trenton had tossed out at the Bono House the week before. "When did you ever kick Cal's ass?" she asked now. Trenton was tough, but Jill could not imagine those two going at it.

"Two weeks after he came back."

"And she actually landed several punches," Heather assured her. "I was there. We went to his uncle's house because Cal wouldn't return our calls."

"Why were you calling him?"

"Because *you* weren't calling us."

"Oh." Jill sat back at the words. She hadn't been returning their calls, because she'd been humiliated and hell-bent on proving Cal wrong.

"It had been two weeks," Trenton reminded her. "And no one had heard from you."

"Cal really told no one anything about that trip?"

When she'd come home, Jill had been floored to discover that no one seemed to have a clue about what had happened in Vegas.

Heather shook her head. "I suppose he could've told Pete. They've always been tight. But Pete wasn't talking, either."

"So, what were you thinking?" Jill asked. "Why go over there?"

Heather studied her quietly for a moment, and when she spoke, the mood in the room shifted. "We didn't know what to think, Jilly. Your phone's in-box was full, you hadn't called us in two weeks."

"We were concerned that something might have happened to you," Trenton added. "That maybe . . ."

Jill's eyes went wide. "You thought Cal had done something to me?" Why had they never talked about this?

And then she registered the guilty look in Trenton's eyes, and she understood *exactly* why they'd never talked about it. "You thought *I* had done something to me?" Jill guessed. Just like her mother had.

Heather swallowed. "We didn't *really* think so, but we also knew how much you'd been looking forward to running off with him."

"To *starting* your life."

They'd known that she'd saved up money and had been planning to surprise Cal with the fact that they could move to LA right away.

"And then *Cal* was back," Heather continued.

"And I wasn't answering my phone," Jill whispered, finally understanding the fear they must have felt.

She closed her eyes. Even when Cal had called her after two weeks, furious because no one had been able to get in touch with her—and equally ticked because *he'd* been worried that she might have done something to herself—it had never occurred to her that Heather and Trenton might have been thinking along the same lines. Maybe Aunt Blu, too.

And it had never occurred to her because Cal had been the only one to know that she'd ever considered doing anything like that.

"I'm sorry I worried you." She reached out and hugged them both. "I'm sorry I didn't call. I'm sorry we grew apart."

Heather squeezed her tight. "And I'm sorry we didn't get on a bus and come out there to be with you."

Jill pulled back slightly, and looked at two of the three people her world wouldn't be complete without. "But we have each other today."

Trenton nodded. "And that will never again change."

~

"That is one impressive swing you've got, Mr. Reynolds."

Cal kept an eye on his uncle as the man showboated for the cameras. Rodney had shown up on the jobsite at the same time Cal had returned from making an ass of himself looking for Jill, and the crew had been following him around since. Rodney had helped to get the new quartz countertops in, then he'd gone to the upstairs bathroom, and demonstrated how to install the underlayment for a heated tile floor. But now . . .

Cal chuckled to himself as he watched the "show" going on in the front yard. Now Rodney stood before an ever-growing crowd, his signature charm on full display, while he demonstrated for the cameras . . . the perfect golf swing.

His uncle was one of a kind.

"Meet me over at the country club," Rodney told Patrick, "and we'll play a round. My treat."

"I might take you up on that."

"I want to play, too, Rodney," a woman called out from the crowd, and when Rodney turned to check out the owner of the voice, the woman's smile let it be known that golf wasn't at all what she wanted to play.

Cal relaxed for the first time that day. This was the Rodney he'd spent his youth idolizing. Charming, fun. Sober. The man had been a step above the rest.

It was a shame days like this were so few and far between, but as Cal stood there watching—remembering—he found himself hopeful that things could change. Yeah, his uncle had been drunk off his ass the night before. But he'd also left when Cal had. Which had been right after coming in from talking to Jill. Cal had offered to give Rodney a ride home, hoping it would save him from having to go back out in the middle of the night to fetch him, and had been pleasantly surprised when his uncle agreed. Cal had considered it a win all the way around since it had also given him the perfect excuse for not hanging around any longer to watch his ex flirt with another man.

Pete's truck pulled up as the crowd started clapping, egging Rodney on to make the putt after someone had located an empty soup can and had positioned it thirty feet away as a "hole."

"Ten dollars says you can't make it," a man called out.

"Ten dollars and you can make it with me," a woman joined in.

Laughter rolled through the onlookers as Pete made his way over to Cal. "Looks like there's a party going on over here today."

"It pretty much is. But that's my uncle for you." This was the first Cal had seen of his friend that day. He edged a step closer and spoke under his breath. "Problems getting out of bed today, Peter? What happened? You needed to sleep in after last night?"

Pete didn't rise to the bait. "Some of us can get laid all night long, *Calhoun*, and still be at work on time the next day. I've been at it for hours. Which is more than I can say about you."

Cal cast him a questioning glance. "You saying I haven't been working today? Or are you suggesting I got laid last night, too?"

Pete harrumphed. "I'm suggesting you *wanted* to get laid last night."

"Yeah." Cal turned back to his uncle. "Well . . ."

"Well," Pete agreed. Neither spoke again for several minutes, until Pete finally said, "You want to talk about it?"

"Nothing to talk about."

"Didn't get laid. Got it." Pete's voice changed, growing more serious. "So, were you *really* out running errands this morning?"

Cal looked at his friend. When he'd gone in search of Jill earlier that day, he'd told the guys at the house that he had errands to run. And then he'd charged around town like a man possessed, refusing to stop until he'd found his ex. Just so he could make sure she'd not had another man in her bed.

He had no idea what he would've done if he'd found her with Doug.

And he was aware that he had no right to care. Jill wasn't his. He wasn't hers.

Only . . . did he want that to change?

"Not so much errands," he finally admitted.

Pete nodded. He'd guessed right. "She alone?"

"She was alone."

"You going to keep it that way?"

Pete had been a good friend over the years, and though they rarely broke the surface of seriousness, Cal knew that when it needed to be done, his buddy would do it. Just as Cal would return the favor for him.

"I don't know," Cal answered truthfully.

They both refocused on the action in the yard, but as they did, Cal discovered that his uncle had worn down. One of the interns was removing Rodney's mic pack while several women stood waiting just across the street, and Cal's slight hope for his uncle's soberness evaporated. With that many women vying for the man's attention, Rodney would be buying rounds before the hour was up.

The workers had come outside to watch, as well, and as Cal turned toward the house, they each made their way back inside. Cal and Pete followed, but before they reached the front porch, Pete stopped them both.

"She talking to you yet?" Pete asked.

"She's talking." Cal didn't let himself show pleasure at the thought. "Broke her down Wednesday night."

"Yet she's still avoiding you on set?"

He'd like to change that, too. "So far she is."

Pete nodded, and when he didn't immediately say anything else, Cal turned for the door. Only, Pete wasn't finished yet.

"You sure you know what you're doing with her?"

Cal looked back. He didn't have a clue what he was doing with her. But he did have sudden clarity on one fact. "I'm flying blind, Pete. But I like the feel of the wind right now."

Chapter Thirteen

"Be a guiding light, even when you don't think others are watching."

—Blu Johnson, life lesson #1

"There's my personal bodyguard."

Jill grinned like a naughty child when Len looked up from where he stood at the buffet table, then she opened her mouth when he speared a meatball and held it out to her.

"'Bodyguard' implies I'd take a hit for you," he informed as she chewed. With his plate already groaning under the weight of the food craft services stocked on a daily basis, he continued piling on more.

"And you're saying you wouldn't take a hit for me?" Jill moved along beside him. They'd both taken a break from filming, and though Len had headed outside on his own, Jill had found herself tagging along behind him.

"Depends on who's doing the hitting," Len confessed. "If the guy is smaller than me"—he looked down at himself, as if to double-check how massive he was, before lifting a shoulder in a casual shrug—"then I probably would."

"*Awww* . . . Lenny." Jill leaned in and hugged up against the man's arm, rubbing her cheek on him as if she were a cat looking for love. "You're such a sweetheart."

He laughed at her teasing, and shoved another bite of food in her mouth.

"Mmmm." She moaned at the burst of cream that spilled from the pastry he'd given her. "Yummy."

She grabbed another cream puff before continuing to trail along behind him, and found the background noises of saws, hammers, and just general construction-site conversation to be comforting. She wasn't used to working on jobs this large, and though they still had almost three weeks to go, she already knew she'd miss it when it ended. And not just the work, but filming. As well as Len.

They reached the end of the food table, and when Len looked back at her, he seemed to realize for the first time that she'd come out of the house alone. Usually, either Trenton or Heather could be found at her side, but Heather had off-site appointments with potential clients, and Trenton had run out to do some errands.

"Just you?" Len asked. He shoved enough food for three people into his mouth.

"Just me." Jill watched him chew. "You have the same manners as Heather, did you know that?" Heather was sweet, but she could be atrocious at the dinner table. "Which means that you're gross, Len. In case you didn't catch on to that fact. That why you have the hots for my friend?"

Len flicked crumbs in Jill's face. "Who said I had the hots for her?"

"Uhhhh . . . Friday night?" They stepped out from under the canopy of the food tent back into the midday sun. "You went out with her, remember?"

"Right. And you went with Little Red." He looked down his nose at her. "That mean you have the hots for him?"

The man had a point. "Touché." She stole a miniature quiche from his plate. "So you're not heartbroken that you and Heather didn't . . ."

She let the words trail off as she looked up at him. He hadn't seemed upset when she and Heather had left the bar Friday night, but she wanted to make sure. This was the first opportunity she'd gotten to speak with him alone.

He gulped half a soda before answering. "Friday night was just a good time. A man and woman can have some fun and still keep it light, you know?"

"I know that."

"Do you?" He looked down at her again. "Then tell me . . . can a man and woman step outside together—late at night at a bar—and keep it light?"

Jill swallowed. She might have known he'd bring that up.

"They can," she answered carefully. Then, without meaning to, she turned her gaze to the Cadillac House, where she could see Cal standing just outside the back door, papers in hand, going over something with one of his trades. "It was nothing," she assured Len. She didn't want him asking questions. "Cal was just trying to get in my head. About the competition," she added hurriedly.

And he *had* gotten in her head. But not about the competition so much as about him. As a man.

But then, she'd gotten into his, as well. Otherwise, he wouldn't have shown up at Heather's Saturday morning with jealousy seeping from every pore. Nor would he have made the first two days of this week a tightly wound tension fest. They hadn't spoken at all, yet everywhere she looked, he seemed to be there.

He glanced in her direction then, not catching her eye, but her stomach did a little flip at the way he did a quick scan down the length of her body.

Then he promptly returned his attention to the documents in his hand.

Jill let out a breath of air, and Len said, "Yep. It was about the competition. That's what I figured."

She ignored him.

The two of them stood together, both eating off his plate, as they watched the rusted metal roof being removed from the Cadillac House. Then Jill glanced at their house, and she pictured the architectural shingles that would be installed later that week. She knew Cal had chosen to stick with metal, which was more in keeping with the original style of the home. Had she and Heather made a mistake in going with shingles?

She'd failed so many times in the past. With her mother. In Hollywood.

With Cal.

She didn't want to let Heather and Trenton down, but she had no idea if they were doing enough.

"I've got to *win* this competition." She spoke under her breath, not realizing she'd voiced the thought until Len glanced at her.

He shoved the last of his food in his mouth. "Why's that?"

"Because I want to win." She tried to blow off the moment. The last thing she wanted was her insecurities showing. "Isn't that why people compete?"

"In this competition?" He tossed the empty plate in the trash. "Most sign on just to be on TV. Or for the benefit the town gets."

Or they might sign on to tick the other off, she thought, glancing back over to search for Cal. She found him on the roof this time, tool belt hanging low on his hips. He stooped to one knee, his jeans pulling taut against his rear, and she forgot to breathe.

Damn. She so wanted that man.

"Earth to Jill," Len said softly, and Jill jerked her gaze from Cal. "What?"

Len smirked. "Geez, woman. Do I need to call the fire department?"

"*No.* Smart-ass," she grumbled. She turned her back to Cal. "You do *not* need to call the fire department. And for the record, I know that winning this competition is really only about bragging rights." She suddenly wanted him to understand. "I'm all for doing it for the house donation the town gets. We're all about giving back. But what you don't get is that we're also trying to reinvent ourselves."

Len seemed confused. "From what?"

"From Queens of the She-Sheds."

"Oh yeah." He snapped two meaty fingers together. "The retreats. The show is considering doing a segment on them."

"What?" *No.* That would only add to the problem. "Can't you talk them out of it?"

"Why would I do that? They're great. Granted, I've only seen them in the B-roll footage that was shot before renovations started, but I have to tell you, that's a niche market you could own around here."

"We pretty much *do* own it."

"Then what's the problem?"

Jill motioned back toward Cal. "That's the problem. I want that. *We* want that."

"You want Cal?" Len didn't even try to hold back his snort of laughter as Cal looked down at them—apparently after hearing his name—and Jill wanted to punch her new friend in the gut.

"I'm going to murder you for that," she muttered. But Cal shifted his gaze to be solely on her, and she had trouble remembering what she was supposed to be upset about.

The naughty sparkle was back in his eyes. He'd been doing that for the last two days. A sparkle that implied that he knew things about her. Which he did. But they were teenage things. He hadn't seen *anything* when he'd been in her bedroom the other day.

Of course, she'd returned her own look—as she was doing now. It said, *I know things, too.* And sometimes it tacked on *I want to know more things.* Which Cal might just be reading correctly.

Jill captured her lip between her teeth, trying her best not to let her mouth turn into a smile, and as she'd caught herself doing all week, she fought Cal for control in the game of who would look away first.

"Earth to Jill, again."

"Shut up, Len."

But Len didn't shut up. Instead he laughed, and though it was seriously hard not to look at him—or to punch him when he *kept* laughing— her eyes remained locked on Cal's.

At least, until Len said, "You do know, Patrick is eventually going to get you two on camera."

She looked at him. "No, he's not."

She turned and headed back to the Bono House without another word. She needed to get to work. And to quit playing games with Cal. That wasn't the smartest move she'd ever made, but nonetheless, she'd found herself unable to stop.

She and Len entered the house together, and as Len retrieved his camera, Trenton's truck pulled into the drive. Jill heard the squeal of the tires and looked up in time to catch Trenton barreling out of the cab, leaving the door open behind her.

Jill rushed through the house. "What's wrong?" she asked the second she hit the front door, but the grin on Trenton's face indicated that "wrong" was the incorrect word.

Trenton held up a notebook in front of her. "Look."

Only, it wasn't a notebook. It was their calendar.

"They're in?" Jill snatched the calendar away from Trenton, and Len and Trenton looked over her shoulder as she stared down at the photo on the front cover.

"What a great shot." Len echoed Jill's thought. "I didn't realize you guys had made a calendar."

"They printed the first batch today," Trenton told them. She quickly explained the reason for the calendars before adding, "I stopped in to check on them, and was handed a full box." She motioned back toward the truck, as if considering returning to retrieve the others, but in the end, took back the one from Jill's hands. She began flipping through the pages, showing off their work, and as she did, Josie—who'd been installing trim in the master bedroom—appeared in the doorway.

Jill motioned Josie over. "Come look."

"I'm October," Josie offered. She crossed to them. "Of this year."

It was an eighteen-month calendar due to the money needing to be raised that summer, and Josie and her retreat had been chosen for the fourth month. Trenton found October, and Jill remembered how special this one had been to build. Unshed tears burned the back of her nose as she studied the photo along with Josie.

"I've never been more proud than the day they came out and took that picture," Josie told them. She traced the outline of the building. "Without you three . . . Without Blu . . ."

Jill swallowed around the tightness in her throat, and pulled the other woman in for a hug. Josie had worked so hard to get where she was, and at twenty, she was doing pretty darned good.

Then Jill realized that Len had lifted his camera and started recording. His lens was pointed at Josie. "Tell me how you came to have the retreat," he prodded.

Jill wanted to tell him to stop. That this would only bring more attention to the sheds. But she couldn't bring herself to do it. Instead, she stepped nearer to Trenton, and the two of them let the younger woman have the floor.

"It's not a retreat for me," Josie told the camera. Her voice was steady, but Jill could see the youth in her eyes. "It's my *home*. I moved in with Blu when I was sixteen. After my dad kicked me out. But when I turned eighteen"—she shook her head as if she were as unsure of the outcome today as she'd been back then—"I needed to go. Only, I had nowhere *to* go."

She tossed a quick glance at Jill, and Jill nodded encouragement.

"I had a job at the grocery store." Josie turned back to Len. "I'd been working there since I moved to Red Oak Falls. And one of the women who'd been there a lot longer than me said she had some space on the back of her property that I could rent. For real cheap. She told me I could put a trailer on it," Josie explained. She licked her lips and stared straight at the camera. "But I'd been watching the Bluebonnet girls since I moved in. I admired them. What they did for women." She glanced at Jill and Trenton again. "And that's what I wanted. I wanted to be a *part* of them."

Jill snuck a glance at Len, noticing that for once, the man's lips, half hidden by his too-full beard, weren't smiling. He stood mesmerized as he filmed Josie's story, and Jill acknowledged to herself that this *would* make a great segment on the show.

"Josie helped build it," Jill said softly. "She worked her rear off to get her home. And she's worked for *us* ever since."

Josie's eyes glistened as she admitted, "I'd probably be on the streets without them. They changed my life. I have skills that can last me a lifetime already, and I'm only twenty. I plan to go to college someday. I *will* be a success. And when I am, I hope I can do something half as special as what these ladies have done for so many others."

Len turned the camera on them as Josie finished talking, and caught the three of them huddled together. Heather had come in while the other woman had been speaking, and they'd silently taken each other's hands. And as they stood there, no one in the room saying a word, Jill found herself standing a bit taller than usual. Because for the first time, she realized that they weren't just building sheds in backyards.

~

Friday of week four rolled around, and with the sounds of a new metal roof being installed overhead, Cal stood in Mrs. Wainwright's room, watching an interview taking place down below.

185

A couple of the producers had been talking with people from the crowd throughout the day. They'd mostly crossed the road, pointing a microphone at whoever got their attention, but occasionally someone would be brought over and wired up. During those times, Cal could overhear most of the conversations. There'd been more than one story relayed concerning how he and Jill never spoke, and how the people in town found humor in this.

Cal knew they'd been placing bets for years on how long Jill would stay in a room once he entered, but as he stood there listening to yet another telling of the situation, the idea of what he and Jill had once meant to each other—faced with how far they'd swung in the other direction—bothered him. He'd never imagined they could have ended up that way.

Thankfully, it seemed to be swinging back. Though just how far he wanted the pendulum to tilt, he continued to grapple with.

He closed the window, unwilling to listen to any more, and searched the crowd for Blu. She was scheduled for an interview today.

After Jill had encouraged him to visit her, he'd called and invited Blu to dinner. She'd insisted he let her cook for him instead, so he'd spent Sunday evening at her place, and when she'd opened her door to him, they'd hugged long and tight. Both of them had understood his being there meant that he'd be doing it again in the weeks to come. Blu had always been like a mother to him, and he wouldn't step away from that again.

A soft knock sounded behind him, but he didn't turn. It would be Mrs. Wainwright. She toyed with him almost every day now.

If anything was left in this room overnight, he'd find it moved the next morning. One day he'd come in to his tool belt—which he'd intentionally placed just outside the bedroom door—hanging over the railing in the landing. She'd actually left the room. So he gave it right back to her. He changed the radio station to ones he knew she didn't enjoy as much, and one night he'd left every light burning downstairs. She hadn't liked that one, though. She'd let him know by not speaking to him for two days.

The rap sounded again, and Cal finally glanced over his shoulder. He wished he could get a glimpse of her. Only, it was Jill who stood at the door.

"Hey." Both surprise and happiness coursed through him.

"Hey." Her eyes made a sweep of the room.

"What are you doing here? Aren't you afraid you'll get caught speaking to me?" he teased. They'd been flirting all week. Mostly from a distance, since she continued to evade Patrick's attempts to get them on screen together.

She nodded toward the window. "Everyone's outside."

"That they are." Cal went over to her. Even if speaking to him was removed from the equation, this was still the first time she'd been the one to seek *him* out. "So, did you want something?" He stopped at the door, but he didn't touch her like he wanted to.

"I wanted to . . ." Her gaze swept the room again. "See if there had been any more ghost activity."

"You came over to check on Mrs. W?"

Hesitation touched her gaze. "I did."

Sure she did. He glanced behind him, as if conferring with the ghost. "Then the first thing you need to know is that she doesn't like the generic term 'ghost.' It's Mrs. Wainwright or lady of the house."

Jill's eyes widened. "You're on speaking terms with her?"

That happiness he'd felt upon seeing her grew. "Only when she calls *me* by the name that I prefer."

"And that's what?"

"Prince Cal is my all-time favorite, but I also answer to Master Reynolds."

That seemed to make it sink in that he was messing with her, and he laughed at the outraged look on her face.

"*Cal.*"

"*Mmmm.*" He leaned closer. "I do love it when you say my name like that."

"Stop it." She punched him in the arm, and he grabbed her hand and reeled her into the room.

"No hitting the competition." He didn't tug hard, but he brought her close enough to feel the heat coming off her body.

"Then the competition shouldn't be teasing me," she murmured.

He so wanted to kiss her. "I like teasing you."

He also got the feeling that she was ready to be kissed.

He twined his fingers with hers. There was no one else on the upper floor, though anyone could show up at any minute. Or spot them from downstairs if they happened to pass through and look up at the right angle. But he couldn't bring himself to stop touching her. Things had changed between them over the course of the week, whether either of them admitted it or not.

"How would you like it if I teased *you* back?" she asked, and his nod came quick.

"I'd like that a lot."

She laughed. "You're incorrigible."

But then she lowered her gaze to his lips, and her eyes turned hazy. In a blink, his jeans grew tight in the crotch. She hadn't looked at him like that in years.

Just as he was about to lean in, to take what he wanted, a grin the size of Texas popped on her face, and he groaned instead of kissing her.

"Seriously? That's not right, Sadler."

She shrugged. "That's teasing."

She pulled her hand from his and went to the window, and Cal missed her already.

"Dang," Jill muttered as she looked out. "I was hoping they'd forget about her."

"Forget about who?" He stepped up beside her to see that Bonnie Beckman and her dog, Winston, were now being interviewed. The animal had on a rhinestone collar that glistened in the sun. "What's wrong with Bonnie?"

Granted, Bonnie was somewhat unique. But everyone loved her.

Jill nibbled at her bottom lip as she continued watching the activity going on below, before eventually casting him a cautious look. "Have you ever seen the retreat we built for her?"

He shook his head. "Never been to her place."

"It's a vacation home for her dog."

He blinked. "A vacation home?"

She wrinkled her nose and nodded. "For her dog. We thought we were building the typical 'man cave' for a woman. You know, a she-shed? Like we do. Overstuffed furniture, lots of natural light. Flowers and blinged-out accessories. That sort of thing. It's as decked out as they come. The woman definitely had money to throw at it. And we knew she'd asked for several extras for her dog. We got that. People love their pets. There's even one of those communication systems that she can connect to with her phone. In case she wants to speak to Winston when she's not there," she added. "Not that she *ever* goes anywhere without Winston. But at the café the morning the show started filming, she comes over and she shares with us—on camera, mind you—that what we really built was a doggie dream home. Where *she's* the guest."

Cal stared. "That's an impression to make."

"Right? See why I'd hoped they'd forget about her?"

"I'm sure Patrick will make sure the story paints you in a nice light."

"*Please.* I'm sure Patrick will exploit either of us in any way that he can."

Soft music started playing from the corner then, and Jill tossed a quick glance in that direction. She then turned a brilliant smile up to him. "Bonnie also predicted that whoever got this house would come out the winner because Winston barked at the house while they were on a walk. I suspect he was barking at Mrs. Wainwright."

Pieces of the puzzle clicked into place. "That's why you wanted this house."

She shook her head. "I never wanted this house."

"Yes, you did. I saw the way you looked at it."

She put her back to the window, still looking up at him, and she graced him with a desperate oh-my-God-I-have-to-have-it look. The same one he'd seen several times the morning of their initial walk-through.

His expression fell. "That was all fake?"

"Every bit of it."

She'd been acting? He couldn't believe it.

He'd had so much trouble with this house. As expected, of course. The wiring. The plumbing. *Mold.* They'd even had to replace several joists under the flooring. At the same time, he'd heard very little of any similar issues coming from the Bono House. The house he'd *intended* to choose. And that had all been because she'd been playing him.

He took a half step back.

"Awww." She pouted. She reached out and patted his chest. "Don't feel bad, Calhoun. I just have skills that you don't."

"You're . . ." He closed his mouth when he realized it was hanging open. Then he captured her hand beneath his, trapping it to his chest.

Damn. He had to admit to being impressed. He also never would have guessed.

And then he wondered what else he didn't know about Jill. Or if he'd ever really known her at all.

He'd once thought he'd known her. He'd thought she was a bit of a dreamer—yet at the same time, grounded in reality. He'd thought she'd loved him. Would stand with him.

He'd *thought* she would fill the hole inside him.

But then she'd insisted on Hollywood. And he'd laughed in her face.

"If it makes you feel better . . ." She tugged at her hand, but he kept it tight in his. Then he retook that half step he'd given up, and she had to tilt her head back to meet his gaze.

"If it makes me feel better . . . what?"

Jill stared at his lips. "Heather and Trenton *did* want this house," she whispered. Her breaths grew heavier. "But I knew it was trouble from the minute I saw it."

Cal nodded. He attempted to keep things light. "Are you calling Mrs. W trouble?"

"The woman's as bad as you."

But there was nothing light in either of their tones. Instead there was something happening in the room. And he hoped it was the reason Jill had sought him out.

"Tell me why you came over here today." He took another step closer, bumping the front of his body against her, and as she opened her mouth to answer, he caught sight of a woman on the ground pointing up at them.

"I came because I wanted to see you."

Cal nodded. That wasn't enough. He shifted them so his back was to the window, so no one could see Jill. "And what else?"

Her eyes searched his, and he saw the plea inside. She didn't want to have to say it.

"Tell me you want me to kiss you, Jilly." He breathed in the same air as her. "That you miss me. That you need me." He leaned forward and whispered into her ear. "I need to know it isn't just me who's this desperate."

She turned her face slowly, and as she spoke, her lips grazed his. "It isn't just you."

Euphoria erupted. It shifted the low buzz that had been humming since she'd first shown up into heated excitement, and though everything inside him screamed for him to take the kiss—*now*—he paused.

He shouldn't have, and he knew it. They'd been spotted. Their time was limited.

But he needed this moment.

He lifted both hands to the back of Jill's head, sliding his fingers through the long, silky tresses. And instead of settling his lips on hers, he angled her chin slightly up, her head away. He wanted to look at her up close. Just like this. He wanted to see that what she'd said was echoed in her eyes. And he wanted to make sure she saw it in his, too.

This was crazy. They were competitors. In this current competition, *and* in their day-to-day lives. They were ancient history. And they were likely still explosive—and not only in the good way.

But Cal couldn't back away from it.

"*Jill.*"

She nodded. It was a barely-there movement, but it was deliberate. "Kiss me, Cal. That's why I came over here today. I need to know, too."

That was what he wanted.

He closed his eyes, kept his hands cupping her in front of him, and he angled his mouth over hers.

"There they are."

They froze at the sound of Len's voice.

"*Fuck,*" Cal whispered. His lips brushed hers. He'd waited too long.

He opened his eyes, expecting to see horror in Jill's. Knowing she would pull back. Or shove him away. But she stayed in his hands instead, her eyes giving nothing away, and together they turned to find Patrick standing inside the bedroom door. Len and a sound guy stood just behind him.

"That's what we've been waiting for," Patrick exclaimed. He spread his arms wide. "Perfect."

It was anything but perfect.

But still . . . Jill didn't move.

The music from the corner had ceased, and Cal looked down at Jill again, to find that she was looking at Len.

"Your mics," Len told them. "They're still hot. We knew you were together."

"Not to mention the crowd outside," Patrick added. "They went crazy when they saw you in the window."

Jill finally put a step of distance between them, and Cal let his arms drop.

"Someone saw us?" Jill asked. She looked over at the window.

"They thought it was the ghost and her lover."

Cal's brow arched at the producer's words. He'd been unsure if Patrick knew the story. No one had brought it up throughout the last four weeks.

"No ghost," Cal told him. He felt protective of the woman who lived in this room.

"No lover," Jill added, bringing Cal's gaze back to hers. He hoped she wasn't implying . . .

But when their eyes connected, it wasn't pushing him away that he saw . . . but laughter.

"I give up," she declared. Her eyes glowed with humor, and she raised her hands in the air. Laughter poured out of her. "I absolutely give up. All this time, I've avoided being caught with you. And I've done a darned good job of it, too. But when he finally does catch me . . ." She let out a laughing sigh and turned to the other man. "*Fine*, Patrick. Sit us down together, if that's what you want. I'll do it. But *then*, will you please leave us alone?" She speared Cal with one last look. "Because I might just want to finish what I started here."

She marched out of the room, and when Patrick swung a shocked expression Cal's way, Cal motioned to the door. "Go. Do what she says before she changes her mind."

And he did *not* want her to change her mind. He didn't give a crap about the interview. The producers could piece together whatever they wanted after the fact, even if they never got Cal and Jill on screen together. But that last part. About finishing what she'd started.

He nodded as he followed the crew from the room. He wanted that a lot.

Chapter Fourteen

"Being a man is easy. Being the *man takes courage. "*

—Papaw Reynolds

Jill sat in the hot seat, hair freshly combed and makeup retouched. She knew Cal remained shocked that she'd simply given in, but when Patrick had found them a millisecond away from a lip-lock, avoiding anything to do with this situation had suddenly seemed silly. She didn't exactly know what was going on between her and Cal, and who knew what would happen with Bluebonnet after the show ran, but for the first time in her life, she felt as if she were heading in the right direction. More importantly, she was driving in a straight line to get there.

So why fight it? She'd decided to try a new approach and embrace the moment, and so far, it seemed to be working.

"We're going to talk about the competition first," Patrick told them. "Compare and contrast the houses, discuss techniques and designs. We want to really make it about you two being rivals so the viewers can get into it and pick a side. We'll pepper sound bites throughout the episodes, beefing it up as we move toward the end. But we also want to cover you *two* today. Your past, and where you are now." Patrick nodded as if asking her to do the same. "Is that okay?"

Cal looked to her for the answer.

"It's why you chose us for the show, isn't it?"

"Also because you're both excellent at what you do," the producer assured her. "But yes, layering in your history was always our intent. It'll make for great TV. So let's get started."

They went through a list of discussion points, doing several retakes when the heat of the competition hadn't been captured right, and through it all, Jill never waned. She was on her game. She was having a blast.

But in the back of her mind, she also knew the hard part was yet to come. She'd been trying to figure out how best to handle it, and in the end, she decided to go with whatever would make the greatest impact. That was the point of the interview, after all.

"Now, Jill and Cal. Let's get into your marriage."

Cal reached over and took her hand.

"You met when you were both teens?"

They discussed meeting at Bluebonnet Farms and becoming friends, all the way up to their first official date at the Rusted Rooster. That had been on her seventeenth birthday. They'd gotten married on her eighteenth.

"And the anniversary of that is coming up soon, is it not?"

"It is," Jill said.

"June second," Cal added.

"And that marriage lasted for . . . one day?"

"That's right." They answered at the same time.

"Something big must have happened to end it so quickly."

"We were basically kids," Cal explained. "I was twenty, but if you've ever been around many twenty-year-old males, you know they aren't the sharpest in the bunch."

"And we both were, shall we say"—Jill glanced at Cal—"prone to quick bouts of anger?"

Several people chuckled, and Jill realized that a group had formed in a half circle to watch. Heather, Trenton, and Aunt Blu were in the group, and all three looked on with concern.

She met their eyes, letting them know she was fine, and she swore all of them were suddenly threatening tears. Jill supposed it had to do with seeing her and Cal in the same space again, and *not* fighting. The two of them had once been unquestionably close.

And she had to agree. It was nice to be around him without hating him.

"And this anger," Patrick said. "It was . . . *prevalent* three weeks ago. Would you say that's accurate?"

Jill and Cal looked at each other.

"I'd say that's an accurate statement," Jill agreed.

Cal nodded solemnly. "Me, too."

She tilted her head as she looked at him. She hadn't realized he'd still been angry.

"And where are the two of you now?"

Jill turned back to Patrick. She ignored the fact that they'd practically been caught kissing, and hoped Patrick would do the same. At least for now. "I'd call us friends," she answered. She hoped Cal felt the same way.

"Friends." Cal nodded. "Definitely."

"No more lingering anger?" Patrick asked.

Jill paused at the question. She could go either way. In the end, she chose the route she felt would play best on television. "No more anger," she said. She couldn't bring herself to look at Cal. He had to be thinking of their no-sex-when-angry rule. "Of course, that's not to say that I'm not still hurt. He's the one who left, after all. I'm not sure if you know that, and I'm not saying I didn't play a part in it. But Cal filed for divorce. He left *me*. After one day," she repeated softly, letting her façade slip and her true hurt show through. "So while the anger may be gone—and it's about time, wouldn't you say?" She let out a humorless laugh. "It does still sting."

The set had gone quiet, and Patrick shifted to Cal. "And what about you? Any lingering issues with the past?"

"None that I'm willing to talk about on TV."

"And do you want to share why you left your wife after only one day of marriage?"

Cal shook his head.

She would have liked to have heard his reasoning.

"Okay," Patrick continued. "Then let's go down another path. We didn't ask earlier, but can you tell us, Cal, how Jill first captured your attention?"

Cal studied the other man before asking, "Ever seen her swing a sledgehammer?"

Jill felt her cheeks heat when every man involved with the show nodded mutely.

"Me, too," Cal added. "She was like that from the moment I met her. She's never changed"—Cal turned to her—"and I wouldn't want her to."

Jill swallowed, aware that the cameras were still on them, then forced a light laugh. "And *he's* the one who first handed me that sledge-hammer. Showed me how to use it."

She feared the mics would pick up her heavier breathing, not to mention the cameras zooming in on the sexual tension popping between them. It was just like Heather and Trenton had said. Get them together in one space and they'd be combustible.

She pictured Trenton standing a floor above her that day, showing with her hands what she meant by "poof," and Jill decided she could use a poof or two about now.

"Are we about finished?" she asked. She needed to put some space between her and Cal.

"Just a couple more questions."

They wrapped up with a benign discussion on their respective companies, and finally the interview came to an end. Patrick stepped over to Jill and shook her hand. "Terrific job."

She appreciated the sentiment.

As they walked away, Blu was ushered forward, and Jill reached out and gave the other woman a quick hug. "Good luck," she whispered in Blu's ear.

Something caught Cal's attention as they waited for Blu's interview to begin, and Jill followed his gaze to see Rodney's truck coming down the road. And it *wasn't* being driven in a straight line.

Cal brought his gaze back to hers, a sense of urgency now coming from within, and she nodded before he had to say anything. "Go. I'll let you know how she does."

Cal headed off, calling out to Pete that he'd be gone for a while, and he slid into the driver's seat of Rodney's truck almost before it stopped rolling. Jill watched until the truck backed out and Cal pulled away, Rodney now sitting in the middle of the seat, then realized that Heather and Trenton had been watching her as she watched Cal. And in their eyes she saw the same questions she'd been asking herself for days. But she had no answers to give.

~

Cal wheeled the truck into his grandmother's driveway and pocketed the keys. He didn't bother speaking to his uncle—nor had he the entire drive home—and he didn't wait to see if the man could get himself out of the truck. He simply unlocked the door to the house and went in.

He headed straight for the fridge, and by the time Rodney stumbled into the room, Cal was on beers seven and eight, pouring them down the sink.

"What are you doing?" Rodney shouted. He raced to the sink.

"What I should have done years ago."

After sitting with Jill and thinking about how they'd hurt each other in the past, as well as how others had hurt them, Cal had suddenly started seeing the world differently. Almost as if the glass had finally been cleaned. Then Rodney had weaved up the street, and that clear glass had shown him something he'd never thought about before. He'd been doing his uncle *no* favors for the last fourteen years.

All this time Cal had believed he'd been taking care of Rodney. He'd been "there" for him.

But he'd only been enabling him by so often looking the other way.

He should have helped his uncle quit drinking *years* ago.

Rodney snatched at the bottles in Cal's hands as Cal continued dumping out the contents, and when that didn't work, he attempted to scoop the foaming liquid from the sink. He slurped at his palms, then he bypassed his hands altogether and leaned directly into the sink.

Cal averted his eyes, but he kept pouring out bottles. He couldn't sit around and do nothing any longer.

"Look at yourself, Rodney."

His uncle paused, head still bent in the sink, and looked up at him. Confusion was clear on his face. "What?"

"You're a drunk. And you're finished living this life. I won't stand by and do nothing anymore."

"What are you talking about? I'm fine." Rodney scooped another spoonful-sized amount from the sink.

"You're not fine. Not even close. And you haven't been for years."

When Rodney started to argue once more, Cal leaned down to him. "You're licking the sink to save a drop of beer," he gritted out, and that finally seemed to get through to his uncle.

Rodney eyed the stainless-steel bowl of the sink, a drop of foam clinging to his lips, and Cal watched as the man's shoulders drooped.

"You're out of control." Cal spoke more gently. "And you know it. You can't do this to her anymore. She can't lose a second son." *Or a third,* Cal thought. "She's your mother, Rodney, and she deserves better. *You* deserve better.

"There's a rehab place on the way to see Granny," Cal continued. He'd passed it multiple times a week for years, and it had never occurred to him that Rodney should go there. "You can check yourself into it, or I'm out. I won't pick you up at the bars anymore. I won't cover for you. I won't keep you from killing yourself out on the roads." He shook his head. "I won't be a part of it at all."

"So you're giving *me* an ultimatum now."

What Rodney didn't say was *Just like your father.*

But he didn't have to say the words for Cal to hear them, and Cal nodded. He was giving his uncle an ultimatum. Just as his father had done to him. "Always knew I was more like the old man than I wanted to be," Cal said.

"You hate him for doing that to you."

"I hate him for being an uncaring asshole. I hate him for not giving a shit that he knocked up my mother—and then caring even less when she died in childbirth. And if you really want to know how I feel, I even hate myself a little for *not* taking him up on his ultimatum."

It had been simple. Go to the college of his father's choosing, or get nothing from Neil Reynolds.

"I could have done better for myself," Cal finished. He'd have hated himself, though. His father would have insisted he leave the area. Leave his grandmother. But he could have had options.

"So now you hate my company, too?"

He would have laughed at the question if the thought hadn't been so sad. "No, Rodney. And it's my company now, remember? I took it over because you were more concerned with drinking than running it. Of course I don't hate it. I'm good at it. I'm *proud* to carry on the business that you started. But I shut down my options simply because my father gave me an either-or choice."

How childish had that been? Kind of like making the decision to walk out on Jill the second she'd said it was her and Hollywood—or it was him and nothing.

As was his norm, he'd taken nothing.

"I also didn't want to leave you," he told his uncle. "I stayed for you, too." He'd calmed down since coming into the house, and he didn't want to leave Rodney thinking he hated him. "I *couldn't* go off and leave Granny, and if I hadn't been here for you . . . you might have killed yourself by now."

He expected his uncle to argue the point, but the other man stayed quiet, and Cal could suddenly see the loneliness rooted inside Rodney. As if he had no one left in the world. Cal supposed three divorces, losing a company, and drinking a hell of a lot of beer would do that to a man.

"She misses you," he told his uncle. Rodney hadn't been to see his mother in months, because he couldn't stay sober long enough.

"And I miss her." Rodney suddenly broke. He collapsed to his knees, holding his head in his hands. "I want to do better," he moaned out. "I've wanted to for years. I'll try to quit again. Just help me."

"I am helping you. I'm going to drive you to the rehab center."

"But—"

"Haven't you tried on your own enough?" Cal shook his head, and Rodney peered up at him. "No more *trying*. This time you do it. And you do it by us getting you the help you need."

Rodney suddenly looked far older than his years. His cheeks were sunken in, his eyes held no warmth. And the man now crumpled on the floor in front of Cal seemed too frail to stand on his own. "But that kind of help takes money," Rodney told him.

Cal nodded in understanding. "And you've drunk all of yours?"

At Rodney's silence, Cal thought of his uncle's other vice, and the full extent of the problem became clear.

"What you haven't drunk, you've gambled away?"

"I gamble to try to win some of it back."

"So you can drink more," Cal accused.

Shame reeked from his uncle as strongly as the smell of beer. "I need help," Rodney whispered brokenly.

He most certainly did.

"And I'm going to give it to you. I'm sorry I haven't been there for you before. Not in the right way. I'll cover the cost of the rehab. For as long as you need." Cal broke off and took in the kitchen before looking down the hall. He hated the thought of selling his granny's home, but he suspected she would be okay with it. Rodney's life was more important than sentimentality. "And if we need more money," he told Rodney, "then we sell this house. You're the priority now."

Cal had the ranch. He'd move Rodney out there if he had to.

Tears streamed down the older man's face.

"Do you want to go tonight or tomorrow morning?" Cal asked, his words gentle but blunt. He wouldn't be swayed by the pain displayed before him.

"I think . . . maybe tonight."

Cal was struck by the fear on his uncle's face. He nodded. "I do, too. Go pack a bag. I'll wait for you here."

As his uncle disappeared up the stairs, Cal dropped into a chair at the table. Exhaustion weighed him down as he flattened a hand to the surface of the table and slid his palm over the twenty-four-year-old fir wood. He and his grandfather had made this table together when Cal had been seven.

"Sorry, Papaw," he whispered. "I messed up."

Noises sounded overhead. Rodney walking around, a TV on that Cal hadn't been aware of before now, and Cal thought about the woman at the Cadillac House who spent all her time in the upstairs room. She'd been waiting in that house for years, unable to move on. Just as he'd been waiting here for his uncle to get his shit together.

Or as he'd been waiting for Jill to come home.

But then, Jill had been home for five years, and he'd done nothing about that, either.

Lily strolled into the room, tail held high, and meowed as if to let him know she wasn't pleased with the noise Rodney was making in her space. Lily considered the entire house her space. She hopped onto the table and sat on her haunches in front of him, and he nodded.

"I know. I've done nothing right."

Lily chimed in again, this time making more of an eye-twitching yowl than a typical meow.

"I know that, too." He scratched the back of the cat's neck. "I've done nothing right with her, either." He looked his cat in the eye. "I'm a fuckup, Lily. Time to face facts. But then, we already knew that, didn't we?"

She agreed with another yowl, and he pulled her against his chest.

"I'm trying," he whispered. "Don't give up on me yet."

Chapter Fifteen

"A man who knocks on your door late at night likely needs one of two things: (1) your help, or (2) you. Whatever his needs are, you're the one in charge."

—Blu Johnson, life lesson #79

The knock was more of a weak tap than a sturdy let-me-in, but Cal couldn't muster the energy to put anything else behind it. It must have done the job, though, because a few seconds later footsteps sounded on the other side of the door, then a light flickered to life. It cast a soft glow through the six panes of glass at the top of the wooden door, and unsure eyes met his through the lower row of windows. Cal didn't so much as offer a smile.

The dead bolt snapped open, and Jill stood before him in black leggings and a navy tank.

"Did I catch you at a bad time?" he asked.

She shook her head, but he didn't miss the questions in her eyes. It was after eleven. Most people didn't knock on others' doors this late in the evening without an invite, and he probably looked as if he couldn't stand upright for another minute. But he knew he'd chosen correctly in showing up there.

"How's Rodney?" she asked.

"Rodney's a drunk." He'd never said that out loud before today, but this made the third time in the last few hours. "I just dropped him off at a rehab center over in San Marcos."

Just looking at her made him feel better.

"He'll be there at least two months," he continued. "My guess is longer."

"I'm sorry." Her soft voice was laced with sincerity. "I know that had to be hard on you." She shifted on her feet before taking a half step back. "Did you want to come in and talk about it?"

"No. I don't want to talk about my uncle." He eyed the room behind her. "I want to talk about you."

"Okay. Then talk."

He brought his gaze back to hers. "You were going to kiss me today."

She nodded. "I was."

"You also told Patrick that you aren't angry anymore."

"I did that, too."

"Did you mean it?"

"Are you asking if we can have sex?"

Her directness comforted him. He didn't say another word, just nodded in reply, and she stepped back and opened the door wider.

Neither of them spoke. She closed the door behind him, he tugged her tank top over her head, and they came together in each other's arms. A groan ripped from him as his arms closed around her, his hands flattening against the heat of her back. It had been far too long since he'd had this. Since he'd had her.

His mouth sought out hers, desperation driving him to move too fast, but she seemed to suffer from the same affliction. Her movements were jerky, the noises coming from her anguished as she tugged at his shirt, the material not freeing from his jeans fast enough to suit her. But when the task was finally accomplished, she shoved the shirt up just enough so that she could fit her bare torso to his. And then it was her turn to moan.

Cal palmed her butt, lifting her to her toes, and she clamped her legs around his waist.

"Down the hall," she ordered.

He turned without another thought.

He soon found the bed, and once he had her on it, he had a demand of his own.

"Light." He had to see her.

She pointed to the reading lamp clipped onto the headboard, and as he reached for the switch, she found the snap of his jeans. Jeans and boxers circled his knees before he realized he'd quit moving to absorb the feeling of Jill's hands sliding over him. The pads of her fingers had a slight roughness to them. A testament to her career. But they caressed with a gentleness that could undo a man.

He finally forced himself to move. He kicked off his shoes, then he rolled to his back and ripped his shirt over his head, while Jill tugged at his jeans. Two seconds later he lay bared before her, erection pointing toward the ceiling, while she straddled his thighs. Her chest heaved with her breaths, the navy bra covering only the bottom halves of her breasts, and his erection neared painful. She was a goddess. Black hair fell over her shoulders, reaching to just inside the cups of her bra, and teasing at what lay underneath. Her lips were lush and parted. And her gaze remained glued to his most active part.

"I've missed this," he confided. "So much."

She was the most glorious thing Cal had ever seen.

She dragged her eyes up to his. "You're not going to miss it for much longer."

The words came out hoarse, and Cal reached for her, unable to keep his hands from her a second longer.

The bra was first. One twist of his wrist, and he had the straps to her elbows.

Pert breasts met his torso, her nipples scraping along the hairs of his chest, and the air left his body.

"Jill," he begged. He buried his mouth against her neck and held her tight.

He wanted this to last forever. Only, there was no way he could wait.

When he eased them apart, intending to rid her of the remainder of her clothing, she stole the lead. She flipped to her back, making quick work of her leggings and the tiny scrap of material underneath, so he dove for the condom in his jeans. When he rolled back to her, Jill rose above him before he could stop her, then she pinned him in place, her toned thighs straddling his once again. With her back straight, her breasts high and proud, and her eyes burning hot in the small room, he once again thought, *Goddess.* She was strength and heat, and so much passion. There'd never been another like her.

"I was going to be the one in charge," he panted out. He couldn't catch his breath.

He couldn't believe he'd knocked on her door only two minutes before.

"Then you should have moved faster."

But he caught her off guard when she made the critical error in dropping her gaze to his dick once more, flipping her so that *she* was now the one on the bottom. And he didn't intend for that to change again. Not until *he* wanted it to.

She was spread beneath him, naked and spectacular, and though he wanted to take his time, to drink his fill, feasting was more important. This was Jill. This was what he'd been waiting years for.

Pink nipples pouted up at him, so he started there, and Jill called out in pleasure at the first touch. Her back arched as his lips raked over her, and he swore he grew another two inches.

"Cal." She breathed out his name. Her fingers buried in his butt cheeks as he continued to work her breasts, and when he squeezed her, sucking a nipple deep into his mouth, she shouted out again. She sounded close already, and he'd just gotten started.

He focused, working her with lips and tongue and teeth, and well before he switched to her other breast, she began to thrust. As her heat ground into his balls, it was all he could do not to bite down too hard on her sensitive flesh.

"Please," she sobbed out a plea. Her eyes were closed tight. "I need . . ."

He needed, too.

But he remained on top of her, not parting her legs and not diving inside, although everything inside him demanded he do nothing else. Instead, he thought about Jill. He wanted to please her. He wanted to make sure she thought of him. Always.

And he wanted her screaming his name as she came.

"I . . ." She gasped. "Can't . . ."

Her chest arched up off the bed, and Cal released her, his mouth retreating only until she lowered and sucked in a breath, then she once again ground herself against him. He gave up the fight. His Jill was ready to blow.

With breaths coming in short bursts and her head rocking back and forth, Cal inched his hand lower.

She gasped again, as if anticipating what was to come, and he kept his eyes locked on her. He wanted to watch her fall apart at his touch.

"Cal," she whispered, the word coming out with a whimper.

"I've got you," he promised.

He parted her with his middle finger then, and her movements stopped. Her mouth opened slightly, as if to speak, but nothing came out. So he pushed in a second finger.

Her body began to vibrate.

He didn't let up. He circled his thumb over her. Once. Twice. Just barely grazing her flesh. Then with one final move, he pressed where she needed it most, and she broke. And she screamed out his name.

Cal held on as Jill shook in his arms, and he fought not to follow her over the cliff. Not yet. There would be time for that later. And only when she finally began to calm did he slide up her sweat-slicked body, and he fused his mouth to hers.

~

Jill fell to the bed sometime later, face-first and ass up, and couldn't bring herself to move another inch. Good. Lord.

The low chuckle that sounded just inches from her ear was both irritating and sexy as hell. The man had improved over the years, and he knew it. But then, she hadn't exactly been a hard nut to crack tonight, either. Pretty much one touch, and . . . poof.

She giggled at the thought and managed to roll to her side. She remained curled in a fetal position, but she could now see Cal. And he looked just as blown away as she felt. After he'd gotten her off the first time, she'd tried to take over, but he'd refused. His theory had been that if he could do that to her that fast and that explosively, then he should be able to do it again. Maybe even faster the next time.

So he had.

But then she'd caught him in a weakened state—likely trying not to come after she'd bellowed out his name, yet again—and she'd pushed him to his back. It had all been over at that point.

She slid a palm over his chest, winding a finger through the narrow patch of hair. "What a way to be greeted at the door."

He made a little grunt of a sound beside her, and she wiggled her way up the sheets so that she lay with her head on her pillow. He turned his face to hers, and she couldn't hold back a goofy smile.

"You don't even *know* how long it's been since I've done that."

"My guess would be not nearly long enough," Cal grumbled. He scowled, but rolled to his side so he lay facing her. "I still can't believe you went out with Little Red last weekend."

She shot him an incredulous look. "Really? We're lying here naked and sweaty, and you want to talk about me and another man?"

"I'm just saying that I can't believe *that's* who you'd choose to go out with. *Little Red.*" He harrumphed.

"*Doug* is a very good guy." She refused to call the younger man by what he considered to be a derogatory name while in bed with someone who wanted to be derogatory to him. "Plus, it was *your* idea for me to go out with him to begin with."

Cal shot to a sitting position. "How in the hell was it my idea?"

"You asked me if I ever dated."

"And *that's* why you went out with him? Shit, Jill. You could have just—"

She couldn't hold in the giggle any longer. "Man, you're fun. Where did this jealous streak come from? And no, actually, lest you decide your actions speak louder than they do, you are *not* the reason I went out with Doug Caldwell. I went because I had to. I was outvoted."

"You were—" His scowl grew even darker. "Is this you messing with me again?"

She shook her head. "Serious as a heart attack. Aunt Blu, Heather, and Trenton all voted yes after Doug expressed his most sincere desire to wine and dine me. So, I had to go."

Incredulity shone back at her. "You let them vote on whether you would go out with the man or not?"

"I didn't *let* them. It was out of my hands."

"The four of you are certifiable. You do know that, right?" He settled back down on the sheet beside her. "Was this, by chance, during drunk rummy?"

"It's whiskey rummy." She rolled to her back and spoke to the ceiling. "And yes, it was. But a vote counts, no matter the circumstance. Just like, if we'd won the coin toss the day we chose houses, I would have had to concede to taking Mrs. Wainwright's house. Because Heather and Trenton had outvoted me."

Cal looked at her again, and she removed her focus from the ceiling to peer over at him. She could stare at his eyes for days.

"You three grew apart for a while, right?"

She nodded at his subdued tone. "We all had to do our thing. Try to prove we were more than orphans, you know? More than . . . kids whose parents had left us," she finished softly. Heather was the only one whose parents hadn't chosen to go, but that hadn't made it any easier.

"Looks to me like you've proven it."

"Some days are better than others. But we don't stop trying."

Cal captured her hand, holding it against the bed, in the space between their hips. "I'm glad you found each other again."

"I am, too. Aunt Blu, as well."

She struggled to believe she'd ever thought she didn't need her foster mother, but she'd go to her grave thanking the powers that be for keeping Aunt Blu there for when she returned.

They both grew quiet, both in their own thoughts. Cal's thumb stroked over hers as he lay there, and Jill ended up scooting in closer and tucking her head against his shoulder. He brought his other hand up and slid his palm over the back of her head.

"I love your hair," he murmured absently.

"I know." She pressed a kiss to his shoulder. "You always did."

"I can always spot you in a crowd. Even when I'm not trying."

She lifted her head. "And have you tried often?"

He didn't let her see his eyes. Nor did he answer her question.

He tucked her against his chest and smoothed a hand down her back, and after several additional minutes of silence, his roving hand stalled at her waist. His thumb began to move over her skin in small circles, and she could practically hear him thinking. What she didn't know was what he was thinking about.

It didn't take long to find out, though.

"So, how long *has* it been since you've done this?"

She hid a smile in his chest. She might have known his ego wouldn't let that remain a mystery. "Do you mean sex?" she asked innocently. "Like . . . with a man? Or . . ."

He lifted his head from the pillow. "Have you had sex with a woman?"

The mixed expression of shock, horror, *and* hope staring back at her was hilarious. She lifted a hand and gave a simultaneous waggle of her fingers and eyebrows, and his eyes rounded with understanding. Then his gaze lowered from her fingers to her crotch, and a low growl rumbled from inside him.

"You're too easy." She patted his chest. "Down, boy. And to answer your question, it'll be exactly twelve years three weeks from today."

The look of reemerging desire disappeared in a heartbeat. "Jill . . ."

He said nothing else. Just looked at her, and she gave a little nod. No one else but him. She'd spent the year after her mother died doing anything and everything with any boy who'd asked—and some who hadn't asked. She'd been trying to prove herself still alive. Or maybe punish herself for still *being* alive. And the boys had discovered that if they got her good and angry first—which hadn't been hard to do—the sex would be even hotter. So they always got her angry.

But the day Cal had given her that sledgehammer, her outlook had changed forever.

She'd also had sex with Cal that afternoon. Only, he'd held her afterward while she'd cried. She'd never done that before, but she'd hated herself that day—she'd hated herself *every* day—and she hadn't been able to hold it in any longer.

She'd hated her mother, the world, and basically everyone who ever spoke to her.

But what she'd detested the most was the person she could see she would be at the end of her one-way path to destruction. She hadn't known exactly who she *wanted* to be when she grew up, but she'd known who she *didn't* want to be.

Cal had said something so simple to her that day, yet it had changed her life.

Then don't be that person.

She hadn't even realized that was an option.

She'd taken his words to heart, though, and she'd never been that girl again. She and Cal had grown as friends after that, and eventually as lovers. As two people *in* love. And she hadn't taken sex for granted since.

Except for one night.

She closed her eyes as she added, "Unless you want to count the one time that I *almost* did."

Cal kept his hand on her back, but she could feel that he'd gone still. He lay as quiet and unmoving as she. "And when was that?" he asked.

"The night I boarded a bus to come home."

She pulled in a deep breath, her chest pressing into his, and let it out slowly. She'd never talked about this before, but she wanted to now. In fact, for the first time, she felt she needed to.

She kept her eyes closed as she drifted back to those six years of her life, but she allowed herself to continue touching Cal. She opened her tightened fist and pressed her fingers and palm to his chest, focusing on the heat of his skin touching every inch of hers, and she pulled in one last deep breath as his fingers covered hers.

"I was so angry," she started. "You know that. I was before I left here, and it only got worse when I headed to California. But I wanted to be an actress so badly. And I thought I could do it. I worked hard to keep my anger inside. I did the exercises the counselor had taught me in the anger-management courses, I took up meditation. I tried. Really, I did. I joined acting classes. I did improv. Whatever I could do to learn the craft, I was there. Of course, I had to get a job to support myself, too. The money I'd saved didn't go nearly as far as I'd imagined. But I was willing to do whatever it took to be someone. Yet the anger . . ." She blew out a breath. "It would work its way out eventually. Something random would set me off. Or someone. Not getting a part. Not liking what my agent reported back about an audition. Irritation over the way a fellow actor looked at me while I was filming a bit part I finally *had* landed."

She laughed drily. "I even lost a few jobs because of something innocuous a customer said. It could truly be anything. I would be good for months, but I swear, the snap always came at the worst possible times. And in front of the worst possible people. But then I got the opportunity I'd been waiting for. A sitcom." She glanced up at him and named a show still running on a popular cable channel. "I was slated for the lead," she told him. "I had a callback, and it was down to me and one other person. I had it in the bag."

"So what happened?"

"To get the part, I had to sleep with the producer."

His jaw went slack. "Are you kidding me?"

"Come on, you know it happens. More often than people would like to believe. And it wasn't the first time the idea had been floated by me. But no other part had been worth it before." She closed her eyes again, and pressed her cheek back over Cal's heart. "This one, though. It was what I'd been waiting for. It would label me a real actress. But along with that, I was just so tired of almost getting there—but then not quite." She squeezed her eyes shut tight. "I wanted it *so* badly."

She'd left Red Oak Falls wanting to prove herself, but she'd also found that she truly loved acting. It hadn't just allowed her to *not* be Jill Sadler, it had given her a self-confidence she'd never known before. Because she'd been good at it. And she'd known it.

"So you slept with him?" Cal's voice remained calm.

"I started to." The corners of her mouth turned down. "I can still remember how he tasted. What he smelled like."

She shuddered.

"He had me down to my panties." She spoke faster now. "His fingers were heading underneath, he'd been rubbing himself all over me. And I swear, it was as if I were standing beside the bed looking down at myself. So, I looked. And I was fourteen again. Brent Cannon was on top of me, humping me for all he was worth. He was my first time, if I never told you that," she said, still keeping her eyes tightly closed. "I didn't even have my clothes off that day. Just skirt up around my waist and panties to my ankles. I was lying on the ground out behind the high school baseball field. We were just out of sight of everyone, and Brent's friends hooted from the parking lot. And as I stood there that day in LA, looking down at this slimy piece of crap who thought he had the right to demand I spread my legs in order to become someone, I realized that I never wanted to be *that* someone." She shook her head. "I couldn't do it. And I *wouldn't* do it. So, I told him to stop."

"And . . . he *didn't* stop?" Cal guessed. She could hear the contained anger in his voice.

"He didn't at first."

A muscle jerked under her cheek.

"He said it was too late for that, and then he yanked my panties to my ankles. Just like that day with Brent. He didn't even take them off me, just down to my ankles, and he shoved my knees apart."

She pushed up off Cal then and sat cross-legged on the bed. She was completely naked, but it didn't bother her in the least. This wasn't LA. It wasn't the year after her mother died.

"I didn't want to be that girl," she told him with no uncertainty. "I hadn't been her in years, and I would not go back. It was bad enough I was already the girl whose mother had killed herself. The girl who couldn't stay out of trouble as a kid. Who continued having anger issues well into adulthood, and likely always would. Who knew it was *her* fault that her mother had killed herself." Her voice cracked, and Cal gripped her hand.

"No," he tried to interrupt her, but she kept going.

"I didn't want to be the girl who slept her way to an acting career, too," she finished.

His eyes never broke contact with hers. "What happened?"

She knew he was trying to help push her through to the end. She knew he wanted to correct her statement that it was her fault that her mother had killed herself.

But she also knew he was wrong. She'd been there that day. She'd been to blame.

"I punched him in the nose," she told him matter-of-factly. And then she laughed.

Her entire body shook with the laughter, and she found herself swiping at her eyes.

"I punched the asshole in the nose," she repeated. "Blood went everywhere. And I swear, if I'd had a sledgehammer, I'd have never gotten out of jail for what I would've done to that man."

She tunneled her fingers into her hair and pulled, tilting her face up to the ceiling.

"He cried like a baby, Cal. Screamed that I hadn't known what I'd just done. But I knew who he was in the business, and I also knew there was *no* way I would ever get an opportunity like that again." She dropped her hands to her sides, and Cal immediately took one again. "I didn't even call my agent to tell her I was leaving. I grabbed my clothes, put them on *after* I got out of the hotel room, and I boarded the next bus home. I was out of money anyway, and I missed Texas something terrible."

She'd stopped by her apartment long enough to grab the only thing she'd cared about before leaving. The African violet Aunt Blu had given her the day she'd left town. She'd taken the plant to Vegas with her, and it sat on her kitchen windowsill to that day. Aunt Blu graced every girl who passed through her home with a plant.

"So you missed home?" Cal asked, bringing her back to the moment.

Jill nodded. "I did. Texas. Aunt Blu." She looked at him. *"You."*

His brows twitched. "You never told me that."

"Well, I also hated you. But I missed you, too. And good Lord, the humiliation I felt. Six years out there, and for what?"

He cupped her cheek. "And I'd told you I'd be here waiting for you to come crawling back to me."

"You did." She'd hated him for those words. "But I never crawl."

"I would never want you to." He sat up beside her. "I'm so sorry I ever said that to you, Jill. It's no excuse, but I had no idea you really wanted to be an actress. I thought it was just about . . ."

He let the words drop, and she gave a small shrug. It didn't matter anymore what he'd said to her that day or what he'd thought when she'd begged him to go with her.

As he'd pointed out in his truck not long ago, they couldn't go back.

"So, did you ever even look for your dad?" Cal asked.

"No." Her dad had only really mattered when she'd still thought she could fix her mother. The man hadn't wanted her . . . she didn't want him. "He'd just been my excuse, anyway. I never let on how badly I wanted to act, mostly because I was afraid I couldn't do it." *Or afraid no one would believe in me,* she added silently. "And, hey, I proved myself right, didn't I?"

"No." Cal pulled her into his lap. "You *could* have done it. You just got a bad break. Wait until you see this show." He brought her face to his. "You're incredible in front of the camera, Jilly. I can't take my eyes off you. Neither can anyone else on set. And honey, that interview today . . ." He shook his head with awe. *"Gold."*

"That interview was a lie," she said softly.

His mouth flattened. "Which part of it?"

"The part where I said I'm no longer angry."

"Jill." He stared at her for a second, dumbfounded, then ran his gaze over the rumpled bed where they'd just had the best sex of her life.

"You left me," she told him. "And you did it *exactly* like my mom's husband left her."

She thought about the day her mother had killed herself. Jill had screamed for her to "just go ahead and do it" as she'd stormed out the door. It hadn't been the first time her mom had threatened to down a bottle of pills, after all. Nor had it been the thirtieth. And Jill had been exhausted from the ongoing threats. Of consoling her mother when Jill knew it would do no good.

She couldn't help her mother. No matter how many times she tried. Only a man could have helped her mother.

But that hadn't been the case, either. Because her mom had finally gotten a man. One willing to marry her and everything. However, a short three months after that marriage had begun, Janet Sadler had arrived home to find divorce papers stacked neatly in the middle of the kitchen table. The man who'd promised to love her forever hadn't bothered to let her know that his forever had already come. He'd simply left. Just as Cal had.

"That was the one thing I asked you to never do to me," she told Cal now. "To leave without a word. And you promised me. You swore you never would."

"I was a bastard."

"Oh, hell yeah, you were."

Her anger *was* still there, but the past didn't hurt her the way it once had. And it was time to talk about it.

Shame filled Cal's face. "I think I might have done it that way just *because* that's what he'd done to your mom."

"I'm sure of it." They'd both been such hotheads back then. "And to tell you the truth, I'm not sure I'll ever get over it. Not completely. But though the anger is still there, it's different now. And that's why I invited you in tonight. It no longer consumes me. It's not eating at my soul, and I refuse to let it do that anymore. I want to live again, Cal. I want to be a woman. I want to have a life. I didn't know that until recently, but I'm finished letting a twelve-year-old action control me."

"What about the sixteen-year-old one?"

"No." She gave a quick shake of her head. "We're not talking about that. We're just talking about me and you. Mostly because I want to do this"—she motioned between them—"again. It was a hell of a good time, and if you want more, then I'm game for it. But there's something I need to know from you first. And we need to talk about it before we do anything else."

His eyes darkened. "And what's that?"

"You also told Patrick that *you* were mad at me. Or that you had been when the show started," she added. "Are you still mad?"

He didn't say anything, and she watched as his Adam's apple moved.

"Is it because of the ultimatum?" she asked.

She'd been thinking about it all afternoon. That had to be it. Because he might have purposefully dumped her in the same way her mother's ex had done to her . . . but by issuing an ultimatum, she'd pushed his buttons, as well.

"You tossed that ultimatum out there because you knew which way I'd go," Cal accused. He didn't pull away, but she felt his muscles stiffen. "And you know it, too. Either go with you to Hollywood—"

"Or return, alone, to Red Oak Falls." She nodded. "And yes, I suspect you're right."

She went back to the day he'd shown up at Aunt Blu's farm after his dad had issued his own ultimatum. Cal had been livid. And determined not to bend to the man's will.

"It was a jerk move," she told him. "I'll admit that. Whether I thought of it consciously or not, I knew what would set you off. And I used that knowledge. But in the end, my words gave you what you needed, didn't they? The perfect excuse to leave? Because we both know there was no other way for that argument to end."

They'd both been so stupid. And so stubborn.

"I suppose it did." Cal's jaw clenched as he looked away from her, and though she tried to be patient, when he continued focusing on something behind her, she whispered his name.

She'd been so wrapped up in her own anger all this time, that she'd forgotten what she'd done to him.

"*Cal,*" she said again, and finally, he brought his gaze back to hers. And he allowed her to see the depth of his anger. She pressed her palms to his cheeks. "I'm *sorry.*"

"I was wronged, too, Jill. You hurt me, too."

"I know I did."

"Yet all this time, all these years . . . it's been about you. Your anger. Your punishing me."

She hesitated. Her punishing him?

He had said he'd entered the competition just to get her to talk to him.

Good Lord, how childish could they have been?

"So you wanted to punish me back?" she asked.

He nodded at her question, and in a blink, the hardness edging his eyes began to soften. "We're idiots," he told her.

"The biggest kind."

Cal's hands covered hers, where they still rested on his cheeks, and he leaned forward to press a kiss to her lips. When he pulled back, he said, "I've held on to this anger for too long, too. I'm ready to move on."

"Let's move on together."

Cal kissed her again then, only, instead of letting him end that one, Jill pushed him back to the mattress. They'd done enough talking for the evening. Enough sharing. It was time for round two—of a different kind of sharing.

Chapter Sixteen

"Never be afraid to push. Friends, family, or lovers. If you don't want the best for the people you care about, then why bother caring at all?"

—Blu Johnson, life lesson #45

Cal made a left, pointing his truck down Dump Road, and worked his lower jaw to stretch out his cheeks. They ached from all the smiling he'd been doing that morning. It was stupid, really, but he'd awoken in Jill's bed, her body wrapped snuggly against his, and he'd been wearing a ridiculous grin ever since.

It would remain on his face for the rest of the day, and again the following day, if he had his way.

He passed a slower vehicle, then he glanced over at Jill.

She gave him a teasing smirk. "You're smiling again."

"I have reason to be."

"Surely not because it's been twelve years since *you've* gotten laid. I'm the one who should be smiling about that."

"Maybe I'm smiling because it's been twelve years since *you've* gotten laid."

That thought *had* added a lightness to his step. He'd listened to her story the night before, and having been there with her as a teen when she'd made the decision to change the path she'd been on, he'd understood why she'd made the choices she had over the years.

But the testosterone-driven part of him had wanted to strut naked in front of all the girls. Because Jill Sadler hadn't had sex with anyone since him.

"Males can take pride in the simplest of things." Jill rolled her eyes at him. "It's not like you ruined men for me, or anything."

"Of course I didn't. You just didn't want any after me."

He laughed at her derisive snort, then he held out his hand to her. "Scoot over here, Jilly-Bean. You're too far away."

Her brows hiked up. "Calhoun Reynolds. Are you suggesting that I slide over there and practically sit in your lap? As if we're nothing more than a couple of sex-starved teenagers?" Her hair was pulled back, and with the wind from the open windows whipping it out behind her, she looked almost like a teenager.

"More like my sex-starved grandparents," he tossed back, and though he cringed at the idea of it, the words made Jill laugh. "Come on." He patted the seat beside him. "Sit by me. Pretty please? Granny always snuggled up next to Papaw on their Sunday-afternoon drives."

"But it's not Sunday, Cal." Jill scooted over, and as she did, she slid a purposeful hand over his thigh. "So, what did your grandparents do on *Saturday*-afternoon drives?"

He covered her hand with his—then he pulled it to his groin. "I don't know what *they* did on Saturdays. But if their days were anything like mine . . ."

Jill giggled as he'd intended her to, and he closed his arm around her shoulders. His chest swelled as she let out a happy sigh and rested her head in the crook of his shoulder, and he decided he'd take that Saturday over most any other. After waking that morning, they'd spent another hour in bed before taking their activities to the shower. With all the upgrades she'd added, Jill's house was nice, but it was only a two-bedroom, one-bath, and he'd found himself anxious to bring her back out to his place.

He made a right and leaned into her as he turned, and when he pressed a kiss to her temple, she let out a sound reminiscent of a purr. He whispered in her ear. "Close your eyes."

She looked up at him. "What?"

"Close your eyes." They didn't have the radio on, and the windows were open. He slowed as they neared his favorite bridge. "Listen to what's around us instead of looking at it."

Jill closed her eyes.

Cal lowered his speed, welcoming the sounds of the outdoors into the cab with them. The wooden bridge creaking beneath them—while underneath the bridge, water streamed over the rocks. A bird chirping as they came off the other side of the bridge. And along both sides of the road, tall grasses whispered as they passed.

Cal pulled the truck over, shifted into park, then rested his head on the seat back and closed his own eyes. He could hear Jill's soft breaths right up near his face. She was as quiet as he as they took in the beauty surrounding them. He made out the pounding power of water from a hidden waterfall he knew to be about half a mile away, and another, softer but steady churning from the dip in the stream that occurred two hundred feet off the road. A cow mooed on someone's farm, and another answered. Bugs of several varieties chittered in the air.

"There's so much more going on out there," Jill said after several minutes. "I had no idea."

"Papaw used to do this for Granny after she started losing her eyesight. She loved Red Oak Falls, but her love affair only increased when she had to see it with her ears."

Jill turned her face up to his. "How is your granny?"

"She's doing pretty well. Fully blind now." She'd begun developing macular degeneration in her early sixties. "Still as sharp as ever, though. Doesn't let me get away with anything. She turned eighty-five last year."

"How often do you get out to see her?"

Jill used to visit with him occasionally. His grandmother had asked about her a few times over the years. "I'm heading out there tomorrow, actually. I usually see her twice a week, more if I have the time. And I call her if I can't make it out."

"Even after all these years, you still make the drive that often?"

"Of course." He furrowed his brow. "Who else would go if I don't?"

"I know Aunt Blu has been out a few times. I assumed Rodney. And I guess I figured others did once in a while, as well."

He nodded. "They do. People from church, mostly. But not as much these days."

"And why did you never bring her home with you?"

"You mean for a drive?" He took in the landscape around them. "I do sometimes. She loves it. I will again once the show finishes filming, but she understands that right now my time is limited."

Jill's fingers touched his jaw, and he turned back to her. "I meant to *live* with you," she said softly. "In her own home."

"I . . ." He stared at her with confusion. That had never occurred to him.

"You said she still has her wits about her, so why not bring her home? I'm sure there are plenty of people who would love a job sitting with her while you're out."

He thought about his and Jill's argument in Vegas. She'd been screaming at him by the time his granny came into the conversation, telling him that they could move her to LA with them. Had that been what she'd meant? Actually *with* them?

And why had he never thought about doing that himself?

"Was it because of Rodney?" Jill asked when he didn't answer. Before last night, Cal had never talked with Jill about his uncle. "Did you not want her to know how much he drinks? I remember you had another uncle—"

"I don't know," Cal interrupted, and before she could ask any more questions, he turned his head and looked out the window, effectively shutting her down.

He'd let all these years pass by being no better than his own father. The profoundness of that sat heavy in his chest. His grandmother could have been with him all this time. In the home and the city that she loved. Instead, she'd lived by herself.

It had always worried him that he might be more similar to his father than he wanted to believe. But those worries had stemmed from concern over not having it in him to care enough about a potential wife. A child. Wasn't that what all the women he dated eventually said when they broke up with him? That he didn't care enough?

Therefore, it shouldn't come as a surprise that he'd never thought to take care of his own grandmother.

Yet it did.

"Let's go to your house." Jill pressed her lips to his jaw. The touch was more one of comfort than sexual in nature. "Show me your home, Cal. I want to see it."

He nodded, still discombobulated at the thought that he'd been as uncaring as his father, and put the truck in gear. And as they drove, both of them lost in their own thoughts, his mind shifted off his grandmother, and played through the night before. Specifically, the part *after* he and Jill first made love.

Jill had confessed that she was still angry with him . . . and he'd admitted the same.

He'd been aware of his anger since she'd moved back to town, but until she'd pushed, he'd never realized that the ultimatum had been his biggest sticking point. She'd gone for the jugular that day, and she'd known it. So he'd lashed back. He'd left. But there had been one thing to come from last night's conversation that he hadn't given voice to. Because it only became clear to him at that very moment. And that was that Jill hadn't loved him enough to choose him. That's the real reason they'd broken up.

They'd had a plan before heading to Vegas. Yeah, she'd talked about wanting to go to LA for a long time, but that had been about wanting to find her dad. At least, that's what he'd always believed. Which Cal had not seen as imminent. They could have taken a trip out West at a later point. Spent time in California instead of moving there. He'd even said this to her on occasion. Because *his* plan had been on track. And his plan would have allowed for *them* to exist.

Rodney had just promoted him to head foreman, and Cal had already talked to his uncle about buying into the business when the time came. Jill had been on board with all of it. At least, she had until the time came to choose. And the reality was, she'd *not* chosen him.

He turned into his drive, and as he started over the ruts, Jill asked, "Why does no one know about this place?"

He looked at her. "Because I didn't want to tell anyone until it was ready."

"And when will it be ready?"

He'd lied to himself for months now. Just as he'd lied for twelve years, pretending his anger had only been about Jill refusing to speak to him. He crested the hill, and as his home came into view, he answered honestly. "Six months ago."

~

Cal led Jill through his house, one room at a time, with each space being more impressive than the one before it. The living room had been massive. Wood-burning stove and rock fireplace, a huge big-screen TV, and a couch and leather recliners, each of which looked large enough to hold a small family.

The kitchen was a chef's dream. Marble countertops, high-end appliances, tons of prep space. The setup had made her wish she were a better cook.

And then there was his bedroom. Jill stepped inside the masculine space and instantly fell in love. A California king sat against a feature wall painted in navy, which sported matching trim in a diamond pattern to give it a three-dimensional look. There was a seating area in the far corner, and even though they'd passed a library down the hall, there were also built-ins in this room, with several books already tucked away on the shelves.

She moved into the en suite bathroom, and literally drooled. Multiple body jets filled the spa shower, with a panel to control the water temperature, and the space was large enough for four. She slipped beyond the glass door and turned her face up to the rain showerhead and groaned.

"I want to move into this spot right here."

Cal's deep rumble reached her ears, and when she looked over at him, she instinctively understood that he was either picturing her naked in his shower right now—or thinking about when they'd been naked in hers that morning.

She wiggled her brows at him and stepped out. "Take me through those French doors I saw in the bedroom, Master Reynolds, and leave your dirty thoughts inside your head."

"Yes, ma'am." He wrapped his hand around hers and led her from the bathroom. But before they stepped into the backyard, Cal leaned in and pressed a kiss just behind her ear. "But you don't know what you're missing," he teased. "I have it on great authority that you like my dirty thoughts."

She shivered at his touch, and let herself get swept up in a kiss. And only when they surfaced for air did she remember they were in his bedroom for a tour—and not for more.

Forcing herself to leave the kissing behind, she stepped across the threshold to the outside world Cal had created for himself, and she shoved all dirty thoughts aside. Because she once again fell in love.

She tried to take in everything at once. The patio was expansive, formed of natural stone, with a dark-stained pergola covering it. It included a daybed swing, a hot tub, and a fireplace. And all of that was nice. Extremely. But the true selling feature was the view of rolling hills, with trees of every shape, size, and color, as well as the pond he'd mentioned her first time out. It winked off in the distance, and Jill could make out deer standing next to it. One even had his head dipped, drinking from it.

She looked up at Cal, feeling as if she'd stepped into a fairy tale. "Why in the world haven't you moved in here yet?"

He returned his gaze to the view. "I don't know."

Those were the same words he'd given concerning why he'd never brought his grandmother to live with him, and her stomach suddenly quivered. What was going on with him?

"Cal?" She said his name as if stepping through a minefield, but when he answered her, he ignored the real question.

"I have plenty of reasons. No kitchen table, for one."

"But you have a bar top and stools." She didn't take her eyes off him. "Try again."

"There's also the matter of no towels or linens."

"Amazon," she volleyed back.

"The basketball court hasn't had concrete poured."

She only harrumphed at that, and he shifted his gaze to stare toward the renovated barn.

"And the cable hasn't been run."

She said nothing else, deciding to wait him out, and when he finally gave up and looked at her, she slipped her hand in his. "You don't actually believe any of those excuses, do you?"

He said nothing.

"Anyone can go without cable, Cal. And honestly, that's the most valid thing on your list."

"You've gone without it for five years."

"I have. And yes, I have issues. We both know that. But we're not talking about *my* issues right now."

"And what if I don't want to talk about mine?"

She kissed his fingertips before letting go of his hand, then she lowered to the swing. "Then I guess we don't talk about them." She set the swing in motion. "But I wish you would. What's going on, Cal? Your house is ready, it's been that way for six months, and it's *gorgeous*. What's holding you back?"

"It's just not been the right time."

She patted the cushion, and when he settled in beside her, she slung her legs over his thighs. "I can understand your reluctance," she told him. "A little, anyway. I know your grandmother's house holds most of your good memories from childhood."

"It holds all the good memories."

She conceded his point. While she'd been busy lamenting the unfairness of her life after her mother had died, he'd shared his burdens concerning the lack of love from his father. She could tell nothing had changed on that front, but something about this situation seemed unhealthy.

"What are you afraid of?"

Cal stiffened at her question. "I'm not afraid of anything."

"Then set a time to move in."

His jaw remained hard. "Fine. I'll do it after filming ends."

"Great. *When* after? The following weekend? A month later?" She leaned into his space and forced him to look at her. "Next year?"

"Back off, Jilly. You're looking for a smoking gun here, and there isn't one."

"But I think there is."

"I've just been busy with Rodney," he told her. "As you pointed out, the man drinks too much. I get calls in the middle of the night on a regular basis. It's easier to pick him up if I'm not out here in the middle of nowhere."

"And easier than being alone?"

He eyed her with suspicion. "What are you talking about?"

She stretched out an arm, taking in the vastness around them. "You clearly love this place, and I can see why. I'd love it, too. Yet you bring no one here. You don't make it a home. You tell no one you've *got* a home."

"I've brought you out here twice."

"You have. Care to tell me why?"

"My God, Jilly." He tried to push her legs off him so he could get up, but she held him pinned.

Then she turned his face back to hers. "*Thank you* for bringing me out here." She spoke from the heart. "I get that's not the norm for you, and I feel special for that alone. So, thank you for trusting me with this. And I also have to tell you I'm quietly praying you intend to invite me to stay the night." She gave him a gentle smile, and she ran her fingertips over his cheek. "I want to lay in your bed with you, Cal. I want to *mess* up that bed with you."

Her words were beginning to shift his gears away from anger, which had been her intent.

"But I also want to be real. I want us to be real with each other. That's what it always was about between us."

He nodded in agreement.

"So, I'll shut up now. I've pushed, but I know when to back off. You've got things you don't want to talk about? Or think about? That's fine. I can respect that. We all need our walls. But I want you to know that I do care, Cal. While I might still be a little bent over our past, at the same time, I care about you. I want you to be happy." She kissed his knuckles. "I want you able to enjoy this spectacular home. So just think about all those things at some point, okay? And in the mean-time"—she tossed a heated glance through his bedroom doors—"offer me a demonstration of your shower, will you? And bring your dirty thoughts in with you."

Chapter Seventeen

"Changing your mind is good for you. It keeps the brain active."

—Blu Johnson, life lesson #17

"Mother's Day!" Heather didn't even look up from the sink full of dirty dishes as she yelled out at their foster mother, and Jill tossed a what-can-you-do shrug to Aunt Blu—who'd been sneaking back into the kitchen. Again.

"I just want to help," Aunt Blu explained. She eyed the stack of pots that wouldn't fit in the dishwasher. "You girls cooked everything."

"And we've already covered this about ten times," Heather replied.

Jill emptied a pan of its leftovers. "What's the big deal with letting us do the dishes? We do this every year."

"But you've done so much today."

Trenton chuckled. "All we did was sit in front of the camera and try to look as cute as you."

"Well, you pulled it off wonderfully." Aunt Blu elbowed her way in between Heather and Jill, and Trenton immediately clamped her hands down on Blu's shoulders and guided her back to the living room.

"If you want your Mother's Day present, you'll sit here and behave."

Jill smiled with Heather as Trenton chastised Aunt Blu in the other room. They'd all gone to mass with Aunt Blu that morning, and afterward they'd come back to the farm and joined their foster mother to show off Bluebonnet Farms to the production crew.

"Trenton *was* pretty cute, wasn't she?" Jill murmured under her breath.

Along with seeing the farm, the crew had filmed a special segment with Trenton. It had been done out in Blu's shed, and covered the calendars slated to go on sale the following week. The show wouldn't air until the fall, so Trenton planned to work with the printer to format a second calendar—one with only twelve months—and *Texas Dream Home* had promised to mention the school's website on the show. Any additional money raised would continue being funneled to the school.

"She lit *up* the cameras," Heather agreed. "I'm glad she talked them into doing that. She's got Aunt Blu's desire to help."

Jill agreed. With all of it. Even if it meant more exposure for the sheds.

But the truth was, she was okay with that exposure. After hearing Josie relay her story last week, Jill's attitude toward how they'd made their name had started to shift. She still wanted to win the competition, of course. She loved the work they were doing on the Bono House, so she'd definitely seek out more projects of that scale.

However, she'd started thinking of their company's creations as more than hideaways in backyards. Bluebonnet Construction built dreams. For women. And that was something she could always be proud of.

Jill put away a platter she'd just dried. "So, you're okay with bringing more attention to the sheds?"

Heather glanced over at her. "Are you?" Her answer wasn't a ringing endorsement, and Jill couldn't decipher the blank look on Heather's face.

"I am," she hedged. "I know we wanted to *shift* our reputation a little."

"I thought we wanted to kill it."

"Well . . . yeah." Jill bit her lip. "But after hearing Josie talking to Len the other day—"

"I know," Heather interrupted. "Right? I came in late, but I heard enough. I started thinking that even though we may not be the business we set out to create, we're still successful, you know? We still *matter*."

"We're not just orphans playing construction," Jill added wryly.

Heather stood to her full five-foot-two height. "We're never just orphans doing *anything*."

"Agreed." Jill sometimes wished for Heather's outlook. "But I still want to beat Cal."

Heather flashed a bright smile. "We always want to beat Cal."

"Speaking of Cal . . ."

Jill turned at Trenton's words. "We were actually speaking of the she-sheds. We're thinking that maybe they aren't such a bad racket, after all."

Trenton's bored look could win awards. "You two are just now figuring this out? We have women calling us from hundreds of miles away, willing to pay a premium, for what amounts to a tiny square footage. What's not good about that?"

Jill and Heather gawked at her.

"I thought you hated them, too," Heather said. She jerked her gaze to Jill's. "Not that we hate them. I just mean—"

"I volunteered us for a photo shoot to showcase our best work," Trenton said drily. "What about that says hate?"

"But . . ." Jill pursed her lips. "You were all for doing the show, too. Just like us. You *pushed* me to do it."

"Of course I was. And of course I did. Because, hello. It's television. When will we get an opportunity like that again? And once the show airs, our work will expand, and the business will grow. I get that, and

I'm all for that. But to be honest, I'm just as fine building retreats. I just want to work. I want to do things that make others happy. And if that's she-sheds . . ."

Heather nodded in agreement. "I feel the same. If that's she-sheds . . ."

Jill looked from one to the other, then in silent agreement, she held out one hand. Heather added hers next, and then Trenton, and at the count of three, they declared it so. "She-sheds!"

Jill laughed at the childhood memory. They'd been the only girls living with Blu long-term for the first couple of years, and as a coping mechanism, they'd formed a secret club. They'd been "The Three." No one else had been allowed—clearly, or they wouldn't be "Three"—and all decisions had been made official via the huddle-type "handshake."

She hadn't thought of that in years.

They returned to the dishes, each with a slight smile curving her lips, as if Jill hadn't been the only one to recall their long-ago club, but it didn't take long for Trenton to change gears. She repeated her earlier words. "Speaking of Cal . . ."

Jill slowed her movements on the pan she'd been drying. "Were we speaking of Cal?"

She hadn't had a chance to tell them yet.

"Yep." Heather nodded. "*Guilty.* I called it. She had sex."

Jill lost her grip, and the pan clattered to the countertop. "What are you talking about?" she hissed. She glanced over her shoulder, checking to make sure there was no sign of Aunt Blu.

"I'm talking about sex," Heather said, this time pumping her fist in and out. "Boom, boom. Bang, bang. You did the dirty. We can tell."

Jill smacked at Heather's fist. "And how in the world can you tell that?"

Trenton pinched one of Jill's cheeks. "Because you haven't stopped grinning all morning, *chica*."

Jill intentionally frowned. "Of course I haven't grinned all morning."

"When you showed up late for church"—Heather counted off on her fingers—"when you were *supposed* to be praying, but were thinking about something else instead. Father Kibby even saw that one."

"How would you know he saw it unless you weren't praying, yourself?"

"When you forgot the words to the hymn." Trenton picked up the game, and Heather pointed to Trenton in agreement, and held up a third finger.

"We could go on," Heather assured her.

"Please don't."

"So when did it happen?" Trenton asked.

Both of them stared back at her, eyes wide and fake innocent expressions on their faces, but Jill also saw their concern layered beneath the surface. And she couldn't blame them. She was concerned, too. She couldn't decide if she'd made the biggest mistake of her life, or if it was simply a matter of her finally growing in the maturity department by letting so much past anger go. "Let's finish the dishes, then take a walk," she suggested.

"Good idea," Trenton agreed. "Because it'll either be that, or we'll talk in front of Aunt Blu. But make no mistake, we *are* talking about it."

Jill didn't argue. She'd actually planned to bring it up herself.

She'd just intended to be out of hearing range of their foster mother when she did it.

They finished the dishes in a hurry, Aunt Blu's soft snores as background noise, then Heather wrote out a quick note telling her they'd be back for presents soon. It wasn't that they got her anything super special, but the woman loved receiving gifts, so they always made a big deal of the day. At the same time, Jill had always wondered if Blu's exuberance wasn't enhanced simply to keep the girls laughing—and *not* thinking about their own mothers. Though not everyone who passed through Bluebonnet Farms had physically lost their mom, none of them were *with* their mother if they were living with Aunt Blu. It could be a tough day. Even as an adult.

It was for her.

They stepped out of the house, and had barely gotten twenty feet before Heather began.

"We know you were home Friday night. We all talked after work."

"I was," Jill confirmed. "But then, Cal showed up at about eleven."

"And you just let him in?" Trenton bypassed Blu's she-shed, and the three of them headed for the open field. They'd spent hours roaming the property as kids, whether on foot or by one of the horses often stabled there, but rarely had they had time to enjoy that simple pleasure lately.

Jill fell into step beside them and focused on the tree-lined horizon. "You said it yourself. Cal and I are combustible." That was the best way she'd come up with to explain it. "He'd had a rough day, and we'd done that interview earlier in the afternoon."

"Where you lied through your teeth," Trenton pointed out.

"I did." She might have known she hadn't gotten that past her friends. "I'm not over my anger, but I really am trying. And I want to be." Jill took in both of them. "I'm tired of that being the focus of my life."

"Good for you." Heather linked an arm through Jill's as they walked. "You've held on to it long enough."

"I think so, too," Trenton added. She turned to face Jill, walking backward as she talked. "But does that mean you immediately needed to jump in the sack? I mean . . . don't get me wrong. I think Cal is great—his past choices notwithstanding—and like I said before, I know you two have fire. But Jilly"—she clamped her teeth together before finishing—"do you know what you're doing?"

Jill had no idea what she was doing.

"I'm thinking I needed the closure?" She made the statement a question. "We had all this unresolved past. So maybe that's all this is. Us wrapping things up. And then the fire will probably recede," she finished on a positive note. She wasn't sure she believed any of it, but it sounded plausible.

Trenton and Heather stopped walking as Jill finished her attempted explanation, and Heather's still-linked arm pulled Jill to a stop. Then Heather stepped forward to stand with Trenton, and both her foster sisters faced her.

"So this was a one-night thing?" Heather asked.

"She wasn't home all day yesterday, either. I went by there three times."

Jill looked at Trenton. "Why didn't you call?"

"Because your car was there, but no you. I went in and made sure."

"Oh." Which meant Trenton had also seen the two damp towels hanging outside the shower. And the two plates and glasses from breakfast. "I spent the day with him, too," she confessed. "And last night."

She wanted to be ashamed, yet she couldn't muster it up.

She pointed at Heather instead. "And no judging. I was doing fine until last weekend. When *you* let him into my bedroom."

Heather held up both hands. "I maintain that I had no choice in that matter. He would have taken out the door if I hadn't let him in." She glanced at Trenton. "I also kind of agree with Jill. I feel like this needed to happen. She's been hanging in a kind of black hole all this time."

"But how long is it *going* to happen?" Trenton questioned. "That's what I want to know. Is it just sex? Was it just for one weekend?"

"I don't know," Jill whispered.

They'd stopped in the middle of a clump of wild-growing yuccas, and she stared down at the pale blue-green spikes. Cal had once told her their color reminded him of her eyes.

She forced her gaze back up. "Am I being totally stupid here?"

"Romance is never stupid," Heather insisted.

"But is it romance?" Jill and Trenton asked the question at the same time.

Heather reached for Jill's hand. "What are you hoping to get out of it, hon?"

"I have no idea," Jill answered honestly. "But it wasn't just for the weekend. I'm going back out to his place tomorrow night. And I'm looking forward to it."

Heather squeezed Jill's fingers, and Trenton kicked at a bare patch of ground.

"Will you promise us something, then?" Trenton asked.

"Anything."

"Be careful. Don't make me have to kick his ass again."

Chapter Eighteen

"Trust a man who feeds a stray cat. His give-a-damn is working."

—Blu Johnson, life lesson #57

Upbeat jazz played from the corner as Cal stared down at Jill. They were naked in Mrs. W's room, with the corner camera covered with a shop rag.

"She is having far too much fun with this," Cal murmured. He pushed his hips forward, sliding deeper into Jill, and as he groaned at the feel of the woman underneath him, he also admitted that he agreed with the woman who'd once found this room to be her favorite in the house. This was his favorite, too.

But Mrs. W had nothing on Cal when it came to enjoying himself that evening.

"I still can't believe I let you talk me into desecrating the place like this." Jill moved underneath him, her body as familiar to him now as his own. "With *her* watching."

"And I can't believe you've become so accepting of her."

"The music doesn't lie."

He chuckled at that, then leaned in and nipped at the corner of her mouth. When she turned her lips to meet his, her body indicating that she wanted the pace to slow even more, he took his time kissing her. He held her head between his hands, and he showed her with his mouth how appreciative he was for the desecration she was bestowing upon the house.

He gave her a slow smile when they came up for air. They'd been in the room for the last hour. First, they'd had a picnic—or they'd started one—then he'd talked her into taking off her clothes. He'd helped, of course, and had returned the favor. And though their lovemaking that evening had been neither rushed nor bursting with energy, it also wasn't lacking in the least.

"This is good," he whispered. And she felt damned good beneath him. "Very."

He continued to move inside her, keeping their pace steady, but when her fingers began to clench at him, he lifted his head and peered down at her. He kissed her nose. "Now?"

She nodded, her eyes glittering. *"Now."*

And just like that, the passion that had been contained exploded. It was always the same with them. Same as it had been when they'd been teenagers. And the same, he suspected, as it would be for as long as this lasted.

He pumped harder, feeling her muscles tighten around him in a rhythm he'd never tire of, and he focused on listening to her body. She was close, but not quite there yet. He buried his face in her neck, forcing himself to wait on her, but give her what she needed at the same time. They'd been together every spare minute over the last eleven days, and had done this very thing during a number of those minutes. It was a time he'd never forget.

"Cal." The single word seemed to fill the room, and he lifted his head once again. Instead of saying anything, though, he put his lips to hers and showed her once more what being with her meant to him. He moved faster, and he held her tight. And when she finally cried out, he let himself go with her, shouting with his own release.

When they were both spent, he collapsed, but he rolled to his back within seconds, bringing her with him. He wanted to keep her tight to his side for as long as she'd let him.

Carpet had been installed earlier in the day, and they lay on a blanket in the middle of the floor. The music filtered back into his consciousness, now a soft piano ballad, and he opened his eyes to stare at the ceiling. What a difference a few weeks could make.

"Did you know she played piano in her husband's church?" Jill said.

Cal looked down at her. "I was going to tell you the same thing. How do you know that?"

A blush touched her cheeks. "I've been looking into her, too. Her husband was the pastor at the Baptist church on Main Street. She not only played the piano every week, but was active in raising money for the church, as well. She and her husband were married for forty-two years before he died in his sixties."

"Yet she waits here for another man."

"I wish I knew who it was."

The music went off then, and they both looked at the corner.

"Do you think she's crying?" Jill whispered. "It feels so sad in here."

"It always feels sad in here." He kissed her on the forehead, and reached for the envelope he'd tucked into his jeans. When he pulled it out, he removed the aged photo stored inside. "Her niece sent me this."

He held out the snapshot of a time in a woman's life when she'd looked to be full of joy.

"Her name was Marie."

He studied the picture of Marie Wainwright while Jill did the same, and felt his heart clench in his chest. The woman in the picture was in her midforties, beautiful, and laughing up at the camera. Everything on the surface read pleasure. Yet there was much more to the photo.

"Look at her eyes," he said.

"I see them."

The eyes in the photo seemed filled with grief.

Jill lifted to her elbow. "I feel like this woman has become your friend."

He felt the same way. "I do talk to her almost as much as I do my cat."

She laughed. "I still can't believe you have a cat. So, you talk to dead women and cats? How did I never know this about you before?"

"Because neither of them had chosen me before." He nodded toward the corner. "She started this, not me. I tried to ignore her for days."

"And then you brought *me* into it." Jill cast a quick glance at the corner, but it remained silent. "And the cat?" She turned back to him.

"Lily showed up at the house one day and insisted I let her in."

"That makes sense. I've heard women do that to you."

He pinched her butt.

"Hey," she yelped. "I'm just calling them as I see them. So this cat—"

"Lily."

"Sorry. *Lily.* How long ago did Lily choose you?"

"Seven years."

"Wow." Jill pushed to a sitting position. "And she hasn't dumped you yet?"

He shot her a "touché" look, and sat up to join her. They weren't in front of the window, so they should be safe from prying eyes. He disposed of the condom into an empty food container, and made a quick dash out of the room to wash his hands. When he returned, he settled beside her on the floor, inordinately pleased that she remained naked, and pulled the remains of their dinner over to them. He tugged apart a bunch of grapes and handed them over.

"I'm sure the day will come when she'll have had enough of me," he said, picking up where they'd left off. "But Lily's got more stubborn in her than some of the females I've known."

"Ah. So, that's what it takes to keep you? Stubbornness?"

His fingers slowed as he popped a grape in his mouth. Did she want to keep him?

"Wait until I tell all the women in town," she continued, and he started to breathe again. "They've been trying to figure out the secret for years."

Cal ignored her, and continued feasting on his grapes. He didn't want to talk about other women. And he didn't want to think about when Jill would be just like them and move along to someone else. Because he didn't doubt that she would. Hadn't she already pushed him away once?

He wouldn't be enough for her now, any more than he had been then.

"Can I ask you something, Cal?"

This time, he popped a grape into *her* mouth. "You can ask me anything."

"Am I the only person you've ever dumped?"

His fingers slowed once again.

"You said Marci dumped you." She kept her eyes on his. "And that all the women you date eventually do. Yet you dumped me."

"I've never thought about it like that."

"So then, does that mean yes?" She gave him a nervous smile. "I'm the only one?"

He didn't want to lie, but she had a point. Even when they'd dated as teenagers, he'd only had a couple of "girlfriends" before that. And both of them had been the ones to eventually move on. "I suppose you are."

"Ouch." She exaggerated the word.

"I wouldn't take it personally."

"Then how would you take it?"

He had the thought that she should take it that he'd cared enough to end it for her.

He didn't say that, though, but the sentiment was legit. His role models were his dad and his uncle. And neither was a catch. His dad had gotten married once, when Cal had been a kid. It had lasted a year. Since then, Neil offered baubles instead of wedding rings. Even upgrading the jewelry if the woman stuck around for a given period of time. But even then, it was Cal's understanding that the women were always the ones to leave.

His uncle had married three times and had promptly run them all off.

So how much *could* Cal truly give a woman?

He wanted to give more. Just as he wanted more in return. Jill had asked why he hadn't moved into his home yet. Why no one even knew about the ranch. He'd brought those questions out several times since she'd put them out there, and he'd even come up with answers.

He'd bought the home because it reminded him of the love his grandparents had shared.

He'd told no one because that kind of love wasn't real. Not for him.

The reality was, he should sell the place. Forget the idea he'd had of turning it into a working ranch someday, pack up his workshop, and make a nice buck after the renovations he'd put into the house. But he wasn't ready to sell yet.

He looked away from Jill's waiting gaze, and he let the other question she'd asked run through his mind. A question he'd been avoiding until now.

Did he have a fear of being alone?

Yes.

He closed his eyes with the answer. He hadn't realized that. And now that he'd put his uncle in rehab, that's exactly what he was. Alone.

He'd dumped Jill years ago because she hadn't loved him enough. He'd dumped her because if *he* hadn't, *she* would have eventually left him. Even if he had gone to LA with her. Because he would never be enough.

He looked at her. "You said recently that you want us to be real with each other."

"I did."

"Then I'll tell you that I left that day because I knew you didn't love me enough."

She leaned away from him. "And how did you come to that?"

"Because you wouldn't come home with me." He heard the accusation in the words, and the adult him knew it wasn't fair. She should have been allowed her own dreams. But dammit, he'd wanted her dream to be *him*.

"I guess that lack of love rolled two ways," Jill finally replied.

He swallowed, feeling as if the last grape he'd eaten had gotten stuck in his throat. "I suppose it did." He reached for his shirt and held it out to her. "Here. Put this on. I feel like I've made you uncomfortable."

She took the shirt and pulled it over her head, and it pooled at the tops of her thighs. She didn't get up and leave, though, and he wouldn't have been surprised if she had.

"*Have* I made you too uncomfortable?"

"No." There was wariness in her eyes, though. As if she was uncertain what would come next.

"Then since we're being so real, can I ask you something?"

She wanted to run. He could sense it in her.

She nodded instead, and he said, "Will you talk to me about your mom?"

That one *did* take her to her feet. *"No."*

"Come on, Jilly." Cal held out his hand to her. "We're being real, remember?"

"And I *really* don't want to talk about my mother. Why would you even bring that up? Plus, you know everything already. I told you the whole story a long time ago."

"But don't you eventually have to *deal* with it?"

"Deal with what?"

She stood there, her arms wrapped around herself, and Cal motioned with his fingers. His arm remained outstretched. He knew she needed to go there. It had been long enough. "Sit with me. It'll be okay."

She chewed on her bottom lip, her eyes not leaving his, but she finally took his hand. She let him pull her back to the floor, and she sat facing him, her knees bent to her chest, her arms around her knees.

"You're still mad at her," he said.

She started to shake her head, and he added, "If you can work on getting past your anger with me, then why not work on this, too? You need to—"

"Stop," she whispered.

So he stopped. He waited.

She pulled in several breaths, and then finally, she spoke. "I've tried to, okay? But I can't move past that one."

"Any idea what's holding you back?"

When she started to look away, he took her hand, and she brought her gaze back to him. She glared at him, demanding he back off. But he didn't budge. She'd do the same for him.

Finally, she caved. "I'm scared that I'm like her. How's that for an answer? She was a needy woman. My whole life, she needed a man, she needed me to hold her hand when she didn't have a man. And she just plain needed everyone to know that she was needy."

Her voice had climbed with her words, and as Cal had listened, he'd stared in surprise.

"You think you're needy?" he asked. "Honey. I've never seen anyone who needs another person less."

"Okay. Then how about the fact that she was prone to trying to kill herself?"

Cal went still. "Are you saying that *you're* like that?"

She gave a little shrug. "I already tried it once, didn't I?"

She'd told him about the day Blu had showed up to get her. The police had called in a suicide at the apartment where Jill lived, and Blu had overheard it on the police scanner her husband once owned. She'd recognized the address and jumped in her car.

"You were in shock that day, Jilly." Cal spoke carefully, hoping she would actually hear the words he was saying. What she'd considered doing in that one moment of time did not define her. "And you were only fourteen. You were a child." He gripped her hands now. "You blamed yourself for your mother's death—which was *not* your fault, by the way."

"But I—"

"No." He instinctively understood what she'd been about to say. "You did nothing wrong. You were not in charge of your mother's actions."

"But I told her to do it." Panic flashed through her eyes. "I left her in the apartment alone that afternoon. I'd never left her before when she was like that. And then she *did* it!"

"And that's a *horrible* thing for a person to go through. But *she* did it, Jilly. Not you."

Jill stared at him, hard and unblinking. Then she jerked her hands out of his grip and rewrapped them around her legs. Her chest rose and fell with her breaths. "I know she was the one who did it," she gritted out. "It's not like this is the first time I've thought about it. I know I was just a kid. She was the adult. I get all of that. But I was all she had." Jill stabbed her finger at her chest. "*Me.* And I failed her."

"Or maybe *she* was all *you* had? And she failed *you*?"

"No." She shook her head in denial.

"Why not?"

"Because I should have been there!"

Tears welled in her eyes, but Cal didn't reach for her. He didn't want to interrupt the moment. She needed to get it out.

"I know she had issues. I get that. She didn't kill herself to spite me. Or, at least . . . I don't think she did. She couldn't handle being let down. And she'd been let down in the worst way that day. Her husband left her. I walked out when she needed my support. And the thing is, I don't handle being let down easy, either." Her eyes went flat. "I lose my shit when things happen, remember? So, what if I have the same issues? The same inability to cope? What if there's a straightedge lying around someday, and I—"

"Jill." He bit the word out hard to get her attention.

"What?"

He hated seeing her this way. She was so much more. "Have you ever tried it again? Since that day when you were fourteen? Have you ever attempted to kill yourself?"

She hadn't actually attempted it that day, Cal knew. But if Blu had been just a few minutes longer . . .

"No." Jill shook her head.

"Not even when I left you? What happened the day I left you? When you came back to the hotel and I was gone? What did you feel?"

"I felt that I wanted to kick your ass."

He cupped her cheek, his heart racing but relief flooding through him. "That's my girl," he whispered. He stroked his thumb over her skin. "No thoughts of suicide that day, right?"

"No, but . . ."

He could see her thinking as her words trailed off, so he let her go with it.

Eventually, he nudged her for more. "And what about when you left Hollywood? Or any time while you were *in* Hollywood? All those nos you kept hearing? All those times your anger got the best of you? Anything then?"

She shook her head.

"That's because you're strong, babe." He pulled her into his lap. "So strong. Not needy. Not unstable." He kissed the top of her head and wrapped his arms around her, and as he held her, he began to rock her back and forth.

After several minutes, she looked at him. "I did *think* about it that last day in Hollywood."

Cal hurt for her, but he also understood who she was as a person. She wouldn't have gone through with it.

"It was a fleeting thought," she explained. "But it did cross my mind."

"Tell me what happened."

"Nothing *happened.* I was already on the bus heading home. I thought about my mother. About how she handled failure." She watched him as carefully as he watched her. "So, it crossed my mind. But really, kill myself on a bus? Who does that? And it would've been doubly insulting if I made it all the way home, let everyone see that I was no better off than when I'd left, and *then* I did it."

He didn't mean to laugh, but he did. He pressed another kiss to her forehead. "You've got nothing to worry about, Jill. You're so strong. So . . ."

Mine, he wanted to say. But he didn't. Because he didn't know if he could keep her.

He tucked her back against his chest, and music once again began filtering out of the small radio. It played "I Got You, Babe," and Cal let out another chuckle. "I'm going to miss her when this is over."

He felt Jill's lips curve against his chest, and he realized he was still naked. "If only you could take her with you, huh?"

Cal smiled with Jill, and then he looked over at the corner. At least then he wouldn't be alone. "What do you say, Mrs. W? We're nearing the end." The Raineses would be back in four days to announce the winner after the parade. "Want to go home with me when this thing is over?"

The piano tune that he found so sad began playing, and the sound of it had Jill catching her breath. "What is that? I heard it the first time I was over here. It's so forlorn."

"I have no idea, but she plays it on a regular basis. I wish I knew what it meant to her."

"I wish she'd never been that sad."

"True." Cal kissed Jill again, suddenly tired of all this "being real." He just wanted to *be*. "Make love to me again, Jilly," he whispered against her lips. "I can't get enough of you."

She nodded without hesitation. She apparently needed no further encouragement.

Chapter Nineteen

"Never settle for fine."

—Blu Johnson, life lesson #50

Be careful.

Trenton's words from almost two weeks before continued to echo in Jill's head, and Jill couldn't say that she'd actually once "been careful." What she'd been was happy. Nothing had been mentioned about futures or feelings between her and Cal, and she was fine with that. Mostly. She'd just been going with it and having a great time.

Only, the thrill of a lust-filled romance had slowly morphed, and what remained in its place was now hope. As well as terror. Because she still had no clue what she was doing.

She didn't know if she was being blind to reality, due solely to her sex life being active—*and amazing*—for the first time in her adult life. Lust had a way of doing that to a person, she understood. Or if there was something more meaningful really going on between her and Cal. It felt as if there was. It felt like maybe they could make this thing between them work.

And when she allowed herself to be as honest as possible, she admitted that she wanted it to work. But it also felt as if their time would soon be up. A choice would have to be made, and she had no idea which way Cal would fall.

She waved at a group of women standing by the side of the road and tossed out a handful of candy. The parade was in full swing, and they were nearing the turn for Pear Street.

"I'm so nervous," Heather shouted beside her, trying to be heard above the high school marching band. Her auburn hair gleamed around her shoulders, and her dimples seemed an inch deep today.

"Nothing we can do now but wait," Trenton replied.

Another crowd of women cheered as the Bluebonnet Construction float passed in front of them, and Jill, Heather, and Trenton, along with the entire group of ladies who'd helped over the past six weeks, waved and smiled. The whole town would soon know who would be named the winner, and Jill couldn't contain the excitement that it very possibly could be them. They'd done an outstanding job with the Bono House. She couldn't be more proud.

Marci lifted a hand from her spot on the sidewalk, and Jill forgot her animosity with the other woman long enough to return the greeting. In fact, she felt for the other woman at that point. Because Jill knew she might be in the he-doesn't-care-enough club along with Marci and the rest of them soon enough.

"We're making the turn," Heather squealed.

Jill looked up ahead. Along with the band, cheerleaders, three Boy Scout packs, and a selection of city officials, Cal and his team were also up there. Behind Jill were more city officials, the Lions Club, 4-H, two Girl Scout troops, and a dance team. And pulling up the rear was everyone from the production crew, as well as Bob and Debra Raines. Bob and Debra stood at the helm of the fire truck, and the majority of the town had fallen in line behind the parade.

Anyone interested had gotten the opportunity to walk through the finished houses earlier in the day, and now everyone was headed back to hear the announcement of the winner.

An empty parking lot had been reserved for the floats and vehicles that had been a part of the parade, and after everyone disembarked, they formed a path to the houses. The crowd parted as the teams made their way down the street, and Jill's heart skipped a beat when she realized that Cal had hung back to finish the route hand in hand with her.

She grinned up at him as his fingers closed around hers, and she had her answer. This was real. It had to be.

And she was certain he felt it, too.

Cal leaned down and brushed a kiss across her cheek. "Good luck."

"You, too."

They stopped, still holding hands, in front of the houses, and she laughed out loud when she caught Len making goo-goo eyes at her from behind his camera. Cal might miss Mrs. Wainwright after today, but Jill would miss Len.

"Ladies and gentlemen," Patrick announced to the crowd. He had a microphone in his hand, and speakers had been lined along the length of the street. "Let me be the one to formally introduce to you the much-loved hosts of *Texas Dream Home*, Bob and Debra Raines."

The crowd roared.

Jill stood at Cal's side, leaning into him, and listened as the couple greeted the onlookers and shared their excitement for the project that had been going on there. They would be walking through the houses next, but would be back out soon to announce the winners and hand over the deeds.

The couple continued talking, while at the same time Bonnie's dog suddenly began to bark. Jill and Cal turned to catch Winston with fangs bared and in his four-pounds-of-dog attack crouch, pulling at his leash. He was doing his best to get over to the Cadillac House.

Cal winked at Jill. "Mrs. W must be watching."

"I'd be disappointed if she wasn't."

The Raineses entered the Bono House first, with cameras following, and the construction teams hung back as they'd been told to do.

Jill's nerves twisted inside her. Then Winston's decibel level rose sharply, and Jill looked over to see a lone man step from the crowd. Whispers reached Jill as the feeble gentleman in the fedora hat slowly made his way into the middle of the street.

"Oh, wow. That's him!"

"He hasn't been home in years."

"I didn't know he was still alive."

Jill glanced at Cal. "Who is it?"

"I have no idea."

"Jerome Jefferson," said Aunt Blu. She'd come out of the Bono House as the TV crew had gone in, and now she stopped at Jill and Cal's side. "He's known as JJ. Blues player from here that made it big back in the '70s. He moved to New Orleans nearly fifty years ago, and as far as I know, hadn't come back home since."

Jill sucked in a breath. He was number two on the list of who'd made it big.

She looked at Cal again. Jerome was a black man, had to be at least in his nineties, and seemed intent on getting to the Cadillac House. In contrast, Marie Wainwright had been a white pastor's wife in Texas in the '60s, who'd played piano and led fund-raisers for her all-white church.

Chills raced down Jill's spine. "Do you think?" she asked Cal.

"Let's go find out."

They hurried toward the house before anyone could stop them, and caught up with the older gentleman as he made his way to the front sidewalk. He was frail. Leaning on a cane with each step, and his arms wiry thin. When they greeted him, he neither glanced their way, nor wavered in his intent. "Ain't gonna stop me from getting in there."

"No, sir," Cal said. "I'm here to offer assistance if you find yourself in need of any."

Jerome Jefferson kept his eyes on the prize. "And who are you?"

"I'm the man who renovated this house, Mr. Jefferson." Cal stayed close to the other man. "And who's spent the last six weeks getting to know the previous owner."

JJ stopped then. And he looked up. His hands shook. "She's really in there?"

"She really is." Cal caught Jill's eyes over the other man's head. "My name is Cal, sir, and that lovely lady on your other side is Jill. She renovated the house next door, but she spent a bit of time here with me, as well."

JJ turned to her.

"Hello, Mr. Jefferson. Could I take your arm and help you up the stairs?"

The older man nodded, his look saying he wasn't 100 percent sure he could trust them, but he knew he could use the assistance. Cal got a grip on his right arm as Jill slipped hers through his left, and together the three of them conquered the stairs. Behind them, someone yelled out that they weren't supposed to be in there. Only the hosts. But the hosts hadn't made it over to the house yet, and there was no way Jill and Cal weren't going to help this man get inside.

Winston continued to bark, and Jill noticed that the crowd had grown quieter. She wondered if others suspected the same thing they did.

"I built those for her." JJ pointed out the built-ins in the front room as they entered. Four feet wide by five feet tall. The details of the workmanship were exquisite. "His car missed them that night."

Jill caught her breath. "So you really are . . ." She couldn't finish her question.

JJ pulled his arms from theirs when they reached the middle of the room, and rested both hands on his cane. His eyes went to the staircase, and then he tilted his head back until he stared straight up. Jill might be mistaken, but a hardness seemed to settle over his features as he stood there. The lines of his face seemed more etched in stone than the previously loose folds of a man who'd lived almost ten decades, and the warmth she'd expected to find in his gaze was cold.

His eyelids closed, and she saw him swallow as the soft sound of jazz began from above.

Cal had removed the radio that morning.

"She loved her some jazz." JJ finally spoke. He bobbed his head with the music. "And her record collection, it was her prized possession." He opened his eyes and nodded to the built-ins. "That's what she kept on the shelves."

He used his cane to point toward the cutout just beyond the shelving, weaving slightly when he lost his support. "Her record player sat back in there."

"How did you meet?" Cal asked.

"Our churches did a collaboration one time. Some fine music, we made." He shook his head, and finally, Jill saw the tenderness she'd been expecting before. "Most beautiful thing I'd ever seen, my Marie."

JJ retook Cal's arm then, and turned to reach for Jill's. "Would you two mind helping me up those stairs?"

As they slowly made their way up, JJ told them the story of falling in love with Marie. He took jobs on the side to support himself while he worked on his music career. He played the piano, he told them. Along with saxophone and bass—in a pinch. He'd been recommended to the Wainwrights for a couple of handyman jobs, and though he'd known on first sight that he had no business being around the beautiful Marie, he hadn't been able to say no.

It seemed she'd had the same inabilities, and in no time, JJ had been trying to convince her to run off with him.

"I've never loved anyone like her," JJ told them.

They reached the landing, and he had to pause to catch his breath.

"I've also never hated another person as much."

Jill looked over to find Cal looking back at her. Her heart broke for the other woman.

Then it split wide open when the music changed to the sad piano melody.

"I wrote that one for her," JJ told them. He remained solemn as he spoke, and he seemed in no hurry to step inside the room. "Never played it for her, though. Wrote it after I moved away." He studied Jill. "You ever been in love, Miss Jill?"

She nodded. "I have."

She didn't let herself look at Cal.

"Then you know what it can do to you." JJ's gaze shifted back to the empty room, and his jaw went hard. "She turned me down, the stubborn woman. Even though she didn't love him anymore. Refused to go with me." He closed his eyes again, and Jill could feel the pain wafting off him. "She loved *me*," he growled out before snapping his eyes back open. "She was supposed to be with *me*."

JJ shook his cane in the air, and Jill held her breath.

Cal slipped his hand over hers.

"But she worried what people would think." JJ's voice became a mix of soft and hard, and he looked between the two of them. His attention snagged on their clasped hands, but he kept talking. "I should have forgiven her," he told them. "Especially when she found me after his death."

Jill pressed her fingers to her mouth.

"But I didn't. Because I'm a damned fool. And though she swore to me that day, I never for a minute expected she'd actually stay here waiting for me," JJ choked out. "Or I would have died and gone home to her a long time ago."

Tears spilled out of Jill's eyes.

Anger and mistakes or not, this was the kind of love she wanted. The kind of love she wished her mother could have found.

Forgiveness for her mother was suddenly all she could think about, and she fought the urge to cry out at the pain her mom must have felt on a regular basis. She'd just wanted to be loved. Jill understood that the need had likely been rooted in something deeper. Depression. Possibly an undiagnosed mental issue. But feeling as if you had nothing to live for couldn't have been easy. And to base your entire being around your need to be loved . . .

She shook her head at the thought of it. How sad.

But how thankful Jill was to know that *she* was more than that. Aunt Blu had done that for her, as well as her friends. She looked at Cal again. He'd done it for her, too. She'd been lucky in where she'd landed.

Jill squeezed Cal's hand, and as they stood there silently waiting, JJ seemed to shrug off the cloak of pain he'd arrived with. He turned to them and announced he was ready to go in.

"We'll wait out here." Cal nodded toward the room. "You take your time."

Cal wrapped his arms around her as JJ slipped beyond the door, and Jill leaned back against his chest. He was solid and strong behind her, and she found herself thankful he'd come back into her life.

She closed her eyes and listened the way he'd taught her. She could hear his breathing above her, the sound of footsteps as the production team moved into the room below them, and low murmurs from Jerome Jefferson just beyond the door. Jerome didn't speak for more than a couple of minutes, and then he was back, and Jill couldn't seem to pull in a full breath.

Cal felt it, too. She knew, because as she stood against him, she felt him struggle to fill his lungs, as well.

The room wasn't sad anymore.

"She's gone," she whispered. And then she realized that Bonnie's dog had stopped barking.

"I'll see her again soon," JJ assured them. "I'm going home now."

Jill barely managed to hold herself together as they got the man back outside, and once they did, he walked away as slowly as he'd come. But he didn't look back. The man had gotten what he'd come for, and he was going to be with his love now.

"I want that," she said softly.

Cal peered down at her, his expression unreadable, but before either of them could voice additional thoughts, the Raineses were back, and cameras surrounded them. All members of both teams moved in, and a hush once again fell over the crowd.

"We've done our review," Debra began, speaking into the microphone, "and we can say that these two homes have come out better than either of us expected. Simply beautiful." Debra and Bob shook hands with Cal and Jill. "It's an honor to have had you as part of our show. But we know everyone here is anxious to hear the results, so we don't want to keep any of you waiting."

Jill took Cal's hand.

"The winner of this year's *Texas Dream Home* competition . . . with only the slightest of margins, is . . ."

Jill locked eyes on Trenton and Heather, and the three of them shared a nervous smile.

"We Nail It Contractors!"

The bottom fell out of Jill's chest. She'd seriously thought they would win.

Cal's hand was still gripped in hers, so she released it, her mind numb, then she reached out to shake it. "Congratulations," she mumbled.

She turned and hugged Heather and Trenton as they closed in on her, each of them murmuring to the other two about how it was fine that they'd lost. Everyone who'd walked through the place that day had seen what Bluebonnet was capable of. They'd been watching them for six weeks. The company would be fine. They'd still grow.

But "fine" or not, Jill had wanted this. Terribly.

She waited until Bob and Debra finished congratulating every contributor to the winning team, then she moved back in to thank them once again for the opportunity. Only, Patrick put a hand to her arm before she could reach the hosts, and motioned toward the backyard. "Could we speak to you for a moment?"

"About what?" Jill just wanted to go home. She looked around for Heather and Trenton.

"Just you," Patrick murmured. He motioned to the executive producer, who'd flown in for the revealing, and who was now speaking with Cal. "And Cal," Patrick added.

Jill remained confused. "What's going on?"

"In the backyard?" Patrick asked again.

"Fine."

Jill followed the others until the group of them were all out of sight, discovering that two cameramen waited in the back, and then a broad smile spread across the executive producer's face.

"What a competition." The man shook Jill's hand, pumping it hard with exuberance. "And Ms. Sadler, may I say, what a charming addition you turned out to be. So much more than we expected."

She smiled tightly. Surely they weren't seriously standing there trying to piss her off? "So, you really were just looking for me to lose my cool on camera?"

"Well . . ." The EP looked slightly embarrassed. "I will admit that we wouldn't have been surprised if that happened. And from what I've seen, it *did* happen a couple of times. That's why we wire the cameras into the house and like to keep the mic packs hot. But your anger wasn't the real thing we were looking for." He nodded at Patrick.

"And we got *exactly* what we were hoping for," Patrick told them.

Cal put a hand to Jill's back. "And what, exactly, *were* you hoping for?"

The excitement on the producer's face was palpable. "We were looking for hosts for a new show that'll go into production this fall."

The air left Jill's lungs.

"What are you talking about?" Cal asked.

"Chemistry," Patrick said. "We're in a fight to up our network's numbers, and *Texas Dream Home* can't do it alone. We want to produce a new renovation show. Still set in Texas, but we'll add a different slant to it. We've found these types of shows work best when the hosts are either a couple or close family members, so one of the things we were hoping for when we sat down to cast the teams was a couple of shining stars we could work with in the future. For instance"—Patrick looked at Jill—"three foster sisters. Or an uncle and a nephew who've grown the business together. Whom the camera loves, by the way. Rodney could have a show of his own, if that's what we were looking for. But then we learned of the connection between you two, and we'd hoped . . ."

Jill stared at the man. She knew she had to appear dumbfounded, but she was terrified to think she might be hearing what she thought she was hearing. "You hoped what?"

"For *you*." Patrick held his arms out to them. "You two are explosive on screen. Not to mention talented at the business in general. Both in your own ways, of course. You complement each other well, and I've got to tell you, you make a dynamic couple on camera."

Jill stared at Cal.

"We had our fingers crossed that the anger between you two was as much passion as anything else," Patrick explained. "And we *hope* we can talk you into accepting our offer of being the hosts of our new show."

Jill's head spun. She might get to do this some more?

On TV?

She couldn't contain her grin, and when Cal looked her way, she knew he had to see everything that she was feeling.

"But there is a catch," the executive producer warned, jumping back into the conversation. He looked from Jill to Cal. "I'm aware it's unconventional to suggest, but we don't want *two* companies for the show. We want two hosts. One company."

"Which company?" Jill asked.

"And which hosts?"

Jill shot Cal a look. Had he not been listening?

"To make it crystal clear," the executive producer continued. "We want you two, but you'd need to combine We Nail It and Bluebonnet."

Neither of them said anything.

Jill's mind tripped over itself as it tried to sort everything out.

Combine businesses? Her and Cal?

Would he want to? Would she?

She wanted to be with him, she had no doubt about that. But she'd worked so hard to get to where she was. To make the company successful. Not to mention, Bluebonnet was an all-woman business. How would that even work?

But that could be adjusted. They could still hire girls who ended up staying with Aunt Blu. They wouldn't have to give that up. And maybe they could even incorporate the she-sheds into some episodes. Especially with *Texas Dream Home* giving them some attention. They'd just hire men, too. With the notoriety of being on TV, the business would continue to grow, so they'd have to bring in more subcontractors. And Cal already had plenty of trades on his roster.

Yes. She nodded with the thought, as her mind continued to whirl. This could work. She and Cal could do this together. She could keep working in construction, but she could also do TV. The best of both worlds. *And* she'd get to do it with Cal.

Her excitement came to a screeching halt as logic finally prevailed. She only owned one-third of the company! And she had no idea what her foster sisters would think about any of this.

"What about Heather and Trenton?" She finally found her voice. She couldn't do this without them.

"There would be a place for your foster sisters if they want it," Patrick assured her. "Unless all parties agreed to a buyout, of course. Another option would be them working renovations, but not being on camera. Not everyone enjoys the spotlight. All of that is negotiable. The part that isn't negotiable is you and Cal. You're the hosts."

"And there's no wiggle room on merging the companies?" Cal asked.

Jill turned back to him. He had to be as excited as her, right? She bit her lip as she waited.

"I'm afraid there's no wiggle room with that," the executive producer answered Cal. "Don't get me wrong, we're not trying to manipulate either of you. Say no, and we walk away. But we've seen something special between you and Jill over the past weeks. *And* from your companies. There are parts of both we'd like to bring into the new production, and given that name recognition will be high immediately after the competition airs, we'd love to go to contract soon."

They were talking as if it were already a done deal, and Jill suddenly couldn't contain her excitement. "Cal?" she asked. He hadn't said much.

When he met her gaze, she nodded and decided to take a leap of faith. What was living if you didn't go for it once in a while?

"I'll do it." A nervous laugh followed her words. "I'll have to talk to Heather and Trenton, of course. I won't agree to anything without making sure they want it, too. But if there's no issue, then I'm in. You and I could . . ."

She stopped talking as she finally began to clue in to the look on Cal's face. That wasn't excitement staring back at her.

"Cal?" she said again. She glanced at the red light on the nearest camera. "Say something."

When he continued giving her nothing but silence, she quickly asked for a moment, and pulled him to the side.

"This could be great," she whispered. "I know it's a big decision, and we can sleep on it. We'll go home and think it over. We'd be crazy not to. But I can really see this happening. You and me." She wrapped her arms around his waist and grinned up at him. "It could be huge. You'd see the business expand the way you've always dreamed. I'd get to stay here, doing work I adore, but still get to live out a dream."

She sighed with unadulterated joy. "And it wouldn't just be the companies I'd want to combine. You know that, right? These last two weeks . . ." She had everything she could ever want right in front of her. "I love you, Cal." She stood on tiptoes and kissed his cheek. "I've always loved you."

~

Cal stared at the woman he'd once married and then divorced, all within a span of twenty-four hours. Until that moment, he'd been questioning if the divorce had been a mistake. Maybe he should have tried harder to find a solution that could work.

Maybe he should have sought her out after she'd come home, and tried to work it out.

But then, Jill had said she loved him. *After* being offered a TV show.

He untangled her arms from his body. "Why did you just now say you love me?"

"What?" She looked toward the group of people waiting on them before turning back. "What do you mean *why now?*" she whispered.

"I mean, why *now* that you just got offered this opportunity, did you then decide to tell me that you love me? Did you say it only because you want to be on TV?"

"What? No."

Was he seriously losing out to her dream of acting again? "I won the competition," he reminded her.

"I know that."

"So maybe if you don't love me, then they'd just offer *me* a show."

Her brows knit. "Do you want a show by yourself?"

"That's not the point."

"Then what is the point?"

He looked away from her. He wasn't exactly sure what the point was, but he was pretty sure everything he'd just begun to think he wanted was once again crumbling in his hands. "I can't just throw away everything I've worked for, Jill. That's all I'm saying."

"But you wouldn't be. Don't you see that? This would only make the company bigger. It would grow beyond anything you've imagined, I'm positive. Everyone would know your name."

"Everyone would know *our* name."

She jolted slightly at his words, then she spoke more slowly. "And that would be a problem?"

"I'm just saying I'm not sure I'm ready to hand over my business. And that you can't toss around words like 'love' and expect—"

"Wait." She took a step back. "You think I was lying when I said that?"

"All I know is you didn't mention it before."

"Because you wouldn't have wanted to hear it before." Her voice began to rise. "And clearly, you don't want to hear it now."

"*I* never said anything about love." He could hear the exasperation in his own voice.

"I'm fully aware of that."

"I'm just saying—"

"Stop." She held up a hand, then she patted him on the chest as if unsure what else to do. "Just don't, okay? You don't have to say it back. It's fine. You don't have to love me."

Did he love her?

He had no idea. And that was part of the problem. Everything was suddenly twisted, with the most prevalent thought being that he didn't even know if he *could* love. Wasn't that what everyone told him?

"I never wanted to hurt you again, Jilly."

"Yet you're straddling that line pretty heavily right now."

"But, why? We were good ten minutes ago, right? So why does my not wanting to combine my company with yours mean that we can't still be fine?"

She stared at him for a full minute, and he found himself wanting to take it all back. He didn't know what "it" was, exactly, he just knew he wasn't going to like whatever was about to come out of her mouth next.

"Because I don't want 'fine' any longer, Cal. I've been 'fine' for years. I want 'great' for once in my life. And I want to be *enough* for somebody. It isn't the thought of you not being willing to combine your company with ours that's the real problem. It's your inability to combine your *life* with mine. It's just like before. I see that now. You were all for us being together. Being married. As long as *I* complied. As long as I gave up *my* dreams and agreed to sit around and let you handle everything."

"That's not what I wanted at all."

"Wasn't it? Your wedding present to me was to surprise me with the knowledge that you were prepared to take care of me. You'd already rented a place for us here. When you *knew* I wanted to go to LA."

"But I had to come back here. We've been over this so many times, Jill. You know that. My father shoved my grandmother into a home and left her there. How was I supposed to do the same?"

"Yet you left *me*. And you had no problem doing that."

"I left you because you never *needed* me."

She sucked in a breath at his words, then she slowly lowered her arms to her sides. She took another step back. "That's what it was about? Who needed you the most?"

"You didn't love me enough to come home with me. To support my responsibilities."

"Yeah. You already tried that one. And you didn't love *me* enough to believe in me. It was only about you." She laughed softly, and the sound felt like a slice through the heart. She shook her head in disgust. "You're pathetic, Cal. I had no idea how much until just now, but I just realized you did the very thing you always claimed you'd never do. You grew up to be your father. A tiny little man who cares more for himself than anyone who might want to care for him."

Rage suddenly colored Cal's vision. "Oh, that's rich, Jill. You can't have what you want—*again*—so you start name-calling. Good thing this is all becoming clear now. Before I was stupid enough to make the same mistake twice."

"Yes, it is." She stepped forward then and poked a finger into his chest. "And for the record, I *still* don't need you," she gritted out. "And I never will. Good luck with your life, Cal. Be sure to carry on that Reynolds tradition with pride."

She paused as she stepped away from him, then she closed her eyes. And when she turned back to the others, it was as if a different person emerged. She'd reverted to calm and collected. "Thank you both for the opportunity to be on the show," she said to Patrick and the executive producer. "It was a wonderful experience, and provided me with memories I'll treasure. I also appreciate the chance to work more with you, but I'm afraid it's a no."

Cal's gaze shot to the cameras as he listened to her. They'd been rolling all this time.

And Jill had known it.

Their mics had been hot, as well. Which meant that the last few minutes had been nothing more than her final act. He'd known she didn't really love him.

Jill turned the corner of the house, heading back the way they'd come, and he saw her lift her hand and wave to the onlookers. He watched until she disappeared, unsure how things had gone from the highest high to the lowest low in a matter of minutes.

He'd found and then he'd lost Jill. Again.

But this time was the *last* time.

Chapter Twenty

"Friends don't let friends hurt alone."

—Blu Johnson, life lesson #10

The sound of Jill's footsteps was the only noise in the small house as she made yet another loop from the living room to the kitchen and back. She couldn't believe what Cal had done to her. Nor what she'd done to herself. She'd fallen for the big idiot. Again! But leave it to Cal. As was his style, he'd handed it right back to her.

Why was it that she was the only woman to ever get dumped by the man? And now she had to face knowing that she'd been dumped not once, but twice.

She stopped midstride and processed that thought. Cal hadn't actually done the dumping this time. She'd been the one to make that decision. He'd wanted to go along, being just *fine*. She growled under her breath and started moving again. She didn't want to be *fine*. And she didn't want someone who half assed a relationship.

Her thoughts stopped her yet again as it occurred to her that she could now join the exes-of-Cal's club. The idea pleased her in a sick way. He hadn't cared enough, so she'd moved on. Nice to know she wasn't alone, at least.

Only, she *was* alone, and she was tired of it.

She quit pacing and dropped to the oversized ottoman, which sat in front of her sectional. Which she'd placed in front of the fireplace . . . which sat below where most normal people would install a TV.

She wanted to be normal again, too.

She flopped back across the ottoman and stared at the ceiling. Cal had told her for a second time that she didn't love him enough. How dare he? He was the one lacking in that arena. She was just fine. She snorted at the thought. "Fine" was going to be her favorite new word.

Her phone dinged from where it lay charging in the kitchen. It would be a text from Heather or Trenton. They'd offered to come over, and when she'd declined, they'd suggested they all go out. It was a Saturday night, they'd pointed out. Why not go out on the town?

But to celebrate what? Her double loss?

She groaned. She hated feeling sorry for herself. But she couldn't help it at the moment. She'd gone from thinking she had it all. *Finally.* To having nothing *at* all. Maybe that was her true commonality with her mother. Her luck with men. Was she destined to always fall for such jerks?

Or only one jerk in particular?

She rolled to her side and pulled her knees up on the cushion, then she stared at the picture of sunflowers above the fireplace. She wanted to watch TV again. She hadn't been able to when she'd first come home. Her experiences had soured her on everything Hollywood, and she'd wanted nothing to do with it. But she had new experiences now. *Texas Dream Home* had done that for her. And she wanted to keep moving forward, keep trying new things. Maybe one day she'd even go out with a new man.

Not today, though. She needed to wallow more. Cal had missed out. She was a fucking prize.

But she was missing out, too. Because she *did* love him enough. He was just too stupid to realize it.

She eyed the plastic-wrapped package of DVDs now sitting on the mantel. Seasons one through four of *Texas Dream Home* had been part of their consolation prize for not winning. She could start her new experiences there.

The phone beeped yet again, and she shoved herself up to go get it. The good thing about having annoying foster sisters who wouldn't leave you alone when you wanted to sulk in peace was that they'd also be there when you wanted to sulk with friends.

She pulled up the text app and typed out a group message.

Texas Dream Home marathon. I need a lot of wine, even more chocolate, a monster-sized TV, and two best friends to do it all with me.

But before she could hit "Send," a knock sounded at the front door. Surprise had Jill going still. It couldn't be Cal, could it?

Her pulse took off. She wished it were Cal. She missed him already.

But as she stared at the door on the other side of the room, reality told her otherwise. Cal would not be standing on her front porch. He didn't want what she did. He didn't want *her*. Not the way she wanted him.

So it couldn't be Cal knocking on her door.

But as she slowly crossed the room, her feet fighting her every step of the way, it didn't matter how much she knew it wouldn't be him. Because she still wanted it to be. She reached the foyer, and with hands trembling, she peeked through the bottom row of windows. Then she heaved out a shaky sigh of relief.

Her two favorite people in the whole world stood on the other side of her door. And they'd brought wine and chocolate.

Jill looked down at her phone as she pulled the door open. She hadn't even sent the text.

She stared at Heather and Trenton, her throat clogged with emotion, and she saw her own pain reflected in their eyes. She needed them. And they'd known it. And then damned if tears didn't spill down her cheeks.

"Oh, Jilly." Heather shoved the wine she carried at Trenton and wrapped Jill in her arms.

"I was just about to text." Jill sniffed. She held up her phone behind Heather's back, as if either of them could see it.

"And we were prepared to break down the door if you didn't let us in."

Trenton leaned in then, her arms loaded with four bottles of wine and two Halloween-sized bags of chocolate, and she inched in as close as she could get. She rested her head against Jill's, and they stood there like that. Jill crying, Heather soothing, and Trenton muttering that all Jill had to do was say the word, and she'd go kick Cal's ass. And Jill understood that whether she had Cal or not, she absolutely would never be alone. She had her girls.

~

"I wish you could see this view, Granny." Cal shifted his truck into park.

"Tell me about it."

They sat at the ridge on his property where he'd first brought Jill, and Cal looked out over his land. It was the day after he'd won the *Texas Dream Home* competition, and he'd officially moved in. There'd been little physical moving to do, of course, since he'd already pretty much furnished his home. But he had brought over the kitchen table from his grandmother's house that morning—as well as his cat. And Pete would be showing up with the concrete truck later that afternoon. He'd offered to help pour the basketball court.

"Green as far as the eye can see," Cal started, wanting to paint not only the picture for his grandmother, but the feel of the place, as well. "And blue sky stretching well beyond that."

He spent the next several minutes showing his grandmother his farm through his eyes, and when he finally moved the truck forward again, he headed for the old barn.

"Before we go into the house, I want to show you my workshop."

His grandmother turned her face toward his, her smile soft and her eyes having long ago lost their color. "You're a good boy, Calhoun. Your grandfather would be proud of you."

"Do you think so?" He navigated the truck into the garage of the renovated barn. "I wish he was here with us today."

She patted his thigh. "Don't worry. He is."

Cal took his grandmother's hand and kissed the tissue-soft skin on the back of it, then he went around to the other side and helped her down. He tucked her arm under his, and walked her around the space.

"I haven't gotten to do much woodworking lately," he told her. "Between renovating the house and this barn, and then the TV show." He looked up at the open rafters. "But I'm going to start again soon. I need new chairs for my kitchen table."

"Why don't you build things to sell, Cal?" His grandmother's fingers trailed over everything she could reach with one hand while she kept her other securely wrapped around his arm. He had several of his grandfather's tools mixed in with his, and he noticed how her fingers took extra time to smooth over the thinner, more worn metal.

"I can't handle a second job, Granny. Running the company is enough. This is a hobby."

"But you've always been so good at it." She released her hold on him when she laid a hand over a small jewelry box. It was made of black walnut, and he'd even installed a tiny dancer inside the lid.

His granny opened the lid, running one hand around to the back to turn the key for the music box, then smiled at the whimsical tune.

"I can imagine her twirling in place."

"She is," Cal told her. "And she's wearing a pink tutu."

"Of course she is. How else would a tiny dancer in a jewelry box dress?"

She set the box down, leaving the lid open, and with both hands, she moved along the shelving that held the smaller items he'd built.

"I hear you messed up yesterday." His grandmother's back remained toward him, her hands moving nonstop.

"How do you figure that? I told you we won."

She shook her head. "You didn't win. You let her get away again."

"Granny." She'd already asked about Jill twice on the drive over. "I didn't let her do anything. She chose her own path."

"Please. Everyone knows you turned that girl down." The tone was one he'd heard plenty of times as a kid. He'd also heard it when he'd come back from his honeymoon without a wife.

"She wanted too much," he explained. He really didn't want to talk about Jill. "I've worked hard to build the company to what it is. I couldn't give her what she wanted."

"And what about the job offer?"

He stared at her. He had no clue how she knew about the offer of hosting a show.

She turned to him, her hands gripping the shelf behind her to steady herself, then she waited patiently for his reply, her pale face pointed in his direction.

"I've already got a job, and you're over there trying to talk me into selling custom furniture and gifts," he pointed out. "Why would I want a third one?"

"Why, indeed?" She asked the question as if only she held some mysterious answer.

"You don't know what you're talking about."

"I know exactly what I'm talking about. I was married for thirty-eight years." She pursed her lips. "Oh, I know all right."

He ignored her. She knew nothing about him and Jill. He led her to where he kept some of the larger tools, making sure the safety was on everything so she wouldn't hurt herself, and when they reached a wrought iron settee that had once been on her back porch, he helped her to sit in it.

"I wanted to talk to you about a couple of things today, Granny."

She nodded and clasped her hands in her lap as if sitting proper on a church pew. "I suspected as much."

He groaned. She'd suspected nothing, but she always had been a stubborn one.

The thought brought a tiny smile to his lips as he realized that her stubbornness was something she and Jill had in common. He wondered if that's part of what had attracted him to Jill in the first place.

"Ever swung a sledgehammer, Granny?"

"What?" Her face scrunched up, and he shook off the thought.

"Never mind." What a moron. He had to quit thinking about Jill. "That wasn't what I meant to say. I wanted to talk to you about Rodney."

He'd decided he should have told her about her son a long time ago. Just as he'd done Rodney no favors by overlooking the drinking, he'd done his grandmother none by pretending it wasn't happening.

"How's he doing?" she asked. "He hasn't been to see me in months. Still busy?"

"He's . . . busier than usual right now," Cal told her. "He's actually in a rehab clinic. He's a drunk, Granny. And I'm sorry about that."

"What are you sorry about, Cal? You didn't make him a drunk."

"I know." He took her hand when she held it out, and squatted in front of her. "But I guess I'm sorry that I kept it from you. I'm sorry I haven't done more to help him over the years."

She patted his cheek. "But I already knew. Rodney's had a problem since his first marriage."

Cal blinked at his grandmother. All this time, and she'd known? Rodney's first marriage had been over twenty years ago. Cal hadn't even figured out his uncle's problem until years after that. "Then why didn't you do something back then?" he asked her.

"Sweetheart. Your papaw and I tried. We wore that boy out trying to straighten him up. But a person can't change until he's ready. Not long-term. So, tell me, is he ready now?"

Cal could see the hope written on her face. He nodded, then realized her hand wasn't on his cheek any longer, so she wouldn't have felt the movement. He grabbed her fingers and pressed her palm to his cheek. "I do think he's ready. I haven't visited him yet, but I get to go next month."

"How long's he been there?"

"Just a couple of weeks. I've talked to his counselors, though. They say he's focused. He's trying."

She patted his cheek again, bringing up her other hand to hold his face in front of her. "I'll write you a check to help cover his expenses."

"No, Granny." He covered her smaller, more feeble hands with his. "You keep your checks. I've got this. It's the least I can do."

"Then I'll have one of the girls knit him a sweater."

By "one of the girls," Cal knew she meant someone at least in the same decade as his granny.

"You have her knit it, but you tell her you'll have to come back and get it, okay?" He stood, pulling her up with him. He wanted to show her his house. "That's the other thing I wanted to talk to you about. I have a room for you here. I want you to come live with me."

She quit walking. "You want me to what?"

"I've messed up for too long. Dad put you away, and I shouldn't have allowed it to happen."

"You were fourteen, Calhoun. What could you have done?"

He urged her toward his truck. "I could have brought you home with *me* years ago, for starters. I don't know why I didn't think of it, but I want to do that now. The house is ready. Let me show you. There's a place for Rodney, too. He'll be out in a couple of months, and then he can live here, too."

She stopped walking again. "Rodney is a grown man. It's about time he acts like one, don't you think?" She shook her head, her intention to not be ignored clear. "Plus, I gave him a house when Neil moved me out. You let him live in it when he gets out. It's time you took care of your own life. And that means quit giving your uncle a salary for doing nothing, too. He needs to find his own way now. He needs to have a purpose."

Before he could argue—or even ask how she'd known he gave Rodney money—she continued.

"And I can't move in with you, are you crazy? I'm fine where I am. Plus, if you have any sense in that head of yours"—she shook a finger toward him—"you'll beg the woman you love to come live in your new home."

"But you're who I love, Granny. And I've not done right by you."

"I am not your responsibility, Calhoun Reynolds." Her strength in refusing to budge surprised him. "And don't you dare lay any guilt about me at your feet. That's hogwash. All you need to worry about now is the fact that I'm not the only one you love. And you need to deal with it." She'd taken on the tone again, and it did the trick. He felt about five years old.

"I never said I love her," he argued, his tone belligerent. At least, he hadn't this time.

She shook her finger at him again. "You messed up with her before, are you really going to do it again?"

"I didn't—"

"You should have supported her. Whatever she wanted. She was your wife." Her voice filled with a strength he hadn't heard in ages. "I thought your grandfather and I taught you better than that."

"Why are you lecturing *me*?" He threw his hands in the air. "I couldn't move off to Hollywood. I couldn't leave you."

"Honey. You've let the woman you love slip through your fingers twice now. You could have visited me a few times a year. I love your visits, but I'm not alone there. I have friends. I would have been fine. But when are *you* going to live? When does somebody get to take care of *you*?"

He didn't want to be taken care of.

"Don't use me as an excuse anymore."

"I haven't been."

"Sure you have. Because you're afraid of what you feel for Jill. Because you're afraid she can't love you back. I get it. You grew up without a momma, and your daddy had issues." She stepped closer and reached up, patting him on the lips. "Your daddy blames himself for Richie," she whispered. "Did anyone ever tell you that?"

Cal shook his head, confused. His other uncle had been killed before Cal had been born.

"What did Dad have to do with it?"

"Richie only had his license for a month when your daddy took him to a party. Then there was this girl." Sadness pulled at the lines on her face, and Cal quickly helped her into the truck so she could sit. "Neil wanted to stay late. Stick around after the party. He liked that girl a little too much. But he knew Richie had been drinking. Those boys of mine"—she let out a weary sigh—"always had a taste for liquor. Your daddy had been drinking, too, but not as much as Richie. But he wanted to be *alone* with the girl. You know what I mean by alone, right?"

Cal hid a chuckle. "I know what you mean."

"So he made Richie go home without him." A tear slipped out of her eye and traced along the line of a wrinkle, and Cal's heart broke. "Richie never made it home that night," she whispered. "And your daddy hasn't been right since. I lost two boys in one."

Cal found himself unable to move. He'd had no idea.

He both wanted to hug his granny to him, and wanted to find his father and ask if Richie's death had played into his disinterest in his own son. Had his father's rejection been about more than just *him*?

"I'm still not going to forgive him," Cal blurted out. "The man should have cared about me."

But forgive or not, something warm tried to seep into his heart.

"And I'm not saying you should." His granny brought her face to his, and she pressed a cool kiss to his cheek. "He should have done better. Absolutely. But stop punishing yourself because of him," she urged. "Go love Jill. I know she loves you. I saw it in her eyes the first time you brought her to meet me."

The first time he'd taken Jill to meet her, Jill had been sixteen.

"She has that forever kind of love for you. Like your grandfather and I had for each other. And I think you might have it for her, too."

Cal shook his head. "You're wrong, Granny. We're not those forever kind of people."

At least, he wasn't.

"I am *not* wrong. In fact, I'm seldom wrong." She pulled her feet into the truck after that, and once again, she sat as she had on the bench. Hands clasped in her lap, face pointing forward. "Now show me this house of yours so I can make sure you didn't mess anything up. And when you get tired of having your head up your rear, you make sure to bring me to the wedding."

He slammed the truck door without comment. There wasn't going to be a wedding, and he wouldn't give his granny the satisfaction of replying.

But as he circled the front of the truck, the music box across the room started playing.

He stopped, and slowly turned. The lid stood open as his grandmother had left it, and the tiny dancer had one hand up, twirling in place in her little pink dress. Only, the music coming out of it was no longer the tune he'd once picked out.

It now played a lonely piano tune. One he'd last heard on Pear Street.

Chapter Twenty-One

"Live enough for two lifetimes."

—Blu Johnson, life lesson #100

Jill's thirtieth birthday had come and gone, Bluebonnet Construction's schedule was filled to the gills, and Jill had spent countless hours interviewing new hires. Additionally, everyone in town finally seemed to see Jill as more than "that little Sadler girl" who'd always been on the cusp of blowing a gasket if anyone so much as looked at her wrong.

And all of this had taken place in one week.

Another surprise to come out of going on the show was that Bluebonnet now took calls daily from people asking for new builds. That had been the dream from day one. However, after much discussion, they'd put it to a vote. And it had been unanimous.

All new builds would *only* be she-sheds. They liked their reputation these days.

As such, Jill was on-site for day one of erecting a new retreat. Only, she was the *only* one on-site.

She pulled out her phone and tried Trenton again.

"Where are you?" she muttered when Trenton's phone once again went to voice mail.

She tried Heather next. Same deal. Even the owner of the retreat they were due to start on wasn't home.

"We don't have time for this," she mumbled to herself.

She checked her watch as she headed back around front. They were going on twenty minutes late at that point, and with so many jobs lined up, none of them had time to be dillydallying. As she took the corner around the back of the house, she pulled up short at the sight of a black four-wheel-drive truck turning in at the end of the two-hundred-foot drive.

It was Cal's truck.

Jill's pulse temporarily blocked sound to her ears as she tried to decide whether to turn and run, or meet the man head-on. She hadn't laid eyes on him since walking away over a week ago, and she didn't want to see him now, either. Only . . . she'd apparently forgotten to tell her heart that.

But as the truck made its way closer, her heart went into a different rhythm. That of flatlining. Because it *wasn't* Cal in the truck.

She waited where she'd stopped, and when the driver emerged, she forced a smile. "Morning, Pete." Pete Logan came toward her. "What can I do for you?"

"The better question is, what can *I* do for you?" Pete held a legal-sized folder stuffed full of papers, which he held out to her. "Seems you're the boss now."

Jill didn't take the folder. "What are you talking about? Are you looking for a job?" She couldn't imagine this man wanting to be known as a Bluebonnet. "And why do you have Cal's truck? Where is Cal?"

"Don't need a job, and I have no idea where Cal is. Probably in his shop."

Confusion reigned. "What shop?" This was why she liked working with women. They might sometimes talk too much—and flirt when they thought it might get them on TV—but at least they talked. "Why do you have his truck, Pete?"

"Oh, yeah." Pete reached into his jeans pocket and came out with the keys. "The truck's yours, too. Cal said to tell you he just had it tuned up for you. He—"

Jill took a giant step back, palms going up, and Pete stopped talking.

"What the—" Jill pressed her mouth closed before she could say more. She didn't get angry for no reason anymore. This was the new Jill. Except apparently where it involved her ex.

Because what the hell was Cal Reynolds up to now?

"Let's take a moment and start at the beginning," she suggested. She held up one finger. "Why are you here?"

"To see where you want me."

"I didn't hire you, Pete."

"Right." He pulled the first piece of paper out of the folder and held it out to her. This time he presented a smile with the paper. "But I still work for you. You're also now responsible for all of these jobs."

She finally took the sheet of paper, and when she looked down at the list, she recognized several projects that she knew for a fact We Nail It had bid on and won. She was a fairly intelligent person, so she was starting to get an idea of what was going on there, but surely her stupid ex hadn't gone off and done something this drastic without bothering to have a single conversation with her first.

Pete looked at her with a drop of sympathy then, and he leaned in a little closer. "He knows he can be an ass," Pete told her, as if sharing a secret. "But he's trying. And he does feel bad about his assiness."

How dare he?

And *then* he sends Pete?

"Oh, hell no," Jill muttered. She tossed the piece of paper to the ground, wanting no part of it, and stomped to her truck. "You'd better move that piece of crap out of my way, Pete Logan," she yelled at him, "or I'm about to ram into it."

"But it's your truck," Pete yelled back, and Jill whirled on him.

"What the hell has he done?" she screamed.

And then she saw why no one had been on-site that morning. Because they all now stood in the front yard of the house next door, smiles from ear to ear. There were Heather, Trenton, the workers who were supposed to have arrived with Trenton, Aunt Blu, a full camera crew—*including Len*—and stepping out from behind Len was Cal.

"I changed my mind," Cal called out, and Jill noticed that he was smart enough to keep his distance.

"No one asked you to," she yelled back. They were only about fifty feet from each other, so yelling wasn't really necessary. But it sure felt good.

The man had thrown her love back in her face, so he didn't get to show up playing hero now.

"That's not actually accurate," Cal told her. He made a face, as if he were a kid being chastised, and added, "My granny asked me to."

And then Irene Reynolds made her way to the front of the crowd, her arm hooked through Aunt Blu's, and she waved toward Jill. "Hi, Jill. It's good to see you again. And I actually told him to get his head out of his rear."

Jill pressed a hand to her mouth. "Hello, Mrs. Reynolds. It's good to see you again, too." She wished she'd gone up for visits over the years. "Your grandson does have a habit of putting his head there, doesn't he?"

Laughter rippled through the group, but no one moved from where they were. Jill and Pete stood in one yard, with everyone else in the other. And cameras and boom mics caught all of it.

"Been working on that one with him for years," Irene told her, and then Cal took a handful of steps forward, separating him from the group.

"What are you doing, Cal?" Jill asked, this time keeping her voice at a reasonable level. She was too mentally beat up to deal with something like this. She'd missed him terribly over the last week, and she'd fully expected to never speak to him again. And not because of anger this time, but because they were finally over.

And it had decimated her.

Cal lifted his hands out in front of him as if ready to ward off an attack. "I messed up," he told her.

"You did," she agreed. "You lost a good thing."

The smile he'd been trying to force dropped, and he let his arms hang at his sides. "Please, Jilly. You've got to hear me out."

A lump settled in her throat. "I don't *have* to do anything."

She glanced around at everyone watching them. What a jerk thing to do.

"I was wrong," Cal told her. "I was an idiot. And I don't deserve to be forgiven."

She said nothing.

"Come on, Jill."

"Come on, what? Forgive you?" She bent and snatched the paper off the ground. "Because you . . . what? Handed me your damned company?"

He nodded, the move jerky and almost desperate.

"I didn't want your company, Cal!" She shook the paper in the air. "Why would you do that?"

"It's called a grand gesture," he yelled back. "When you mess up as bad as I did, you have to make a grand gesture to get the woman back."

"Who told you that?"

All eyes turned to Heather.

"What was I supposed to do?" Heather squeaked out. "He threatened to knock my door down if I didn't let him in."

Jill stared at her foster sister. "You have issues."

Heather smiled then, and the ridiculous dimples that had probably gotten her far too much in her lifetime finally began to ease the pain in Jill's heart.

"You're too romantic, Heather."

"I know. But he loves you, Jilly."

"Well, he has yet to tell me that."

Again, all eyes pivoted. This time to Cal. And that time, when he looked at her, he no longer seemed like a man fearful that his grand gesture was five seconds from being rebuked. He stood taller, and he nodded with confidence, and Jill saw in his eyes what she knew was in her heart.

"I love you, Jilly-Bean. And I'll give you everything if you'll just give me one more chance. All of me. All that I have."

"I don't want all you have. I just want you. I want *us*."

"I want that, too, baby."

She stared at him, wanting to call him over, but did they really have to do this in front of cameras? And then she remembered that Pete stood behind her, and she turned to the other man.

"I know what your first assignment is, Pete."

"Yeah?" Pete stood at attention. "What can I do for you, boss?"

She nodded toward the other yard. "Get rid of them. All of them." She looked at Cal. "Except for the idiot."

"Consider it done."

Pete jumped into action and, surprisingly, managed to herd everyone but the idiot out of hearing range, and as he did, Cal inched her way. She stood her ground, making him come to her, and when he finally reached her side, she lifted her brows in question.

"Come on, Jill. Are you seriously going to continue arguing with me about this? Haven't we done enough arguing for one lifetime?"

"Maybe I want two lifetimes."

A light lit behind his eyes. "I could consider that." He took a step closer, and dipped his head to meet her eyes. "How's the anger? Calming down yet?"

"You're not seriously trying to finagle sex with me right now?"

He angled his head. "Is that an option?"

She blew out a breath, and looked over his shoulder. It was hard to hold on to outrage with the man she loved when he stood before her, begging for her forgiveness.

"Maybe," she finally muttered, and he broke into a grin.

"Maybe?"

"Stop it."

He reached for her hands. "I can't stop it, Jilly. I love you. I want a life with you."

"Did you really give your company to me?"

He nodded, and she shook her head.

"You can't do that, Cal. You've worked too hard to build it. Plus, I have my *own* company."

He inched a half foot closer. "And now you have my company and a third of your company. We're going to combine them, and *you're* going to continue building it."

"But . . ." What was wrong with the man? And then something else occurred to her. "What about Rodney?" It had been Rodney's business to begin with. He'd started it. "You can't just give your company away without talking to your uncle first."

Cal slid his thumb over her knuckles, and his eyes turned serious. "Rodney is fine with it. I promise you. And I did talk to him. I got to call him the other day, and he's on board with the change one hundred percent. He's happy about it, actually. And he's already coming up with ideas for how *he* can be on the new show."

Jill chuckled at Cal's words, because he sounded exactly like his uncle. "And what *about* the show?" she asked softly. "They want two cohosts. Remember?"

She didn't see how this could even work.

"We're going to give them two hosts," he told her. "I'll still be a main part of the show, just in a slightly different format. You're going to run the company, and I'm going to build custom pieces whenever you need them."

"Your shop?" she murmured, recalling what Pete had said about Cal being in his shop. She hadn't even thought about the workshop on his farm.

"Yes. And Heather and Trenton will be a part of things, too," Cal added before she could ask. "They're negotiating their contracts now. We're going to incorporate the ranch into the show, as well. If you're on board with that. I'm going to have cows and horses."

She stared at him, unable to speak. He was going to have cows and horses?

"If you'll have me, that is." He smiled at her then, and squeezed her hands in his. "What do you say, Jilly? Will you have me? Think you can ever forgive my faults enough to marry me?"

"Marry you?" Everything was happening so fast.

"They'd prefer a married couple for the show," he explained. And then he grinned at her visible outrage over the thought of *that* being the reason he'd asked her to marry him. "But *I* told *them* that our marriage had to be a part of it," he assured her. "I brought it up first. They didn't tell me."

"It's a darned good thing."

"I know. I have learned a thing or two over the years." He closed the remaining distance, and tilted her face up to his. "Tell me, baby. Tell me you love me. That you'll do this with me. And that you'll never ever leave me, no matter how many stupid things I do in the future."

"I don't get a stupid limit?"

He shook his head. "I've proven I can keep doing the same dumb things over and over, so no. You take the good with the bad." He touched his lips to hers so lightly that she shouldn't have even been able to feel it, but though she'd closed her eyes as he'd leaned in, she knew.

Her heart knew.

"Say yes," he pleaded, and she opened her eyes and finally smiled at the man she loved. This was all she'd ever wanted.

"Yes."

Acknowledgments

The funny thing about this new series is that it came about because of a bad experience with a contractor. A male contractor. Who had a team of males working for him. Who showed up to work at ten in the morning, took two-hour lunches, and left at three thirty in the afternoon. And during the hours that they actually were there? They stood around a lot. Doing nothing.

These people just about drove me crazy!

So, as I sat in our new house one day last year (about five weeks after our backyard-fence installation was supposed to have been completed) and I watched this team of male workers spend yet another day screwing around more than putting in legit work . . . I turned to Terri Osburn (a great author friend, who was visiting at the time—and whom this book is dedicated to!), and I said to her, "I'm going to write a series about an all-female construction crew someday. And those ladies are going to know how to get a job done!"

Thus . . . the Deep in the Heart series was born. And I have to say, I'm completely in love with these ladies. They're tough, they take crap from no one, and though things might not always turn out the way they'd hoped . . . they know how to get a job done! So, thank you to that male contractor and to all those inept male workers. You inspired me!

(And for the record, the fence did turn out looking great. But still . . .)

About the Author

Photo © 2012 Amelia Moore

As a child, award-winning author Kim Law cultivated a love for chocolate, anything purple, and creative writing. She penned her debut work, *The Gigantic Talking Raisin*, in sixth grade and got hooked on the delights of creating stories. Before settling into the writing life, however, she earned a degree in mathematics and worked for years as a computer programmer. Now she's living out her lifelong dream of writing romance novels. She's won the Romance Writers of America Golden Heart Award, been a finalist for the prestigious RITA Award, and served in various positions for her local RWA chapter. A native of Kentucky, Kim lives with her husband and an assortment of animals in Middle Tennessee.